ALIGHT

A.H. CUNNINGHAM

COVER ART: NIZZYARTS
COVER DESIGN: JACK HARBON
DEVELOPMENTAL EDITOR: GABRIELLE BROWN
COPY EDITOR: KATRINA CARRUTH

For Briana and Sandra.
We miss you Wade.

CONTENT WARNINGS

Please scan the QR code for the most updated content warnings. I'm always updating them based on reader feedback so if you have anything you recommend to add please email me at:
ah@ahcunninghamauthor.com. I want the reader experience to be safe and consensual!

CHAPTER 1

ALICIA

Alicia Powell Torres wondered if she could trade in her adulting card for something else in return. Like a puppy, or the ability to eat without her hips going wider than the seats in domestic flight airplanes. No one tells you that being an adult comes with a host of responsibilities that require your mental gymnastics with no feedback from anyone else. Lately, she wished she could bring back time to the moments when she wasn't so lost.

"Alicia," Reg, her realtor pursed his lips, "we continue to get the same feedback from the buyer's inspectors when they show up and see your home." Reg was the second realtor she'd commissioned to sell her parents' home. The process had been exasperating and lonely. She shook herself from her sad thoughts and faced Reg.

"There has to be someone," she struggled to keep her frustration at bay. Alicia needed to find a buyer that didn't need frills. She refused to believe that wasn't a possibility. In order for her to leave Florida, she needed this house sold. The sooner, the better. Every time she came to this house, a mixture of emotions overwhelmed her.

She wouldn't say the house was haunted but it sure felt like it as she walked each space. The energy of the house hadn't been the same since her mother had moved to Panama, unable to cope with living there after losing her husband of thirty-five years.

Her childhood home always brought bittersweet reminders. To be the one in charge of selling it weighted heavy on her, regardless of what it meant for her bank account. There were so many memories here. The smell of her mother's Arroz con guandu y coco, the complexity of her mom's Afro Panamanian abstract art, the sounds of her dad's favorite Beres Hammond tunes, the keepsakes from her summers in Panama or Ocho Rios, the sheer bleakness of the inevitability of her father's diagnosis.

"How many inspections have you had since you listed your parents' home?" Reg asked her. Having a close family friend as her agent was a plus. He knew how to deal with her, a double-edge sword, but she needed the best person on the job, and Reg was that person. When things weren't working out with her previous realtor, she thought it was a problem of incompatibility, not the house itself. She had scoffed and barreled through the entire process and lost a couple of months in return. To hear Reg confirm all the things her previous agent told her stung her pride.

"I don't understand why that matters, Reg." Alicia responded. Reg stared at her with patience and skepticism, both shining through his otherwise passive face. The man was gifted in non-verbal communication.

"Fine, five inspections, but I thought my old realtor was full of sh… crock, I assumed she was trying to pull fast one," Alicia said.

"Which is why you left work, to supervise the inspection, instead of trusting me. Mhm." She looked down at her fresh Nikes, looking incongruous with her tailored red suit, then back up again to Reg. She'd taken a long lunch break and rushed to the house, changing to sneakers for comfort. Heels are lovely, but they aren't useful when you are a big girl and need speed on your side. Reg was right though, she should trust him. He was a friend and had nothing to gain.

"Are you sure you want to sell the house? It was giving you good money while you were renting it, I don't understand the sudden change of heart." Reg asked.

"Since Mama left I—I just don't feel at home in Florida anymore. I think moving to Brooklyn, closer to my dad's side of the family, will be a wonderful change of pace. I loved living in New York when I was a kid, and I was so mad at them when they moved me here. I was such a brat to them." She smiled in memory of how gentle her parents handled their move when she was twelve. "Maybe I was meant to stay there. Who knows? I want a clean slate in Brooklyn, and the money from the sale will allow me to buy an apartment there. I must sell the house." She shrugged, feeling oddly vulnerable by his questions.

He wasn't asking anything she hadn't heard already from her family. Everyone questioned her sudden need to move. But she knew herself, she needed a drastic change. Lately, she'd been waking up at night, sweating and in tears. Five years had not been enough for her to get better about her father's death and her mother's abandonment, and now it seemed her grief had decided to physically manifest itself.

She didn't want to live her life in a state of nothingness, she deserved to be joyful, and her current situation was not cutting it anymore. Making a move to Brooklyn sparked hope in her, looking at a future where she wasn't surrounded by jolts of sadness, and peaks and valleys of emotions. She visualized Brooklyn and saw the golden opportunity to rebuild her life on her terms. She firmly believed in clean slates.

Reg stood, patiently waiting with a gentle smile. She shook her head and focused back on the house sale. She trusted Reg as much as she could trust anyone. *Always be wary, even of those close to you.* She'd learned that lesson the hard way.

"Walk with me, likkle Alicia," Reg said, his nickname for her a reminder of her summer days visiting her grandparents in Ochi.

They walked towards the front door, and she basked in the light sifting through the tall windows and high ceiling of the room. Her hand lingered on the cream and blue furniture left behind because of memories better left unexplored. The house was a two-story single home, with cream-colored walls and dark brown trimmings, your typical south Floridian family home in any middle-class gated neighborhood.

As they left the house, Reg pointed to the top of the roof. "I have nothing to gain or lose. I'm doing this because you're Clinton and Juanita's pickney, and he wanted to make sure you receive the best value for your property. So even though you doubt me, you have to trust me. This place needs a new roof and hurricane-proof windows. Most comps in this market have these updates, so what happened today..."

"Ok Reg, I need the money from the house, so I can get out of here and move to New York. Lay it on me. What will all these updates entail?"

REG LEFT AFTER GIVING HER AN OVERVIEW OF WHAT SHE needed to contract to get the house in top shape and ready to sell. Feeling overwhelmed, she made a list of things that she could tackle, and that gave her a sense of peace. She trusted that sense of peace. She welcomed the feeling.

Work had been her solace on the first years after her father had passed away, but lately whenever she stepped into the office, a wave of extreme dissatisfaction and regret came over her. She had worked for her company for many years as the VP of Finance for a hospitality management company. Corporate America at its finest. During her college years, it had been her dream job, and now she was one of the top executives in a company that managed over fifty hotels in the area.

Colleagues respected her in and outside her company, but it all meant nothing. What was she contributing to society, she wondered, outside of making a few men wealthier than she could ever imagine?

She went back inside to turn off all the lights and adjusted the air conditioner temperature. Standing in her parents' house with all their things was an assault to her senses and the peace of mind she'd briefly attained.

The house was still full of them. Somehow, after her father's death, she'd found the perfect tenant who didn't mind having the house furnished. The guy had been a super commuter, traveling between Florida and Boston, and had been amenable to living surrounded by her family's assorted knickknacks.

She glanced around the living room, eying her mom's Mola art on the beige colored walls. On one side, and her father's bookcase full of books on African Liberation, Economics, and fantasy novels— his guilty reading pleasure —on the other. She stood gazing at family photos of the three of them, and of few of her and Gabo, her old friend. Her very best friend.

Ages ago, Gabo understood everything about her. He would have realized something wasn't right with her. He would have been here to help her, holding her hand through life's stress.

But life wasn't fair, nor it was easy, and they lost touch. Years of separation had allowed her to think of him with fondness and tenderness. She'd learned to compartmentalize her disappointments better than a Jedi master.

There were many reasons she wanted to leave Florida. Gabo had been smart, he'd left as soon as they graduated college. Even though he'd left, their old friendship still had a heartbeat in this house. Here, time hadn't passed and they still smiled at each other and were each other's favorite person. Here, she allowed herself to feel all the things she kept buried deep inside.

She couldn't help but smile at his goofy expression in one of the photos. Even after all these years, her breath caught in her throat, and her heart beat twice its normal rhythm just looking at him. She wondered what it would be like to have him in her life, but this wasn't the time for thoughts without solutions. She put Gabo back in the mental drawer of unsolvable things, where he belonged.

GABO

Gabo hadn't been touched with such enthusiasm for a while.

"Ohh, you are such a good boy. We don't have many gentlemen anymore." Ms. Doris pinched his cheek and went back to rubbing his arm up and down. "They don't make strapping young lads like you anymore; my Fred and my John have grown tall like you too. They get it from their daddy. How tall are you, 6'2", 6'3"?"

"Yes ma'am, I am 6'2". You're right on the money," Gabo said.

"Thank you so much for helping me pump my gas. I hate getting my hands dirty, and well, I ain't as agile as I used to be."

"Please. I saw how fast you were moving from the pump to your car," Gabo winked at Ms. Doris and she winked back in return.

Weariness and a nervous current ran through him as he approached the last pit stop before arriving at his childhood home. As he exited his car, he saw an older Black lady, silver lavender braided hair shining in the sun. He recognized her as Ms. Doris, the neighbor around the corner from his parents' house. Pleased to see a familiar face, he offered to pump her gas as he escorted her to her car, and she happily accepted.

"So Gabo, you've come back. I knew I recognized that handsome face." Ms. Doris looked ready to glean a shit ton of information with the efficiency of a CIA operative, that was nothing new. She was the resident eccentric, vidajena old lady of the block. Always around with an unexpected observation and getting all the gossip from the street.

"I have ma'am. It was a good time to return."

"That's good my boy. And you're moving back to your old house," she said, leaving Gabo shellshocked at how quickly she was getting the 411 of his move out of him.

"Yeah, my parents moved out not too long ago, to one of those fancy retirement communities." He confided.

"Smart move. They host the best sex parties," Ms. Doris said.

He almost dropped the nozzle and had to readjust it before he kept dispensing the gas.

"Oh, Ms. Doris, you ain't going to get me with that one. You think you scandalous, don't you?" he smiled.

Ms. Doris cackled while she patted his cheek like you

would a small child. She smiled and told him, "If you don't believe me, ask your parents' next time you see them."

"I'll do no such thing Ms. Doris," he shuddered comically, knowing she would love to see the terror in his eyes. She patted his arm and cackled again. She was nothing but trouble.

"No, *Ms.* Doris, I'm a young eighty-five years old. I let all my suitors call me Doris. Now, child, I'm nosy. I have to ask the why? It is lovely for you to want to live closer to your parents, but I always thought you were going to settle down in that big city up north, based on all your mom told me about your job and prospects." Curiosity shined in her eyes as she awaited his answer.

"I just sensed it was right time. I'd always planned to come back. And a free house until I settle don't hurt nobody," he said.

"That is very generous of them. Good for you for taking a risk. You are young, my boy. It's time to make leaps of faith. That project you have helping kids in the community.... your parents must be proud." she nodded sagely.

"Thanks Doris, coming from you it means a lot." Hearing her say that reinforced all the reasons this was the right time to return to Florida. He needed to trust his instinct for once and allow himself to go with the flow. Taking risks didn't need to be a scary proposition anymore, and even though he had been reticent to take the last leap, he knew his project with his best friend Mason would not flourish with him working remote from Manhattan. The student center they wanted to open required a personal touch and his full presence.

She raised her eyebrows and a mischievous grin came through, "But don't think I don't realize why you're really back. I always ask your mom why you and that lovely Alicia on the other street haven't gotten together, you both were inseparable when you were teenagers." And just like that Doris' ninja skills made all the nervousness from moving, flood back again. *Damn.* He wondered if he would ever not react to the sound of her name, Alicia.

He'd promised himself not to make decisions based on emotions when looking at the pros and cons of moving back home. For the most part, he'd succeeded. He had a work plan and solid financial plan, and even though starting this new non-for-profit might seem risky on paper, it well positioned him to focus on this venture and give it his all. But he would be lying to himself if he thought that was the only reason he had taken the plunge.

He wondered if Ms. Doris knew anything about her. He knew in broad strokes what she was up to, courtesy of his mother's weekly updates or Mason's oblique mentions; but he tried his best not to cyberstalk her, or check her updates. After all, they hadn't communicated in years, and it would be some sad shit to be pining for a friend that no longer talked to you.

"Ms. Doris," his stern look didn't deter her, instead, it had her smirking. "You are fishing for extra info, and I've none to give. I'm just back to start this new project and be closer to my parents."

"Sure, child. And I was born yesterday." She sucked her teeth in disbelief.

"I see you're not buying what I'm selling," he said.

"Not one bit, my boy, but it's fun to see you try!"

Bumping into Ms. Doris on his way home helped him run things through with someone that had no stakes in his move, and he welcomed her unvarnished bluntness. It didn't hurt to talk about Alicia even if only for a brief instant. He finished with the tire pressure valve and assisted Ms. Doris in getting back in the driver's seat.

"It so good seeing you, child. You make sure to come visit old Doris when you aren't too busy, alright?"

"Thanks, Doris. I'll visit you soon. Make sure you go straight home though, no stopping at any sex parties on the way, ok?"

He heard her cackle as she drove away.

CHAPTER 2

ALICIA

"Entonces Licy, are you really going to move back to Tia and Uncle's home?" Mariana, her first cousin on her mother's side, looked at her while deftly braiding her freshly washed hair. The smells of wrapping foam and essential oils permeated her senses and Alicia tapped her feet to the rhythm of Reggaeton playing in Mariana's salon.

A small two-chair storefront decorated with white and black stripped walls, with motivational phrases in gold cursive such as "You're not a Basic B," "Black Girl Magic," and her favorite "Black AF." All that she could need to tend to natural black and brown folk's hair , she could find in this inner sanctum of TLC.

"Yeah, it sucks, but I need the cash flow. In order for me to sell the house, it needs work. Work that requires money. I don't want to be paying rent in my apartment, when I could at least be saving rent money by living there during the repairs. Once we finish the repairs, I can put it back in the market and move to Brooklyn," Alicia said. The sense of emptiness expanded every time she thought of leaving her modern two-bedroom apartment close to the beach and to work. The thought of going back to her parents' home, even if only for a few months to reach her ultimate goal of moving out of Florida, brought emotional gut punches at unexpected times.

"Mija pero, you have bread with capital B in that bank account. You've been saving the rent you collected from the house for five years! If my parents went back to the mother-land, God forbid, and leave me their house to do whatever I wanted with, girl, I would capitalize on that."

Mariana scowled when Alicia twisted around with eyes full of outrage. As they stared off, Mariana pushed back her big, beautiful coiled curls from her forehead, where they framed her deep brown skin like a halo complementing her statuesque black beauty. Alicia was her opposite in many ways, favoring her father's side. Shorter, with light brown skin, and a body that loved to keep every single empanada she ate as a cherished gift to her curves. Their family resem-blance was all in the face: the same eyes currently shooting daggers at each other, dimples that were the trademark of the Torres family, and the full lips they both loved to adorn with bright smiles and deep-set lipsticks.

"Quedate quieta! Stay still, girl. You are worse than Mili-ta," Mariana complained.

"Oye, that hurt! I'm not as tender-headed as my little cousin, you're just mad rough. Don't be an ass. And yes, Mari, that money is accounted for. I plan to take that and the money I'll make from the sale of the house as the down payment for my apartment in Brooklyn."

"Here we go again with this moving away from home, plan," Mari said as her hands went through each section of hair at the speed of a well-oiled machine."I don't understand why you're so pressed to leave. You have a good job, a nice apartment, you own property, a family that loves you, no entiendo. You have fulfilled the single girl American Dream."

Alicia stayed quiet. This was a recurring conversation she had with Mariana. They both were unapologetically proud of their single-hood for different reasons. Mariana abhorred gender constructs and had not found a partner that was not intimidated by her determination. Alicia had thought she had found love until she realized maybe love was not for her. Things didn't work out for her even when she gave her all. Telling Mariana about what she thought were panic attacks would just freak her out. Mari had her own shit to deal with, she didn't need Alicia's baggage on top of that. Alicia recognized that a change of pace was what she needed, she was sure of it. Sometimes you just had to get out of the place that brought you horrible memories. She'd given herself time after her father died, thinking it was going to get better, that she would navigate life smoothly again but, it was not working. Nothing was working.

"Maybe you just need to get laid. Those toys may do the trick, but sometimes you just need a warm body to hold you after a good orgasm." Mariana said.

"Ya vas! My toys are doing the damn work, thank you very much. You wish you had a collection as pretty as mine. And if things get dire I have a few phone numbers I can call..." Alicia said laughing, but inside she wasn't amused. Even her libido was suffering lately, and demanded immediate attention. She didn't play when it came to her orgasms.

Mariana just did not understand how lonely and stuck Alicia had been for the last couple of years. Life was a chore, and she worried if she did not make drastic changes, she would only end up bitter and disconnected from life. She rubbed her eyes, tiredness from it all descending upon her.

"Ok, Licy, you've explained this to me in the past so that I won't harass you anymore. But you have to live with the fact I don't like the idea of you moving to New York. You aren't the only one that gets to be stubborn about this," Mari said, not pausing to breathe once during that statement, sassiness dripping like ice cream on a hot summer day. A long sigh escaped her lips at the underlying hurt threaded around her cousin's words.

"Mariana," she said in a soft voice, conciliatory. An olive branch.

Mari's eyes rolled then smiled through the mirror, things between them ok, for now. It hurt Mariana that Alicia no longer wanted to stay in Florida. She could not explain to Mariana the knot of emotions and memories that made this place no longer feel like her home. The lack of direction, the claustrophobic trap of her job, the longing for what used to be and will never be again. She changed the subject before melancholy and hurt feelings dampened her wash day like salty waves on a sandcastle.

"Did you ask Tío if he can help me? If he could take up the project for the roof and the windows and the landscape, it would happen quickly and the right way," Alicia asked.

"You are pushing all the buttons today, huh?" her cousin asked. Alicia flushed, knowing that the change of topic was not the best avenue to make peace with Mari, but she needed to see if she could count on her tío.

"What makes you think Pa is going to drop everything to help you, huh? When is the last time you called him just to say hello?" Mariana asked while she continued to braid her hair methodically.

"Ay ya Mari, estas intensa today!" Alicia exclaimed.

"Do you want my help or not? Or do you prefer to call your Tío Padrino on your own?"

The thought of asking Tío Toño for help brought a familiar tension in her stomach. Her mother's twin had an abrasive personality with a heart full of gold. The two of them stayed on each other's wrong side for many reasons.

"I can call Tío if I need to. I just thought you could say something to him next time he comes by the salon. He's here all the time," Alicia said.

"Like you used to chiquita. I miss that. I miss you trusting us to do right by you."

Alicia stared at her hands, refusing to look at Mariana.

"I just need a change of pace, Mari, don't you see? Daddy's death and Mami leaving..." Alicia trailed off. Her cousin knew her too well, that comment about trust stung, so she kept quiet. Soft hands caressed her hair, and Mari leaned towards her giving an affectionate peck on the cheek.

"Ok prima, whatever you say. I'll link up with Pa and get you on the docket for the project."

GABO

There was nothing like the sense of complete and utter uncertainty that he made the wrong decision to move back home to get his day going. He looked around his parents' backyard and across their pool to the house behind theirs, and his stomach swooped down, momentarily breathless. That house and its occupants had once held a very special place in his heart.

Life had its seasons, and those years were the happiest of his life. Sometimes he wondered if everything he remembered was through rose-colored glasses because of the way things had ended...

Gabo made his way to his car and drove to the supermarket to pick up supplies for the week. He'd arrived late but had the presence of mind to detach the U-Haul from the pickup truck before turning in for the night. The balmy morning made his body instantly break into a sweat as he walked to his car, his body still adjusting to the area's humidity. His cellphone rang, and he pressed the Bluetooth car button to answer the call.

"Yo, yo, yo! You here, my dude!" Mason, his best friend since high school, said.

"Bruh, you have too much energy for me this morning," Gabo replied.

"You bet I have energy. We are moving forward with our plan, and it cannot be better timing. I'm proud of you, man. You took the plunge. I was afraid you would stay scared and not make this move," Mason said.

Mason and Gabo had been working on this non-for-profit idea for many years and had always planned to make it their life's mission once they'd established themselves financially. A year ago, they had both hit their financial goals and prepared to take the plunge. Gabo was hesitant, wanting to study his decision from every angle before moving. His parents moving out of their home and allowing him to live there rent-free, had been the final push he needed. It had been difficult to leave his property behind in New York, but he planned to put it on the market in the next few months. It also didn't hurt that his ex-girlfriend was a realtor and had promised to take care of the sale.

"I'm no flake. This has been in the works too long for me to back out. This is as important to me as it is to you," Gabo answered.

"I know, I know. You had me worried for a while, though. You're too cautious sometimes. Maybe it's time to be fearless," Mason said. Gabo's muscle memory allowed him to navigate the familiar streets with enough attention to follow the conversation with ease. His eyes absorbed all the sameness and the difference in the landscape. The taller palm trees at the end of the road, the gatehouse now light brown instead of yellow, the brightness to this area that New York could never give him.

"It took you less than a minute to introduce that subject. But we are not going there today." They were not going to talk about her today. A chill raced up his hands, to his arms and down his spine at the mention of her. All these years later, she still elicited such a visceral reaction; the one that got away.

When he thought about being fearless, something he'd been working on the past year, it was always about Alicia. When they'd been friends, he thought the best thing was to keep things strictly friendly and platonic, at times it caused friction between them. Now he saw the errors in his ways, but it was all too late.

"Alright, you can ignore me, but by moving into that house, you are going to bump into her eventually. Didn't your mom say the Powells still own it? Then what are you going to do? Be all awkward and shit? That's what happens when the women come to you. No game. I still remember when the girls at school used to slip notes in your backpack, 'do you like me, Yea or Nah.' You were still oblivious though. You were the most oblivious with Alicia." Mason said.

Mason continued, rarely needing a response from him to carry on a conversation. "I never told you this, but, if she hadn't been my friend too, I would have been jealous as your second choice best friend," Mason said seriously.

Silence echoed through the speakers.

"Get the fuck outta here. Jealous? You are so full of shit. You had way too many friends to be worried about Alicia and I being best friends. Wait till I tell Malik about this." Gabo said, shaking his head. Malik was the third friend in their trio, but spent most of his time abroad as a merchant marine. He heard Mason laughing his ass off on the other side of the line.

"Also, I doubt I will see her. From what Ma told me, she owns the house but doesn't live there. She rents it out, so there's no reason for our paths to cross," Gabo replied. Now all he had to do was convince himself he didn't want to see her. But that would be lying to himself, and he rarely did that anymore. He'd been working on himself, so he couldn't afford not to be in-tune with his feelings.

"Whatever you have to tell yourself to sleep at night. Of course, you want your paths to cross, among other things..." Mason's suggestive tone and subsequent laughter had his finger hovering over the end call button.

"You ain't shit," Gabo said with no heat in his voice.

"And you love me just the way I am. I'll come through tonight to see you. It's good to have you home.

CHAPTER 3

ALICIA

Alicia sat on the top floor of the downtown Fort Lauderdale building, looking out of the ceiling to floor windows at the view of the city and sparkling water of the sea beyond. The sun shined bright and the sky a beautiful blue that accentuated Fort Lauderdale's greenery.

Her mind wandered away from her work for the eleventh time that day. She thought of what her life could look like in Brooklyn. She had been researching non-for-profit organizations that could use someone with her skill set, hoping to make her transition out of the corporate world smoother. She wanted her work to make a difference. Not for a few rich people, but for those who needed it the most. People that look like her and needed assistance because their socioeconomic status didn't open golden doors for them. She was certain she could throw all her dissatisfaction at her work into something good, something positive.

When she pictured her future she saw herself working

doing good, she also saw a nice place to live, time to be with family, and hopefully for traveling. She'd not been able to travel much since college, and she wanted to see the world outside of the United States. She had a map in her room where she highlighted places to visit. Just picturing herself in a plane headed somewhere far from here made her smile.

"Alicia Maria! How are you today, my friend?" A flash of bright blue and the clack of stiletto heels were the only warning she had.

Alicia's arms crossed over her chest, an involuntary response, her mouth transforming to a perfect straight line. She took a second to rearrange her face to a pleasant noncommittal smile. Forget code-switching, she was the master of demeanor shapeshifting. By the time she composed her face, Jennifer Winters sat down with a delighted and fake smile.

Jennifer was her equal in the company, Alicia was the Head of Finance, and Jennifer was the Head of Operations. Jennifer was a contrast you did not expect. She was a forty-year-old white single mother of one, that had worked her way up the corporate ladder and took no bullshit from anyone. To Alicia's puzzlement, she disguised that ruthless-ness with sweet smiles and fake platitudes that did not fool Alicia one bit. She liked straightforward people and Jennifer was anything but that.

"Good Morning Jen, please call me by my name." Her serene smile was at odds with the blunt words coming out of her mouth.

Jennifer flipped her brown hair back, making it fall over her shoulder, and a sigh punctured the otherwise quiet office. "Alicia, I swear I have no idea how you work in hospi-tality. You can be such a sour patch kid."

"I assume you are in my office because you need something from me?" As she leaned back in her chair, her fingers crossed underneath her chin, her body language betraying not one bit of her annoyance.

"If you saw Jack's email, you are aware we are meeting the board tomorrow, and he thought it would be good if we pulled some of the key metric reports, as well as the performance overview and the Payroll deck to review before the meeting," Jennifer said.

"Jenny," she had scored a point in their odd childish competition when she saw Jennifer flinch. She hated when she called her Jenny. "When you say *we*, it sounds like an army will be pulling these reports, but last I checked, you haven't worked on those reports in a few years now."

"Well, girl, I have offered in the past, and you have always preferred to run it on your own," said Jennifer with all her sweet fakeness. Point for Jennifer, it drove her wild when non-melanated people called her "girl". She had overheard Alicia say it to Janina, a fellow Black colleague who was Haitian American, at lunch once and remarked how she would "do better" in the future. Alicia guessed the future was not today.

"You're right. I prefer to run all the documentation to ensure synchronicity between all comparisons across the board. Did Jack mention what comparison scenarios we will be discussing?" Alicia asked.

Jennifer had the grace to look contrite. "I missed that key detail." Both of them realized that there was no going back to ask Jack for the answer. He was the type of leader who considered his time more valuable than anyone else's. Anything that caused him to repeat something he said would put him in an unpleasant mood.

"I will ensure I have all the key comparison scenarios, just to be on the safe side; run your comparisons against the earlier forecast, one year, three years, and five-year trends, and the proposed budget. I foresee this being a precursor of our meeting in November to discuss the budget in detail," Alicia sighed. No matter what, this meant more work for her.

She hated that Jennifer was making her have to do all this work. Based on all that she had on her docket for the other properties and closing, she would not be done until late tonight.

"Oh, another thing… he mentioned you had approached him about us doing more philanthropy work in the community?" Jennifer asked, crossing her legs and relaxing back in her chair.

Her heart lightened considerably, glad to learn Jack had paid attention a few months ago when she explained she wanted to spearhead an opportunity to partner with non-for-profits that may need help, not just with funds but with ground-up work. Their little company had fifty hotels they owned and operated throughout the state. Working in the communities of the people who worked in those hotels would be impactful not only for said communities but also for the company's turnover and retention. In corporate America, there always had to be a business reason to extend a lending hand. Jack had been dismissive at the time, another nail in the coffin was her motivation.

"Yes, well, apparently he thinks you might have been on to something, so he asked me to tell you to bring the numbers of what we could donate to the board meeting as well as a preliminary plan," Jennifer shared.

"Ok, I will prepare a small deck for that as well," she said calmly.

Secretly, anxiety made her chest a little tight and her hands a little clammy, but she could handle the workload.

She did not know how much longer she could take the negative physical reactions her job brought out of her every day.

"Mami ¿Como estas?" Alicia asked over the phone.

Alicia approached her car. Most days, she tried to call her mother once a day. The calls were short and hid a thousand little hurts they both inflicted without meaning through the years.

"Mi chiquita, how was your day at work?" Her mother asked.

"Ugh, the worst, Mami, I'm just walking out now." Her heels clicked and clacked, the echo reverberating in the quiet parking lot. After such a long day, she struggled to keep her posture from mirroring her turmoil. Long days at the office had become a too common occurrence.

"Ay mamita, that is no time to leave work. That boss of yours is overworking you," her mom said in concern.

"Mami… I remember the long workdays when you were a General Manager, ok?

"Bueno, but I tried to be home by dinner every day. It is 8 o'clock on a Monday chiquita, that is no way to live," the sadness in her mom's voice something she was used to hearing, especially when talking to her only daughter.

"Mama, you worry, too much. I'm going to the new Jamaican joint by my apartment, I'll be choosing violence because I already know the lady will tell me they ran out of curry goat, then get cuddled up to watch Netflix before bed." Alicia said.

"Ay, what are you watching now? I need a new show."

Alicia sensed her mother's alertness as she closed the car door and pressed the bottom to lock the doors before doing anything else. There is a saying in Spanish: *Mujer precavida vale por dos*— a cautious woman is worth double.

"Nothing good," Alicia answered. "If I find something, I'll let tell you."

"Are you in the car already?" her mom asked, confirming what the sounds of Alicia's car already told her.

"Yes, I'm in the car now driving out the garage," she responded. The sounds of La India blasting for a second as the phone switched to Bluetooth.

"Good mamita, I worry about you, leaving late and nobody at home to receive you…." her mom trailed off.

"Mami, I don't want to go there. I made the right decision." Alicia held back her annoyance.

A sigh was her mother's only reply. She wouldn't rehash her decision to break things off with Tariq, her ex and quasi-fiancé. Her mom had always liked Tariq since he had started hanging out with her in high school. He'd been in the same school as Mariana, and had a crush on her since he met her. It took her a time to warm up to him but she gave him a true chance during college. It had been two years since they broke up, and one since he'd moved away. Like everyone else.

He was a good man, but things were not meant to be between the two of them. They tried for years, did the on-off relationship thing, tried to be compatible because on paper they made so much sense. Unfortunately, she was never able to give him her trust and love, which was on brand for her, one of the many things she wished could be different.

"Ok, mamita, but now you are all alone, and it is not because I want you married, I want you to have your people close to you. You keep shutting people out."

"I wonder why…" her voice was low and her jaw and neck stiff. Inevitably, they always got to a sore point between her and her Mother.

"Alicia! Con respeto," her Mom warned.

"Si Mama. Let me let you go, I'm going to get this dinner and head on home."

Another sigh, this one full of resignation.

"Ok, drive carefully, talk to you tomorrow."

"Love you, Mama."

"Love you too chiquita."

"Mija, slow down. I thought we were just going to have a couple of drinks and head out. At this rate, I'm going to have to drive you home," Mariana warned her while she sipped her drink. Instead of going home after work and stress eating, Alicia called her cousin and planned a happy hour before heading home. It was a cute after-work spot full of thirty somethings looking for a place with pleasant music and great vibes. They were regulars.

"I'm fineeee. Besides, I need my car. Tomorrow is the big move day, remember? Bleh," Alicia said. What was she to do with a four-bedroom, three-bathroom home full of memories and no warmth? She reminded herself throughout the entire week that this was the wisest decision to make. Saving money was paramount for her move to New York.

"Honey, that's why I ditched the hot piece of man candy I'd lined up for tonight and came to meet you instead because I recognized you were in your feelings."

"Que feelings, I'm fineeee. Big girls hold their liquor," Alicia complained.

"Sure," and Alicia could sense the epic eye-roll that Mariana gave her.

"Perate, were you not dating that girl Asia, last you told me? She was super-hot. What man candy? Estoy confundida nena."

"No need to be confused. Asia and I are friends. Things

didn't work out. She wanted a girlfriend, I wanted a lover." Mari shrugged and finished her drink with the same finality she ended her so-called relationships.

"You wanted a sneaky link." Alicia nodded wisely.

"What have you heard about sneaky links, cus?" Mariana said with outrage. Alicia just laughed and kept drinking.

"So... I heard Gabo is back," Mariana said, pretending to be calm about it.

"What? Is he visiting?" The alcohol must be affecting her organs because her heart skipped a beat at the sound of his name. He had been in her mind a lot these past weeks as she kept going to the big house. She guessed those pictures were making her recollect their time together, the way they could complete each other's thoughts, how she used to beg her parents to shorten her summers in Panama and Jamaica just so she could come back to hang out with Gabo, how he would come over and hang out not just with her but with her dad after he was home from teaching class, how Gabo was the first person she would go to when she was sad or upset. Had she conjured him?

"No. From what I heard, he is back-back," Mariana said while sipping her drink, eyebrow raised. Her cousin tried to trick her into saying more than she would typically say when Gabo's name was mentioned, but she was on to her. A whole-body shiver ran through her at the news. After so many years, he still affected her. She was just good at pretending he did not.

"Where did you hear that?" Alicia hoped that her tone sounded innocent.

"You know me... I have my sources," Mariana said mysteriously.

"Yea right? That man candy's name for tonight starts with M and ends with ason, huh?" She replied and retreated to her drink.

"You think you're slick. No changing the subject. Are you going to link up with Gabo?" Mari asked.

"Nah, that ship sailed a long time ago," she said as she shook her head and felt a little woozy for it. For all her longing there was zero to minus ten chance of Gabo and her reuniting again. She wasn't opposed to the idea if she hadn't been planning to move. Fifteen years had done a lot to blunt her pain, and she was an expert at keeping her feelings in boxes. If the boxes were threatening to collapse around her, well, she was also handy with packing tape.

"For real? You aren't even curious to see how it could be now?" Mariana's face of mischief was a bad warning sign.

"No, besides, I'm not trying to link up with anyone right now. I'm focusing on getting out of here. He is just moving back. That spells drama to me." Alicia shook her head, remembering she needed to order some water.

Mariana looked at her for a minute, then sucked her teeth. "Aya tu. Last time I saw him, he was looking fine, with a capital F."

Alicia had a high tolerance for alcohol and had only had three whiskeys on the rocks, nothing she couldn't handle, but it seemed she was drinking her fourth a little too fast, so she slowed down a bit. The fact she was speeding through her drink to blunt the news of Gabo's move, was something she'd have to revisit when she was alone.

"Ok, chiquita, don't turn around, but there is this adorable guy that has been making puppy eyes at you the whole night, and his name is Tariq."

"What? My ex?" Alicia exclaimed, and her eyes widen in shock. What was in the water that all her past men were creeping back into town?

"Girl, shush your mouth. Can you at least try to pretend we ain't talking about him?" Mariana rolled her eyes.

"You're right," she whispered back. Mariana looked at her

with mild disapproval mixed in her smile. "Whatever you are doing right now is not a whisper. Look, just say hello, and that's it."

"Maybe I shouldn't say hello. I don't want to send him mixed signals after our breakup..."

"To quote a drunk cousin, 'That ship has sailed.' You broke up almost a year ago. You can say a cordial hello. But, you need to get laid," Mariana replied.

"No, I don't," she scoffed.

"You do. You barely go out. And you're always working. Live a little."

Another sip of her drink. One more for courage. The music volume had increased exponentially. The 10 p.m. crowd liked more of a party atmosphere than your casual conversation and drinks. Top 40 hits were playing, and Alicia trained her eyes around the crowded bar with its dimmed lights and understated decor.

"Ok, I'm going to turn around now," she whispered.

She glanced over her shoulder, and her eyes connected with her old boyfriend. He had laughing eyes with wide lips that turned into a sexy smile when he saw her looking. A warm tingle between her legs signaled its need for attention.

"Maybe it is ok just to go and say hello."

Whoever left the curtain semi-open needed to die a slow, painful death, similar to the current throbbing in her head, along with the one in her soul. She needed to get out of this place with the same urgency as she wanted to move away from Florida and start anew.

Unfamiliar white and beige walls surrounded her, and a warm body with a broad, muscular back laid next to her.

She sat up on the bed, clutching the sheets to her naked

chest, then dropping her head to her hands. That turned out not to be the smartest of moves, when she felt like the Atlantic Ocean had taken residence in her brain— the turmoil of things left unsaid and feelings left untouched.

One-night stands weren't typical for her, but they happened from time to time. Her sex drive had always been high, a nine point five on scale from one to ten, so being without a boyfriend meant trying to keep herself occupied with her variety of vibrators and the occasional hookup when things were in dire need of attention.

Last night was one of those nights. But was it a good idea to use her ex-boyfriend to scratch an itch?

Tariq had been in town for work, and took advantage to visit his Mom. They had both been sober enough to have a conversation about consent but buzzed enough to ignore all the red flags about getting together.

Thoughts of the night before ran through her head:

"Are you sure you want to do this, Tariq? I'm not looking for anything else," she was able to say between kisses.

"I can fuck and not catch feelings...again. I just want you, baby, one more time, ok?"

She could not fault her decision, because Tariq had given it to her just like she needed, but looking at things in the bright light of the morning, she was not sure that had been the best of ideas. No matter how clear and honest she had been with him, she suspected Tariq had not moved on one hundred percent.

Her phone vibrated. It was Mariana.

Mariana: Oye, are you ready to head out? I want to have some arepas from the Colombian place by my house.
Alicia: Yeah, I'll just get dressed and hopefully say a short goodbye to Tariq.

And that is how she found herself doing the walk of shame with her cousin Mariana. The guilt had nothing to do with the good sex she had last night and all to do with the way her life seemed to be floating around with no direction, no true north.

CHAPTER 4

GABO

The secret to an everlasting friendship is to understand when to keep your mouth shut. Gabo read that on a fortune cookie, or was it on a wall in a bar restroom?

"Gabo, turn a little to the right, yeah more, there, good."

He owed Mason. He had given up his Saturday to help Gabo finish the move. Gabo brought some items with him in the small U-haul trailer, but he purchased his larger furniture in South Florida. That included his new bedroom set, which he bought in IKEA. He could have done without Mason's eye-rolling though, he recognized he had made a mistake there.

Mason, being an outstanding friend, gave him shit the entire morning. He gave him annoying directions as they navigated the load in and promised to dial it up once they started assembly. Because Gabo had not paid for assembly. Again, he had no need for Mason's excessive eye-rolling when he learned that news.

"Dude, you are doing well, right? Like your coins?" Mason asked voice strained. Sigh. There was no need for his answer in this conversation, Gabo already knew that much. He navigated the last landing and walked straight into his bedroom. This was the last of the items that needed to come up. Thank you, Jesus.

"You are doing good, like pockets good. You could have just paid for the damn delivery and assembly," Mason complained.

Gabo stayed quiet, as he bent his knees to put down the mattress on the already assembled bed.

"At least I don't have to go to the gym today. This sexy body does not take care of itself." Mason turned to look at himself in the mirror against the wall.

Objectively, he knew Mason was a handsome man. All the awkward limbs when they were growing up had converted in muscle, girth, and height. Mason was an in-lust-at-first-sight type of guy with a bright smile, deep brown skin, wide-open chiseled face, and dark brown eyes that made his flavor of the week go wild. He would go for any person who attracted him, whatever their gender identity.

"Now that you are here, I can help you bulk up a bit. You're looking mad scrawny," Mason said to continue on his quest to annoy him.

Gabo ignored the slight. He wasn't skinny, his large build developed years after college. He took care of himself by swimming daily, if he could swing it, and going to the gym for some lifting when he had time. He had a body that was a combination of muscle and comfort that suited him well. Swimming also helped him to decompress and disconnect from his busy schedule. Now that he was consulting while they worked on the beginning stages of their project, he would have more time for both activities.

"Sure, man, I would love to work out with you," he smiled

at Mason. For all Mason's messing with him, Gabo was grateful for the help today.

"Ok, ok, now you are getting all mushy and soft on me. What's next in this day of free labor and toil?" Mason shook his head, still admiring himself in the mirror.

Gabo clapped Mason's back and guided him to the door. "Come on, let's grab a beer, and I'll order some pizza. Hopefully, after that, some of your *hangriness* will go away."

AFTER SOME COLD BREWS, A HOT PEPPERONI PIZZA, MORE joking from Mason, and a couple of extra assembly pieces he didn't know what to do with, they were done. Mason went to the toilet while Gabo stood inspecting the space.

The minimalistic furniture fulfilled all his needs for now. He'd decided to keep his old bedroom versus taking over his parents'. One of the best features of the neighborhood, was that the houses had dual main chambers with a walk-in closet and ensuite bathroom. The slightly smaller square footage still allowed him to stay in his old space and equip his parents' old room as a working space for him and Mason until they started renting a location.

He stretched, his body ached with the discomfort of standing and bending in unusual positions to get the damn furniture together, when a frisson of awareness made him look towards the window. Early evening crept in, the sun still up and bright, the long days of the summer lengthening the days.

His body must have known before his eyes were able to register what he was about to see. His body went cold, then hot the sensation resembling an utter change in matter where your atoms and molecules rearrange themselves as they recognize that your life is about to change, and your body could not stay in the same state of inertia.

Something called his attention by his window, and there she stood. Their houses were far enough to not see all details, but he recognized her essence even after all these years. Alicia Marie, his once best friend. A lamp in her room illuminated from behind, but his most fanciful thoughts made him think that the light emanated from within. Her warmth reached out from there to fill him up with all the sense of possibilities. His heart kept beating, blood rushing through his veins, the metamorphosis done. He was back home. Honesty also compelled him to acknowledge that there stood the true reason for his move.

ALICIA

Today was not the day for trading in her adulting card. Today was a day someone should've snatched it from her hand stomped it into the ground in front of her. She wondered who'd dare to give her the card in the first place. An anvil and a loud hammer had taken up residence in her head, and she was doing the annoying celebrity trait of wearing shades indoors. Her excuse? Why remove them when she had to inspect the load in?

The movers arrived at her apartment at 8 a.m., and she hadn't been ready. Hours later, and she still felt the weight of last night. What was she thinking, doing this to herself?

Mariana, the angel, had come around with some food from her Mom's Saturday fish fry.

"You look like death becomes you, girl," Mariana was clearly not an angel, not one at all. "What exactly are you wearing, honey?" Mariana continued.

Alicia looked down and saw her comfy pink leggings, favorite fuzzy slippers, and oversized black off-shoulder sweater. Her hair struggled half up and half down, some braids trying to escape the ponytail. She'd inherited her mom's sense of fashion and always strived to leave the house well put together but had given zero fucks today.

"Did you leave your apartment in chancletas?" Mariana pressed her.

"What's wrong with them?! Besides, you slept for a while, right? I got two hours of sleep, and it cost me. The movers will charge me overtime as I was late letting them in the apartment."

"You right, you right," Mari said, noncommittally, while she enjoyed her own plate of food. Mariana pressed on again. "But still, girl, chancletas? I mean, you are head of finance for a hotel conglomerate. Why are you walking around in them?"

"Whatever, Monique. Why are you trying to read me right now? Let me and my chancletas live our best life," she answered back.

They burst out in laughter as they sat in her parents' kitchen. The arroz con coco y guandu, fried fish escabeche, and green salad were sitting warm in her belly, giving her a sense of well-being, even though it had been an otherwise crappy day. Fried fish escabeche was one of her favorite dishes and her Auntie, Mariana's mom had killed it today. It made her think of her dad's fish escabeche.

Her Mom's kitchen was one of the places she felt her father the most. She'd learn to live with the jolts of sadness, and the sparks of joy she could feel here. Happiness and grief were always present in an odd choreography that was never-ending in her life.

"Ms. Powell, we are all done with the items. Would you please come with me to see the empty truck?" the leader of the moving company startled her out of her thoughts. Mariana took advantage of walking out with her, enveloping her in a warm hug goodbye, the smells of lemon verbena and incense surrounding her.

After walking all the rooms and making sure all was in order, she sat in the family room watching TV, her sectional and TV set up to her liking, her fridge stocked with everything she needed for the week. She rearranged the bookcase in the living room, adding her baking books and her romance novels, and still had more stacked in a corner in her room. She'd placed candles all over with her favorite scents, sandalwood & lavender, to dispel some of the fantom memories that hit her in unexpected moments.

The familiar sounds of a building settling after the intense heat of the top of the day were all oddly comforting. In the areas where she would spend most of her time, she'd put in the effort to personalize them, every other room she'd emptied except for a few things she wanted her mother to check. She looked for some of her reality TV love shows but found no new episodes, so she turned off the TV.

She jerked to a stop, an odd pull, a sensation of slackness that gone suddenly taut, came over her, pulling her...

She dismissed the weirdness and took a quick shower, getting herself ready for bed. Early evening announced its appearance, but her body was weary, and at soon to be thirty-five, she was paying for her night of drinking, so an early bedtime was just what she needed right now. After a nice hot shower that cleared her head and eased some of her aches and pains, she put on her pajama shorts and tank top and let her braids down from the bun she had placed during her shower. She put her sad reggae playlist on, nostalgic for her father more than ever.

"Girl, what's that ruckus?" Her dad stopped short in front of her room. "Oh please Daddy, you think reggae is only those old tunes but reggae is evolving!" She said laughing. Now that Alicia was fifteen, she had enough money to buy her own CDs and rushed to

get some in Jamaica before traveling back from her summer break at her grandparents. "You say that's reggae? Nah, Licy, I'm going to play you some good reggae. Come, I got some of my LP's down-stairs." Alicia groaned in mock frustration but deep down they both knew she loved hearing his music. He smiled at her show of reluctance, leaning on the door frame while he waited for her, "Alright Daddy. But you have to promise to listen to my new CD, too."

"Ya hear that Juanita?" He raised his voice so that her mom could hear him from downstairs. "She tryna negotiate with me! That's alright Licy, I'll listen to your CD, and I'll learn all them songs too." And he did. He listened to all her CDs and together they did a mashup of some of his songs and hers.

Alicia always thought of her dad when she heard this playlist, a mix of old and new, a mix of him and her. She walked out of her childhood bathroom and stood by the window, the one she loved sitting by during her younger days. She ran her hand over the cushioned window seat, a small sigh escaping her, and her eyes closed for a minute, letting all the weariness of the day out with her breathing. When she opened her eyes, she looked out to the house she had avoided paying attention to in the past, and did a quick double-take.

Gabo.

She had a knot on her throat, her heart racing. She could not believe her eyes. Somehow, they had managed to miss each other most of the times he came to visit in the span of fifteen years. Both their parents could not understand their estrangement, but at the same time, they respected their kids' decision.

Her mother had ensured she understood when not to come around, casually mentioning when Gabo planned to visit his parents. Alicia had stayed close with the Millers, exchanging holiday cards and visits through the years, but somehow everyone understood not to push too much about their friendship. They hadn't completely stopped being cordial with each other the few times they could not avoid contact, but it had all been so different from what they had before.

Lord, he stood broad, tall, and sexy, and he was looking right at her. That beautiful smile that blossomed at the sight of her had her breath caught in her throat. Memories flooded her mind, but a nagging thought brought her back to the present. Like an alarm she had forgotten snoozed. Suddenly, she remembered she wore skimpy PJs and panicked.

Oh shit, shit, shit. If her heart was racing before, it was practically trying to escape her chest now. Her cheeks warmed up, until they were hot to the touch. Then she did the most stupid shit she had ever done in her life, and that was saying something. She dropped down with more agility than she had shown in a long time and fell flat on the floor.

ALICIA TWELVE YEARS OLD

It was so hot. "Daddy, can you please turn the AC higher?" She couldn't believe that Mami and Daddy had moved to South Florida. Who does that to their twelve-year-old? Her parents were super selfish and inconsiderate, and she hated that. Now she had to start a new school and had to meet new friends. This was all just extremely stupid.

"Mi Vida ya llegamos, mira que linda esta casa nueva." Her mother turned around from her front seat and looked at her with kind eyes, eyes that pleaded with her to be happy with this pretty new house. Her mom knew her well enough to know she was upset and hurt and most of all, nervous.

"The neighborhood is pretty nice. Most families have kids around your age, and you can walk to school." Now, her dad attempted to convince her this was a good idea. She hated when her parents tried to team up and talk to her like she was toddler instead of a teenager. They tried to make her seem unreasonable. As if moving all the way to South Florida for Mami's General Manager promotion wasn't pure crap.

She grunted noncommittally, "That's nice, Dad, and yes, it is a cute house, Mami," They were giving her some leeway. She could get away with some sulkiness, outright rudeness would never fly in her home. With a Black Panamanian mother and first generation Black Jamaican Father, there were some things you just did not do. On the flight here, she had seen a white girl a little older than her, go off on her mother because her mom had not gotten her the right seat for the flight. The mom had just asked her to calm down, and that was the end of the conversation.

Alicia glanced at her mother and found her serving the *look*. Every kid in the diaspora knows what look that was. The face that told Alicia *in no uncertain terms she should ever try that type of freshness with her— by the way she did not like the way Alicia was looking at her right now, so she had better fix her face ASAP* look. Yep, THAT look could be used for any occasion and situation.

As they pulled up, she had to admit the house was very nice. They lived in a two-bedroom apartment in Brooklyn, so this was an upgrade in space. She could have invited her entire homeroom class to a party here. She ran around the house looking at all the rooms, exploring the lay of the land. The big airy living room, the bedroom upstairs with large windows and lots of natural sunshine.

Alicia picked her room the instant she saw it. The room had yellow pastel walls and white trimming. It faced the backyard and pool. Her excitement threatened to overflow, but she wouldn't let her parents see her smile until maybe two hours from now. She could see into the street behind, with its line of houses, their backyards against this row of backyards. Every corner of the room was illuminated by the sun. It had a large window, and the main reason she fell in love with the room, a window nook for reading.

"I was sure you'd pick this room, ya know. I can already see you sitting there reading until late at night."

Her dad's accent was a fast barrage of words. Along the years of living in New York, it had melded to a pleasant mix of Brooklyn and Jamaican patois, so familiar to her. He also learned Spanish after meeting his mother to convince her to marry him, so it all blended into this cadence that was purely her dad.

"You were right, Daddy. It's a very nice house, and a wonderful neighborhood it seems. It's just a lot. New school in the fall, new friends, all the family back at home," Her eyes started watering, the sadness of the day overwhelming her. Her dad enveloped her in a big warm hug. She was grateful for him not using words instead of comfort. His mix of berg-amot and tobacco clung to him, and she inhaled, feeling home for the first time since they walked away from their Brooklyn apartment.

———

It had been a couple of weeks since they had moved and Alicia held on to her disappointment. Her parents were still giving her the patience and leeway to feel her feelings but today her Mother had put her foot down when Alicia had tried to beg off meeting the family that lived behind them. She had no interest in sitting down and being polite, she preferred to be on the phone calling her cousin Aayala or hanging out with her cousin Mariana. In the end, here she was outside of the neighbor's door with her parents.

"Good evening! Welcome to our home," Mrs. Miller opened the door, her husband standing right next to her with a warm smile on his face. He was a tall white man, taller than her daddy, with dark straight hair with streaks of silver, especially in his temples. He had blue eyes with thick eyebrows and the kind of face that makes you stand a little straighter. Mrs. Miller was a beautiful Black woman. She seemed to be a little younger than her husband and was as tall as her Mom, with abundant coily hair and dark mahogany skin. Her eyes held genuine warmth, and that set Alicia at ease.

"Thanks for having us." Her father was doing that thing men do when they greet each other with handshakes and firm pats on the back. They moved away from the door to welcome them in, and there was Gabo, the boy she'd heard plenty about these past days.

"This is Gabo. Gabo, say hello! And this must be Alicia. You are so lovely!" Mrs. Miller gushed at her, and she smiled shyly back then turned to Gabo standing by the stairs of the house, one foot still on the bottom stair like he was ready to bolt at the first opportunity.

"Hello, Mr. and Mrs. Powell. Hi, Alicia." Gabo was tall for a kid his age. He had brown smooth skin and if she hadn't just met his Dad, she wouldn't have guessed he was mixed. He was all his Mom, handsome with the same approachable smile, and big ears that made him look adorable. The only thing from his dad was the shape of his eyes. They were dark brown like his mother's but had the same quality as his dad's. Her mami had said Mrs. Miller was originally from Colombia, and Gabo also spoke Spanish. He smiled wide as she stood staring at him, like he caught her and now had a secret of hers. That smile made her stomach flutter. She stopped smiling, and Gabo frowned at her.

"Hello Gabo, hello Mr. and Mrs. Miller, very nice to meet you," she greeted politely. She wanted this night to end as quickly as possible. Alicia didn't want to have a crush on a kid she'd just met, especially one who lived right by her and was going to the same school.

The dinner was pleasant enough. She stayed quiet most of the night, though her parents tried to include her in the conversation. She could have told them that meeting her neighbor would fix nothing. She just wanted to go back to New York but understood that wasn't a possibility.

"Why don't you two go to the terrace and hang out for a while? I'm sure you don't want to be talking to us old people." Mrs. Miller read the situation and gave her a kind look. Gabo, who had short but funny things to say during dinner, gestured toward the sliding doors outside and the patio furniture. "Wanna chill for a bit? It is nice outside, and we can play some music if you like."

"That sounds good, thanks," she replied. Music would be good. Maybe she could just sit and listen because she didn't have much to say. She got comfortable in the seat outside, the heat of the day had decreased by a few degrees.

"Sometimes, when there is nothing good on TV, and I get tired of video games, I come out here and just chill for a while," Gabo said. His voice was on its way to full baritone. She stared at his Adam's apple, a clear sign that puberty was visiting him the same as it had visited her two years ago.

"Do you really get tired of playing video games?" She asked, unconvinced. He laughed, which was less deep and that made him more endearing. It gave her a little thrill to make this handsome boy laugh a little.

"Nah, not often, but it can happen," he shrugged and flopped his body onto one of the patio seats after he saw her sitting down.

"So you are pretty bummed about moving here, huh?" he cleared the silence that was gathering around them, both their eyes trained on the lighted pool in front of them.

"What could make you think that?" she said with a slight smile on her face.

"So, she does talk," he said. His eyes on her, he made her nervous but in a pleasant way.

"I do, but don't tell my parents. I'm planning to milk their worry until at least the beginning of the school year. I haven't done any chores since we moved," she said.

His laugh was sudden and infectious. It filled the patio and a little place inside of her that thought she would be lonely at school started to crumble. She couldn't help but join in with him.

"So are we going to listen to music or what?" she smiled when he'd calmed down.

"I think you and I are going to get along just fine," he smiled back.

Two hours later and she was back in her room after a wonderful night with Gabo. They had listened to his CDs, shared some of their favorites, and promised to swap CDs during the summer. He seemed to have overreaching access to popular American music and Colombian music from his mother, and they chatted about their favorite Latin-American artists. When she told him she adored "Pies Descalzos" by Shakira, he pulled out the CD, and they listened in companionable silence until her mother came looking for her.

She pulled a book from her little bookcase and sat down to read when she saw movement across the backyard. It was Gabo, standing by his window, which was directly in front of hers. She could see enough to notice he was also in his PJs and smiled at her, signaling her to go to sleep. She lifted her book and waved it in his direction, and he nodded in understanding. Then he walked away from the window, and her shoulders slumped. All of a sudden, he was back with a note on a large cardboard.

WILL YOU BE MY FRIEND? YEA OR NAH.

She burst out laughing at the note. She scrambled off the window seat, quickly looked for the largest pad on her desk, and wrote in big capital letters:

YEA.

CHAPTER 5

GABO

Did she just fall?

The door to the bathroom opened, startling Gabo from the intensity of the moment. It felt like he hadn't seen Mason for days, but in truth, it had only been a few seconds, a minute at most. An eternity had passed since he'd seen Alicia again.

He turned and walked right out of the room with purpose, taking two steps at a time down the stairs. Impatience coursed through him, and he wished he could just levitate to the Powell's house.

"Gabo. Gabo. Gabo! What happened?"

Mason put his hand on his shoulder and realized he was already by the sliding door leading to the pool, unsure how he had gotten there so fast.

"Gabo stop, why are you looking so pressed? What happened while I was in the toilet?" Mason's voice was low and urgent. Whatever energy he was putting out, it worried Mason. He stopped and breathed in and out, oxygen filling his lungs, working to calm the riot of thoughts and emotions coursing through his brain, slowing the fast beats of his heart.

"I saw Alicia." There was no additional explanation required.

"Oh, *oh* shit, she's home then?"

"Yeah, she was standing by her window, and then I think she fell." He wanted to go, but Mason would not let him out without an explanation.

"You think she fell? So, what's the plan? You're going to bust into her house and rescue her from a… tumble?" Mason's tone was measured.

"I want to make sure she's good, then I'll leave her alone," Gabo shrugged. He was just mildly concerned for an old-time friend.

"You know," Mason said like he was about to give a lecture. "I've known you since we were six years old, right?"

"You're really going to bust my balls right now?" An aggravated sigh escaped him, the sense of urgency still coursing through his veins. Mason just raised an eyebrow.

"Fine. I'm tripping from seeing my friend, the only girl that has ever known me inside and out. I still don't under-stand what went wrong between us. So, what if I want to go check on her?" Gabo asked.

"Now that sounds more like the truth. Imma ignore the part where you said you have no idea what happened with her. What I will say, is walking through her back door like you used to—not a good idea,"

Mason was right. He ran his hands over his hair in slight frustration at the delay. The Powells and the Millers had bonded through their children's' close friendship, which lead to a quick cosmetic change to their fences that created a pathway between the houses to ensure the children could just walk back and forth form their backyard versus having to walk around the block to access the front door. They usually left the access open even though both gate doors had a lock. At the pinnacle of their friendship, they used it daily to hang out together after school or during summer breaks. However, Alicia and Gabo were not best friends anymore, and walking through that gate, even if it was open to him, was no longer his right.

"Ok then, let me get my car keys." Gabo said and changed track to walk towards the front door.

He heard a very heavy sigh behind him.

"Right behind you, bruh."

HE KNOCKED ON THE DOOR RIGHT AWAY. HE DIDN'T WANT TO second guess his decision to come here.

After what felt like hours, he heard her voice from inside. "Who is it?"

"Alicia, it's me," Gabo said. Mason stayed in the car, claiming that he had only come with him in case Alicia needed to be driven to the hospital because of severe injury. His sarcastic tone left much to be desired concerning his sincerity. The asshole.

The door swung open and there she was, closer and oh, so beautiful. Her expression was cautious, her eyes talking to him as they always did, telling him she was nervous. His heart calmed for the first time since he saw her earlier this evening, recognizing her.

He spoke. "Hola, I came over because I wanted to make sure you were ok."

She'd changed. He registered little of what she was wearing. He had trained his eyes on her face, but now he couldn't help but look down to see all of her.

Alicia had grown into a stunning woman. Her eyes were

as expressive as ever to him, her dimples on full display and her lush lips framing her beautiful smile. Her hair was up in a ponytail and she had a silk wrap around her braids reminding him of many nights they sat in their respective rooms, talking on the phone once her curfew for the night had forced them to go to their respective houses. She had a long sleeve t-shirt and sweatpants. The clothes hugged her body and revealed that the promise of what was to come when she was twenty had been fully delivered. As teenagers, he'd tried to avoid looking at his friend with any other type of interest, but it had been a losing battle. Now at thirty-five, she exuded sensuality, and the force of it was hitting him hard.

He could not deny he had always been attracted to Alicia but did a stern mental shake, now wasn't the time to go down that route.

"Bueno Gabo, are you done checking me out?" She smirked, the devil. She cocked her hips, resting against the doorframe, and by God, those hips. By the way she stood, she wasn't ready to let him inside the house. She cocked her head to the side in curiosity. He tried his best to look at her face, and not let his eyes wander all over her body.

"I'm ok, I promise. You didn't need to come running over. I forgot you are a gentleman through and through," she said.

"Of course I had to come through. I didn't have your phone number, so this was the next best thing. I also just wanted to say hello." She was amused, but there was still a current of nervousness below it all. She was still his Alicia though, outspoken even when put in the spot.

He was aware of her air of caution and tried to respect that. He wanted to barrel head-first to this reunion. Gabo had pictured this occasion so many ways, and in every scenario he'd been slow, cautious, feeling her out. Now he couldn't help his eagerness. He was, at last, talking to her and he wanted to make sure she knew how momentous this occasion was for him.

"I'm good. I just wonder what you were planning to do if I didn't answer, though?" She asked.

"Mason is in the car and Plan B was knocking down your door with our impressive combined strength, rescuing you from your room, tending to your many wounds, and gallantly driving you to the ER."

His answer startled a laugh out of her, and his chest expanded. To hear her voice, and her laugh, to see her eyes sparkle with joy was more than he could have asked for tonight.

"No has cambiado. Same old Gabo with the hyperactive imagination." Her face, always in motion, now had a gentle smile, her eyes nostalgic.

"It's good to see you Gabo, I would invite you in, but I'm in PJs and we haven't talked since..." she trailed off, a sad smile on her face. "So I confess I'm nervous." she finished. He leaned against the arch entrance, taking all she said in. He relaxed his posture, wanting to set her at ease.

"So you recognized it was me before I told you?" he asked, circumventing all the old baggage she dumped in front of him with a couple of sentences. He perceived that if he tried to address it right away, she'd shut down. Unless she'd drastically changed from the Alicia he knew from before.

"Yeah, Gabriel Ernesto, you used our special knock," she said.

"So you are going to use my entire name, like that? And yet you still opened the door? Not that I'm complaining." He cocked his eyebrow at her, surprised when she flushed.

"I wasn't 100%. You know what they say about asses who assume," she said.

"That's not how the saying goes Alicia," he shook his head in mock despair.

"Sorry English police, I'll do better next time," she smiled back.

"So there will be a next time?" he tried his best to not betray too much enthusiasm.

Just like that, the spell broke for Alicia. Her eyes dimmed, and she sighed.

"I've got a lot going on right now. I'm trying to sell my parents' house. I barely have time to breathe in between that and work and…" she trailed off and he could tell she was trying to pump the breaks on him.

"I was more thinking like a drink or two in a bar close by. Two old friends catching up. Not another Alicia & Gabo Olympic Hangout of '03." he said.

"I can't believe my parents let us put a tent in my back-yard that long weekend," she laughed. Then… "I must admit I'm surprised you are inviting me out, as friends," she empha-sized. "Just guns blazing. Let me think about it Gabo, I don't want to be rude but, there is a lot going on right now."

He inclined his head, recognizing when to bow out, ignoring the disappointment coursing through him. The adrenaline of the moment was wearing off and it surprised him how quickly he'd moved with her. All his plans of being careful, out of the window. "I get it. Look, I thought it was high time we reconnected. I also wanted to make sure you were ok, and you are. So I'll let you get back to your evening,"

She opened her mouth, poised to say something, then closed it again and did a quick head-shake.

"Good night Gabo, say hello to Mason for me please, it was great to see you again."

All her thoughts were on display right now. She was conflicted and looked like she carried the weight of the world on her shoulder for all she'd been friendly tonight.

ALICIA

Making a decision to go for drinks and a hangout shouldn't be this nerve-wracking. Gabo, again, in her life. The gut punch of emotions that surged at the thought of connecting with him again had her reaching for some rum to chase the chaos away.

It was Friday night, and she sat in the family room, listening to her latest audiobook, an erotic fantasy novel which was also staring at her accusingly from the bookshelf in the living room. She had a whole budget set for her books, and every month she blew it over. She allowed herself to splurge on books, baking utensils, and clothes. With everything else she was frugal, her budgeting and meticulous attention to spending was why she'd gone into finance.

Work was an afterthought right now, as was living what she considered her best Florida life. Which was mediocre. Platanitos, Appleton and Ginger Ale were her companions as she listened to her book.

Mari had called her to link up at the bar again, but she was in no mood to socialize. Most Fridays it was an internal tug-of-war with herself where she worried that she was going to die alone. Her Panamanian side always came out with a vengeance, voice eerily like her mother, telling her staying at home to drink on her own was no way to meet new people. But, she countered herself, this place was not home anymore. Not since Daddy passed and Mami left. What was the point of creating new bonds if she planned to leave soon, the sooner the better?

She'd loved socializing before her dad had passed. Every fish fry, island fete, and bashment you could find her there. But since his passing she'd fizzled out to occasional outings where she made dubious decisions. Like sleeping with Tariq. And now Gabo was in town, so she was certain she would make even more dubious decisions if she accepted his invitation, no matter how platonic they meant it to be.

With Gabo, what was the point of going out for drinks to reconnect if she planned to leave? She'd be cutting things short before they could grow close again. After all these years of seeing him in pictures that Mrs. Miller shared with her, quick sightings from afar when they bumped into each other during his visits, and during her light social media cyber stalking, the reality of seeing him in person had been a lot to her senses.

The man was built like a dream come true. He was taller. His body had been lanky before, now he was solid, having filled out during the years, all shoulders and broad chest. He probably was still swimming, based on how he filled the T-shirt he wore last week. And his ears. Still big and adorable.

All that aside, her favorite thing of the night was seeing his eyes and those lips that could not help but smile at her in excitement. It was contagious and for a second; it swept her away. Then she remembered all they had been through and something deflated inside of her chest.

If anything were to happen between the two of them it would be friendship only, beyond that she was not interested in getting into anything romantic with anyone. Not now, and based on how things were looking in her life, never.

The audiobook stopped and her ringtone for her Powell side of the fam came through, her cousin Aayala calling.

"Wa gwaan baby girl," Aayala said.

"Nothing nah guwaan gyal," her cousin loved greeting her in patois to test her Jamaican commitment to that side of the family. She thought she was cute.

"Are you home?" Aayala asked, her voice clear through the background noise.

"Yes man, nothing to do tonight," she replied.

"You could go out with Mari if you wanted. What's my

firecracker cousin doing home on a Friday night?" Aayala pressed her.

"Mari called, but I wasn't feeling it today. Who is there with you?" Aayala could read her too well, so she tried to deflect.

"Tina, Juju and Laurie. Ladies say hello to Alicia!" A chorus of hellos came through the phone, the fact she already had them on speakerphone spared her ear. She could imagine them all dressed to the nines because her family was like that. Never basic, always extra.

"So, you not going to tell me about seeing Gabo?" And there was Aayala with her mind reading qualities.

Aayala had lived in Miami during her high school years before moving back to New York with her parents. Because of that, they were closer than the rest of her cousins, who spent their teenage years knowing Alicia as the Florida cousin. Aayala was part of their high school crew and regularly came to Florida because of her work.

"Mari runs her mouth too much," Alicia answered.

"Nah, we just have a separate chat where we talk hair tips and she told me you had seen Gabo last week, and that he asked you out for drinks and you turned him down."

"Nooo, I didn't turn him down Aayala, I said maybe." Alicia played with the popcorn in her hand, it had gone cold and sad just like her Friday night.

"Ok then. Say yes. I heard the wack story you told Mari, so I'll save you time. I want you here in New York so bad. Yoo! Bring the music down, no? You're so loud," Aayala said and Alicia could hear some commotion in the back and then Aayala was back on the phone.

"Look, we are about to go into this fish fry but, friendships like the one you had with Gabo don't grow in trees, ok? Don't be stubborn cousin, live your life! New York isn't going nowhere and there are things like internet and cellphone." Alicia hated when Aayala talked sense. Aayala was the wisest of her cousins, but something deep down told her she was right to be cautious with Gabo.

"Ok, ok, get off my back, sheesh. I'll figure it out, don't worry." Alicia replied "Oh! I forgot to tell you I applied for a non-for-profit finance job that starts four months from now," she said with excitement only to be met with silence on the other side. "Aayala?"

"That's good, but think about what I said. A new job, even if its non-for profit, might not be the solution you think it is," warned Aayala.

"How could you say that, though? You are doing what you love. I'm just existing right now,"

"Babe, if I believed the move and a job were going to solve all your problems, I would pack you up myself, but I don't think it will solve anything. Just think about what I said, ok? Bye babes," Aayala said.

Alicia's shoulders slumped at the weight of Aayala's words. The lack of support was disappointing.

"Ok, bye." She replied, dejected.

Why did no one support her decision?

GABO

Moving to Florida with his freelance consulting job and a dream project was like bungee jumping without a safety cord. There were days he was plagued by the free fall sensation deep in his stomach, other days, it was exhilarating. Seeing Alicia last week solidified his decision was the correct one. The sense of certainty a welcome change.

Even though she'd shot him down, and he was dealing with the hangover of the courage it took to ask her out, he realized their paths would soon cross again. It would be hard to avoid her with their houses located behind each other. He wanted the opportunity to catch up and hear about her life these past years. See that smile again, spy those dimples. Be a part of her life, as her friend.

The week was filled with consulting gigs and he had little time to focus on their non-for-profit plans, so he dedicated Friday to put together all the research Mason and he had gotten through the year. They both sat in a large two-person desk in the middle of his old parents' bedroom, now their office. The table was wide enough that each of them had a good amount of space and leg room and they had ergonomic chairs.

"Ok, so, the idea is to place The Gifted Athletes Center of Broward in an area that is accessible for the youth that need it the most," Mason said while typing on his laptop.

"Yes, I saw you scouted a few locations close to our old high school."

"The center should be easy for the kids to walk over after school I want it to be their hang out space. We can mentor and support their sport scholarships efforts and help them with academics, job opportunities if they don't get into college."

"You don't have to preach to the choir," he said, knowing all the reasons Mason felt so passionate about their project. "I'm thinking we look at some of these locations before we work on grant proposals."

"That sounds good. I have to rearrange my schedule in the restaurant, but I can make it happen," Mason said.

"Now that you say restaurant. When are you going to invite me to have dinner?" Gabo sat back.

"Whenever you want to come through, my dude. When you are best friends with the Executive Chef, you are well connected. But, there is a condition. If I buy you dinner, you have to tell me all about seeing Alicia again. You were giving nothing on the ride home last week." Mason said.

Gabo had been out of sorts after being with Alicia and getting to connect with her, if only for an instant. After hearing her turn his invitation down, all the reasons he berated himself for not trying harder to reach out to her after their fall out came back to his head, crowding his memories and put him into a pensive mood.

"Yeah, it was a bit of a mind fuck seeing her again. I was happy to see her, though. I invited her for drinks and she turned me down."

"Mhm, it seems you both know how to hold a grudge," Mason said with slight exasperation.

"Nah, is not like that man. She explained she was busy with work and apparently she is selling Mr. and Mrs. Powell's house."

"Oh man, that would be the end of an era. I always thought the two of you would find a way to end up together, not sure why the two houses were part of my master dream for you two."

"What are you trying to hook us up? Nah, you have it all wrong." He shook his head, his heart tripping a little.

The reality was, he always understood he and Alicia were meant to be friends and friends only, even with him secretly wishing they could be more. He recognized this and was very careful not to confuse the two. True lasting friendship and romantic love had no compatibility. He had yet to see a successful friendship evolve to more without things going wrong along the way.

"Alicia and I are meant to be friends and nothing more." He pushed his chair back and stood, restlessness attacking him after sitting for the better part of the day. Mason stared at him, waited for him to crack, and he refused to say more.

"So you aren't going to tell me if she's fine as hell then?" Mason asked, chiseled eyebrow raised.

"I said we were to be friends only, not that I had grown blind after my visit to her." He matched Mason's eyebrow.

"So spill."

Gabo sighed, then ran his hand over his hair.

"She was, just beautiful, man. I don't have words for it. She is just perfectly Alicia"

"Yeah," Mason's eyes followed him as he paced back and forth, "you always had a soft spot for all that ass and curves."

He turned around and scoffed when he saw Mason was playing around, trying to bait him into saying more.

"Stop, she was my best friend I was smooth about the rest. I wasn't thirsting," he said.

"I'll get you the definition for 'smooth and thirst' for our next meeting because you clearly missed that lesson day in school." Mason's laugh carried on for minutes.

CHAPTER 6

Another week flew by in a rush of meetings, reports, and over analysis of the state of her life by every family member close to her. Everyone and their mother had an opinion on what she should do about her lack of friends outside of her family, the sale of the house, and her potential move to New York. She'd been close to visiting Gabo so many times, but at the end, she'd held firm to her conviction that attempting to rekindle their friendship was not a good idea. Things happened for a reason, and she was in a forward trajectory. There was no space for what if's in her life.

She needed a break this weekend and couldn't stand another stay-at-home Friday with thoughts of the house, memories of the past or her non-existing friendship with Gabo stressing her out. She hoped to link up with Mariana for some drinks at their usual spot she frequented when she was in the mood to go out, after her work day was over.

Alicia: Fidler tonite at 8?
Mariana: I'm down! Gives me time to dress up!
Alicia: Yeah I don't see myself leaving until about 6pm from here and I want to go home first
Mariana: Sounds like a plan honey, see you tonite!

Alicia put down her cellphone, a slight smile on her face now that she had some type of plans for the evening then dove back to her work. She was deep into a report due at the beginning of next week when her cellphone vibrated on her desk. It was an email in her personal account. The sender was from the organization she had applied for last week hoping to speed up her move to NY by having an incentive to push through the last steps of her move.

Her hands tingled. This was a nationwide organization that provided pro bono law support and guidance for Black people immigrating from any country in the world, due to financial hardship, or geopolitical safety reasons. The organization did tremendous work to keep family together in the United States that otherwise would be separated because of their lack of knowledge of immigration laws.

She opened the email:

Ms. Powell-Torres,

We received your application for our Director of Finance open position and would be thrilled to set up an interview with you this upcoming week. Please reply with your availability for an hour video-call next Wednesday, Thursday or Friday from 12pm EST onwards.

We look forward to your reply,

Angela Garcia

VP of Human Relations and Community Liaison.

Her heart skipped a beat and that fluttery sensation in her stomach bust out in full force. She couldn't believe they contacted her so fast. Her hand hovered over the phone screen keyboard, wondering if it would seem too eager to answer the email right away. Who cared? This was her ticket out of this state of nothingness she was living every day. Doing this work would ensure she was putting her talents to the right use.

Dear Ms. Garcia,

I am honored to have been selected as a candidate for an interview. I am open to meet next Thursday at 1:00pm EST. I look forward to the details of our video call.

Warm Greetings,

Alicia Powell Torres

TONIGHT SHE WORE A BLACK SHEER MESH YOKE WITH HER DARK wash skinny jeans. She had her hair in a high bun, her braided ends tucked in, all-natural eye makeup accentuating her eyelashes, and her lips in deep burgundy matte lipstick. The lipstick was a new buy, and she was living for it, she looked good and the strain of self-consciousness that hit her sometimes was not present at all today.

After much debate, she had decided not to tell her family about the interview. Her mother would fret, Mariana would get pissed at her for pushing through with the plan to move, and Aayala would only try to psychoanalyze her to see if this was what she needed right now, while assuring her she couldn't wait to see her in New York. They all meant well, but she just needed to do this for herself and she could not find the words to explain to them why it was so important to her. But she realized she needed the change, sleeping was getting harder at night and she was drained all the time.

She went downstairs, put on the red dark high heels of the night, and walked out to meet Mariana in her car.

"Oye prima, you are looking good!" Mari shouted above the reggaeton blasting from her sound system. Mari looked incredible, her coils popping and beautiful around her face, and her purple jumpsuit, from what she could see of her in her car, was hugging all the curves. Alicia got in and brought the volume down.

"Why are you coming to this peaceful neighborhood making all this noise, que escándalo tú tienes." She shook her head.

"Ay please, I need to listen to my tunes before the bar just to amp up," Mari smiled and winked at her and Alicia could only shake her head.

"Thank you prima, you look great too. Love that body-suit! I wish we were the same size we could exchange clothes."

"Mija, I would kill for your rack and those hips of yours… uff I'm gonna to have to keep them off you tonight."

"I can't with you! Vámonos que es viernes y el cuerpo lo sabe! Turn up the volume!" Alicia said with a big smile on her face.

GABO

Gabo was looking forward to a couple of drinks with Mason and some of Mason's colleagues from work. The night lights of South Florida flew by while he and Mason sat in companionable silence, beyond the radio sounds filling Mason's car.

Today, they'd received some disturbing news that brought an additional sense of urgency to their project. The kids of the school they wanted to pilot their first year had heard some of the big college scouts were reconsidering coming to see their varsity teams after their marquee teams had a couple of tough seasons in the past two years.

"Dude, we need to get the rent settled on the location we choose ASAP. These kids need a place where they can get counseling and guidance if the scholarships they had been working all their lives fall through." Mason broke the silence, putting in words their concerns.

"I have been working nonstop on the grants applications, but the process is lengthy. I don't see us having access to any funds from grants in the next couple of weeks. I've been doing my homework about sponsorship and funding, but we had that set for the second stage of the project," he said, matching Mason's concern. This was all his responsibility, grants, fundraising plans. It all fell under his current role.

They worked through the years with youth living in low-income areas of the city, that were departing high school with no sports college scholarships after working their asses off to get into college. Many of them had no other avenues and ended up in jobs that didn't match their skill set or passion, just to make ends meet for their families. They had sponsored scholarships through other friends that were in different industries, as well as provided vocational education access. But they wanted to do it on a bigger scale, reach out to more youth.

"I don't want to fail them." Mason hit the steering wheel in frustration.

"Yes, same here. I'm visiting my parents early tomorrow and will get some insight from Pops, and let you know what trees he can shake with his connections, we'll make this happen."

Mason sighed, "Sorry for the worry. We had said we

would enjoy tonight and tackle this tomorrow. Let's have a good time."

The bar Mason brought Gabo to was a cool little spot. People their age congregated in small groups around the patio, and the tables and booths inside. A large dark bar was on the end of the indoor space and opposite to that were a row of booths where Mason lead him as they walked inside the bar.

"Yo, yo, yo! Everyone can relax. I made it and the fun and games can start now!" Mason boomed to his coworkers, who all exchanged handshakes, hugs, and kisses. There were at least ten people in the group and he did his best to learn everyone's name as they shouted it to him over the music. He was definitely not in New York anymore. The affection Mason's friends gave him via friendly pats on the back and warm welcomes were not something he was used to back in his old city.

"Everyone, this is my best friend Gabo. We have known each other since we were six years old he just moved back from New York, so treat him kindly!" Everyone waved and cheered.

"I don't understand how all of you keep up with this guy, but for those of us who put up with him for free, I thank you from the bottom of my heart." More laughs and banter continued as he got to meet all of Mason's coworkers.

He stood next to Mason and asked, "You sure you don't want me to drive tonight?"

"Nah bruh, go get your drink. Enjoy."

Gabo waded through the room. The crowd had grown since they had arrived. He was able to get a spot on the corner of the bar and asked the bartender for a whiskey on the rocks. The music was getting loud enough that you could still hear someone if they were speaking close to you, but loud enough that you could shimmy by your table and vibe to the music.

The bartender served him a glass of Glenlevit when he heard a voice close to him, "I'm so glad to learn you have good taste in spirits."

He turned around and Alicia was standing right behind him, her hand on the bar. She signaled the bartender, "another one Manny please."

Her luscious deep red lips were all he could see at first because his eyes and his brain refused to focus elsewhere, then his eyes traveled over her, taking in what he hadn't last time he saw her. This is how he would think of her from now on instead of the nineteen-year-old young woman he had for his mental picture of her. She was stunning. But he reminded himself only friendship would ever work for them. So instead, he focused on her eyes again.

"So, you're in first name basis with the bartender?" He asked.

She cocked her head, eyes suspicious. "Yes, Manny is Sra. Gloria's youngest down the corner of my street."

"Oh, I remember him as a little kid!" He nodded in recognition.

"Yes well, he does this on the weekends while he goes to college to FIU so Mari and I frequent the spot," She shrugged as if it was normal to come to a bar, because the neighbor's youngest kid needed tips to support himself during college. "That, and the fact that the average person here is thirty versus nineteen."

"Yes, I noticed, that was my only condition when Mason said we were going out today. I did not want to be in no early twenties joint. My ears nor my liver can keep up with that type of partying anymore." He took her drink from Manny, the bartender-neighbor, and gave it to her while she laughed at his old man joke.

"So you're here with Mason," she smiled up at him, "maybe later Mariana and I'll stop by and say hello."

"Sounds good, and then we can have that drink together." He smiled at her with friendly attentiveness. Or so he hoped.

"Gracias Manny! Ahora doy otra vuelta." Her fingers twirled in a circular motion, telling Manny she would be back.

Manny smiled at her, gave him a nod, and then turned back to the next person vying for attention. When he turned around to look at her, she was already walking away, back to where he could see her cousin Mariana waiting. Giving in to the moment, his eyes followed Alicia as he indulged in looking at her until he saw Mariana staring at him, smile wide. Fuck. He was helpless.

ALICIA

"Come on. I haven't seen Gabo in a long time so we are going to their table to say hello. Why are you acting like you don't want to go over there?" Mariana did the chin point every self-respecting Panamanian knew how to do.

Alicia was dancing to the music, her body swaying to the beat. She had been blessed as all the Torres, with undeniable rhythm and a love for dancing. She looked over the table where Gabo and Mason were chilling. All of them were laughing loud, dancing and singing along to the '00 tunes. It looked like fun. Dammit.

"Vamos Chiquita, here we are, only the two of us, when we could hang out with them!" Said Mari over the music.

"I can't stand you sometimes, you know that?" Alicia said

with a smile. She looked over again, then back at Mariana "Ok, ok, let's go over there, but nada de show!" she warned.

"Quién, me?" Mariana's mock innocent face was too much for her as she walked past holding her hand out so they could navigate the crowd without being separated.

They walked up to the group just as Mason was pushing Gabo to dance with a white girl with a pretty smile and kind eyes. She looked at them, then turned to Mason.

"I heard the devil was here, so I came to pay my respects," she told Mason, who turned around and smiled at her.

"Ms. Powell Torres! I'm honored to have you come to our little table." Mason's mocked bowed with a smile then he looked behind her winced for a second. Then was back to smiling. Had she imagined that?

"Ms. Torres Charles, always a pleasure." Mason's eyes twinkled when he greeted Mariana.

Mari stepped from behind her and gave Mason a kiss. Mason stood stock still, barely moving or breathing while she leaned into him. The same expression, not quite pain, maybe longing, appeared over his face.

"Hola, guapo." Mari smiled and moved on to say hello to everyone at the table without waiting for introductions. All the while, Mason stood there like a lightning bolt had hit him.

She scanned everyone's faces until her eyes connected with Gabo, who had somehow extricated himself from the brunette by gently guiding her to her friends. The girl was tipsy and the gentleness he used was one thing she had forgotten about him.

She could tell Gabo saw the entire interaction with Mason and Mari, because as he approached her, he just shook his head. He stood beside her and looked at her for a minute while she enjoyed his gaze in ways she couldn't explain. Then he gave her a soft, lingering kiss on her cheek.

His short beard grazed against her cheek, making her shiver. He smelled delicious and she could not help but close her eyes, taking it all in.

"I wasn't able to say a proper hello earlier. Took you long enough to come over." He whispered against her ear as he stood far too close for comfort. After all these years, he made her experience things long forgotten. His gentle baritone stimulated her. She would even venture to say he'd overstimulated her and her body, just by one kiss on the cheek as greeting, and a few words whispered in her ear.

"Yeah, Mariana didn't leave me much of a choice. I was enjoying our little party of two we had going on, and staring at this fun group with contempt. How dare y'all have a good time?" she said.

"I could sense the daggers from over here. I tried to scale back on the fun after that. Made sure we weren't showing off too much." his tone full of laughter and deep warmth. His voice drifted through her like warm whiskey on a chilly night, something she adored. The way he set her at ease even though they hadn't talked in such a long time was not even surprising to her. They'd always been like this, even after arguments they bounced back to their reset mode, Alicia and Gabo. The rest button had been stuck for fifteen years, but now that they released, the same ease of the past came rushing back.

"So, how come you moved back after all these years, huh?" She tried her best not to put too much weight to the question.

"Why? Are you curious?" A slow smile bloomed on his lips. He took a sip of his drink, eyes never leaving her.

"You can keep your mysterious reasons."

"No really, what do you want to know? I want to answer all your questions." The emphasis he placed on "all" didn't escape her attention. The way it made her heart pound wasn't missed, either.

"I was just wondering why you moved back. You've been in New York for so long."

He shrugged. "It was time. Maybe I got brave enough to come face to face with you again..." The playful smile of his remained, but his eyes were over-sharing, telling her much more. She wasn't sure she wanted or was ready to know.

"Nothing was stopping you before."

"You right. But now, the time was right."

She realized they were leaning towards each other. The music was loud now, pumping through her veins and her insides were on free fall. She hated rollercoasters, and this was too close to that feeling of complete suspension; Gabo around her again. He was gazing at her, face intent and open. She felt that draw, the evermore sensation she translated to being near to him.

Goddess, I cannot do this again.

She broke his gaze, needing a second to compose herself. Being this close to him after such a long time... She looked around to Mason's friends all having fun and she realized Mason and Mariana were nowhere to be found.

"Oh shit."

"What, what happened?" Gabo sipped his drink, gazing at her.

"Your best friend and my cousin, happened. I think one or both of us might need a ride home tonight."

GABO

Alicia had been right, but Mason had the decency to leave his keys with one of his friends, after telling the group he did not want to interrupt Gabo and Alicia while they "made up".

Gabo had only had one drink, and he was more than sober, which was the good news.

The bad news was that the connection he had with Alicia dissipated the instant she realized they'd been left behind. He wanted to be glad for the interruption, but couldn't shake the impression that she'd also been affected by how close they had been.

"Man, I can't believe Mason made me come out here to then leave me behind. I'm gonna give him so much shit tomorrow." He was cruising on the highway, the exit for their community looming in the distance.

"With those two, I don't ask questions anymore," she said.

"Does this happen often? I mean, Mason doesn't speak about it a lot, but he mentions whenever he's seen Mariana. I didn't realize that this was a recurring..." he left the thought unfinished. His best friend and Alicia's cousin's private life were not for him and Alicia to analyze.

"I'm not one to tell tales, and I don't think you are asking me to," she looked at him sideways, "so I'll say that next time that Mason mentions Mariana, casually try to dig a little more. Who knows, he might open up."

"I may try that. Did she ask you about us?" He left his voice casual.

"Yes, you are the only thing we talk about. My whole life revolved around wondering about you," she said, her voice droll.

"You always resort to sarcasm when you are nervous. Good to know some things haven't changed," He volleyed back.

"Nervous. You wish. My entire family is ecstatic you're back. I swear they thought we would get married and have babies. When we stopped talking, they took that as a personal insult." She shook her head, making her braids sway from side to side. "My mom couldn't understand for months what happened."

He glanced at her and back to the road. She was playing with a braid she had tugged out of her bun and had removed her heels and tucked her legs under her, the picture of comfort. Listening to her talking about the past was harder than he expected. It was a wound that should have healed a long time ago, only to realize it was still in need of stitches.

"Neither did I Alicia. It took me a long time to understand what went so horribly wrong that day. I mean, I understand why you were upset, and I think I understand why you didn't want to talk to me after. But during those months, when you weren't picking up my calls and couldn't be bothered to even answer my text and emails… it was hard missing you, and I was low key angry at you,"

"You were angry, at me?" She looked at him like he had just grown horns. In theory, he was the bad guy at the end of their story. He had not wanted to touch on this subject tonight, not when he had her attention and her tentative acceptance. He just wanted to start over. There was no use bringing up the past. It was all done.

"Look, I don't want to rehash everything that happened back then. What I want to say to you is that our friendship meant the world to me. I cherished it always. I don't know if we can go back to what we used to be, but I would like to be your friend again." He slowed down for the gate access and gave time for Alicia to absorb what he was putting out. After fifteen years, there was a lot to absorb.

He parked next to her car in the driveway and turned to her.

Her face was pensive now, her hair all down from the bun, falling over her back and shoulders. Eyelashes hid her eyes, and he wished he was privy to her thoughts and silences.

Alicia's lips pursed in thought, still vibrant after all these hours, her breasts full under the mesh material of her top that covered her soft belly, large hips and thighs arranged for her comfort and not to intentionally draw his eyes; but he could not stop admiring her.

"I'm tired, I've a lot to do tomorrow." Her soft husky voice punctured the silence that had lulled them both. She continued, "Thanks for driving me home. I need time to process. I don't know if this is a good idea."

He sighed in frustration. Gabo didn't want to rehash the past, and regretted saying anything earlier. He just wanted her as a friend again. "Would it help if we agreed not to speak about the past?" he asked.

She shrugged "That might work. It is late and it's not right to keep you here while my mind is in a million different places. How about we exchanged cellphones?" she handed him her phone, an olive branch he would hold on to tonight. He placed his number in her cellphone and called himself from it, prompting his phone ring.

"There, now we are connected." She reached forward, and he thought she was reaching for her phone but she was leaning for a kiss goodnight, her soft full lips touched his right cheek and the same scent he smelled earlier of coconut, lemon and something earthy that called to him, enticed him again.

"Have a good night Gabo." She left his car in a whirlwind of braids and lemon.

AS HE PREPARED HIMSELF FOR BED, HE STOOD IN THE DARKNESS by his window and looked across. Since they'd seen each other, Alicia had been very careful about keeping her curtains closed. Tonight they were open and there she stood, a quizzical smile on her face.

She held a large cardboard that read:

WOULD YOU BE MY FRIEND: YEA OR NAH

He picked up his phone and texted her while standing still watching her:

Gabo: Yea, every single time, yea.

CHAPTER 7

It was mid-morning and Alicia was wearing her favorite apron with the words "Whatever happens, we are eating it". She hadn't stopped baking since she woke up at 6:30 a.m. on Saturday.

She used to love to wake up early on the weekends. Her mom used to sleep in on Saturdays as it was the only day of the week she could afford to do so, her father and her would wake up at the crack of dawn and sit in the kitchen talking about everything and anything and cooking up salt fish and akee or porridge for breakfast. Mornings were their special time together and when he passed it became one of the hardest times of the day. She'd learned to keep busy now, she did yoga, if the spirit called her to move, or she would clean up the apartment top to bottom and be done by 9 a.m.. Today she was doing one of her favorite pastimes: baking.

The house smelled like pineapple goodness from the upside-down cakes that were in the oven. Next, she planned to bake mini rum cakes. The cinnamon cassava muffins pan she had made first had already seen some casualties.

Having spent time with Gabo, talking to him, being near him had been nerve-wracking. The short time they'd been together had been enough for him to peel some layers off her well-constructed armor, and she was vulnerable. He'd been so earnest about being friends again and she'd been lured by how easy it had been to banter again with him, laugh and bask in his presence. With a few sentences, Gabo had managed to make her rethink her stance about keeping him at bay. It was the familiarity of him, his quiet reserve that disappeared when she was with him, and the way she was so relaxed around him. She missed that old Alicia, the one that looked at everything with excitement and optimism.

If Alicia were to go to a therapist, they would say baking was a coping mechanism for her, as she tended to bake extensively when stressed. If you were to ask Alicia, she just loved sugary baked goods, and no one could tell her different. Above all, she loved gifting her creations to her friends and family. Today's lucky recipient of her bake goods: her Tío Toño and his crew.

"Buenos días familia!" Alicia said, now free of flour and sugar after taking a shower before bringing her boxed goodies to South West Ranches. Mariana, the angel, had cursed her to hell and back when she had called at seven asking where she could find her father this morning. Alicia assumed she regretted some of her decisions from last night, so she took pity on her and asked no questions, but her cousin owed her some answers come Monday. Alicia hadn't missed the fact that she and Mason didn't seem surprised to have bumped into each other at the bar last night.

"Sobrina, what a miracle to see you this morning." The site was a new build, what looked like a six-bedroom house with a lot of land around it. The project seemed to be half done, all the walls had been erected, and roof and window install seem to be the projects of the day.

She hugged her tío then gestured to her car. "Come, help me get all these boxes full of yummy cakes and muffins.

Her uncle's eyes sparkled at the news of cakes. "Did you make my volteao de piña?"

"Of course, how could I bring you goodies and not make your favorite?"

After unloading all the boxes and placing them by the trailer where the team took their lunch, her uncle turned around and bluntly said, "Bueno, I'm glad you came personally to ask me for your favor."

She should have guessed Tío Toño would not make this easy for her.

"Mira Tío, I'm sorry I sent Mari to ask, but you and I don't always see eye to eye."

"Understatement of the year, como dice Milita" her uncle scoffed, "I think you're wasting time waiting for life to turn a corner and suddenly become perfect. The world doesn't work like that. Moving to the north ain't going to fix your problems. But what do I know? I'm just an old man."

Looking at her uncle, it was hard not to think of her mother. They were paternal twins and had very similar mannerisms and movements. It made her miss her.

"Mira mija, I will do the job. I don't want any arguments with you, and your mom has asked me to stay out of it, so I'll stay out of it. You are my family, and no matter what, family looks after each other. Pero, I cannot start until the beginning of December."

Panic raced through her. December was too late, the work from what she understood would take a few weeks, and after that, she needed to speak to Reg to put the house back on the market. To wait so long in limbo made her anxious. Meanwhile, her interview was next week, and if she moved on to the next round and got the job she would need to move to New York end of December at the latest. She was getting ahead of herself. She needed to do things one step at a time.

"December? Is there anything I can do to help speed up the process?"

"Unless you can finish this project for us and the roofing projects already contracted after this one, I don't think so. The weather hasn't been our friend this month, so this project is behind. I've another crew out doing a significant renovation, but my roofing guys are all booked up.

"Could I at least start something on my own?"

"Bueno, your cousin said you need to do some upgrades to the landscape outside and in the front; if you are adventurous, go for it, that will help with timing."

She wasn't sure she could do it, but she could at least give it a shot, anything to speed up the process and get her out of here and into her new life. A life that would put her away from Gabo...

"Ok, Tío, if anything moves up?"

"Of course, chiquita, if anything moves up, I'll be there with the crew to do to get that house ready for the market."

GABO

Gabo drove into the community his parents lived in and couldn't help but laugh remembering Doris and her deadpan comment about sex parties. The community was large, with winding roads and clubhouses full of senior citizens living their silver years in style. The landscape was impressive, with beautiful tropical plants and flowers interspersed between properties and large manufactured lakes creating paths to walk and relax.

John and Mercedes Miller had a loving relationship

rooted in traditional gender roles. He was the kid with the stay-at-home mom who always had lunch ready for him after school and took care of the house and all his father's needs. She was fiercely intelligent, having studied engineering in Colombia, and met her dad while studying for her master's degree. They fell in love, and the rest was history.

He never understood why his mother decided not to work, but it seems she was content with her life, and that is all he could ask for, but sometimes he wondered if she would have done it differently if she had a chance.

He parked the car outside the bungalow and grabbed the flowers he brought his ma and the whiskey for his pops.

"Gabriel Ernesto, mi niño!" His mom enveloped him in a warm fierce hug.

"Gaby, so good of you to visit us this weekend," his pops said an undercurrent of chastisement in his voice, utilizing the nickname only his parents used for him. Gabo hadn't had time to come and visit them until now, and it seems the old man was making sure he felt the sting of his disappointment. It was always like these passive-aggressive undercurrents that made him think he was not quite what his pops had envisioned for a son.

"Stop it, John. He has been busy, and he'd let us know all he has been working on. Ven, I made you some arepitas for you to eat."

"POPS, I WANTED TO ASK YOU FOR A BIG FAVOR IF YOU COULD." He had spent a pleasant day with his parents. His mom made him dance with her, as his dad had two left feet, and she took advantage anytime he visited to dance salsa and merengue with him. After a couple of beers, they were all sitting in the backyard.

"Mason and I were planning to make sponsorship and donation requests in stages after we had started the organization and we're doing the groundwork. However, we found out that the two colleges that do most of the scouting for the school where the students go are going to potentially pull out this year." "That is horrible, mijito," his mom interjected, looking outraged.

He nodded. "It is, so we are looking to accelerate our timeline of the actual brick and mortar building where the students can come, get the center up and running."

"And I'm guessing you need my connections?" His dad was sitting back in his recliner, beer in hand.

"Let me ask you this before I answer. Do you think this was the right time for you to leave your director position at the college?" his dad asked, sparking an ongoing debate since he'd moved.

"I think I made the right decision at the right time. My skill sets make me the perfect person to partner with Mason, and this is something we have been working on for many years. This is not a surprise, and I hope you can respect that," Gabo said.

His dad nodded pensively. Whenever he used words such as respect, that was code for his dad to step back for a while.

"Ok, yes, I have some connections that I think would be useful for you. Let me make some calls and play some rounds of golf, and I'll let you know what comes of it." His dad took another sip of his beer. His mom sat next to him and placed her warm hand on his shoulder, her way of telling him she would make sure the old man followed through.

"Ven Gabo, help me inside to clean up," his mom asked.

He followed his Mom inside while his Pops dozed off on the porch. She looked over to make sure he was not listening and then turned around to Gabo. "I spoke with Juanita a few days ago."

Ah, here we go.

"She said Alicia is back in the house and trying to sell it," his mom continued.

"Yes, your sources are good, Ma." He kept washing the dishes and passing them to her to dry. He gave her a plate and was met with air. There she stood, hands crossed over her chest.

"And you weren't going to tell me all of this?" she protested. He sighed. His Ma always dreamed that Alicia would be her daughter-in-law. She refused to believe it wasn't going to happen, so when he saw Alicia again, he didn't tell his mom. He didn't want to get her hopes up for nothing.

"Yes, Ma, I was planning to tell you. Let me just say that I'm not planning to date Alicia. We are just trying to reconnect as friends."

His mom scoffed then said something in Spanish under her breath that sounded very much like, "Friend is the cheese to the rat, he eats it."

"Ma. No one is eating anyone," he said with a mock stern tone.

"Are you sure? I would bet on that," she answered back.

"Ma!"

"Ok, hijo, I won't say much, but I'll say this, Alicia is one of those rare true friends, and whatever happened between both of you, you fix it, and you make sure she stays close to you, ok?"

He kept washing the dishes, and she kept drying, her point made.

CHAPTER 8

GABO

> Gabo: Good Morning, Alicia
> Alicia: No jodas, it's too early. Go back to sleep
> Gabo: It's ten...
> Alicia: I regret giving you my number. I'll be going to Verizon first thing tomorrow and changing it.
> Gabo: Want some Arepas for breakfast?
> Alicia: I'll be there in 10.

"Mmmm, this is so good." Alicia was slaying the arepas and huevos he made for her. The arepas were his mother's recipe. He was enjoying himself too much watching her eat his food. Also, the moans. He was enjoying her moans. He'd been nervous while texting her in the morning, worried she'd be weary of coming over. Old Gabo would have let the nervousness win, and let things happen naturally, hoped for the best and wait patiently. But one of the things he'd learn these past few years was that you couldn't wait for life to happen, you needed to make it happen.

"If you say 'that's what she said' I'll walk out of that sliding door and take all the arepas with me, ok?" She looked at him while daintily wiping her lips with a napkin.

"Do you want one more?" Gabo sat across her on the tall table in his parents' kitchen. The morning light illuminated her face, and contentment shone through.

"If you insist, I don't want to insult the chef." She shrugged as if she didn't care.

"Oh right. Thanks for your sacrifice."

"Someone needs to do the hard work, and I'm here for it. Mrs. M's recipe is the best."

Alicia looked lovely today. Her hair vibrant this morning, plunged in tight coils over her shoulders. No makeup. She'd taken a quick shower, put on leggings and an oversized t-shirt, and ran over for his mom's famous arepas.

"What? Do I have a booger on my face?" She asked. She used to ask him all the time when they were young, and she caught him staring. His neck heated suddenly, and he moved to the kitchen to clear the sink.

"Of course not. If you did, I wouldn't have allowed it to stay there for long. I'd have swiped it off your face."

"Ew, no, we aren't that close yet, sir. You keep your booger swipes to yourself," she said with mock disdain.

"So, do you have any plans for the day?"

"Why Gabo, you are making me lunch too?" she said around a smile.

"I'll make you anything you like." He peeked a look and was pleased when her face dipped down, and that dimple appeared. He wanted to have a love affair with that dimple.

"Nah, thanks for the offer, though. I have to go to Home Depot to get gardening tools and a ladder."

He turned around, wiping his hands on the kitchen towel.

"Tell me more…" The Alicia he remembered was not very manual work oriented. She was great with arts and crafts and baking, but housework wasn't her favorite. At least, it wasn't before. Her dad would try to get her to help him with the gardening, and she always managed to find something she had to do and get out of the chore.

"Yes, I have to start working on the landscape in the back of the house for this sale. I have to spruce things up." Hesitation was written all over her face. He moved closer and leaned against the counter facing the table she was still sitting at.

"Well, if you need any help, I'm your man. I can go along with you for the ride," he shrugged nonchalantly. But inside, he wanted her to say yes. This was him, making life happen.

She stared at him for a minute, then smiled. "Ok, let's do it, Miller, let's go to Home Depot."

ALICIA

"I really hate hardware stores."

Gabo chuckled at her disgruntlement as he drove her car back to their neighborhood.

"Why? It was a productive trip," Gabo asked as if he was indeed intrigued and hadn't listened to her complain for an hour and a half straight.

"I hadn't any idea on what to get. I'm in over my head with this project."

"Why are you doing the landscape? I thought you mentioned Toño was going to work on some home repairs for the house?"

She sighed. She didn't want to get into too much detail with Gabo while so much was still up in the air. Every time she thought about her interview on Thursday, she got a stomach cramp. The day had been so lovely so far. The promise of their friendship made her hesitant to explain too much about what was happening with her move. When he'd reached out this morning she had trusted her instinct, which seemed to need a good polish versus trusting her head. So far, her instinct was proving to be correct. She enjoyed every minute of their time together and could sense the seeds of their old friendship attempting to sprout again.

"I'm trying to get the house sold by the end of the year. I've been exploring some opportunities to work off state, maybe closer to my family in New York, nothing set in stone but getting the house squared away would be a weight off my shoulders."

"I can help you with the landscape if you want. I'm, no expert but the two of us can figure it out."

She sighed in relief, thankful that he wasn't going to make a big deal out of her move. She glanced at him while he was focused on driving.

"I guess you expected me to have more to say about you moving away?" Busted, it seemed he'd become more perceptive with time.

"Look, I just came into your life again. I can't expect to know all these details, but I think I know you, even after all this time. If you think moving is a good step, then there must be a damned good reason. I'm sure you made a list of pros and cons, maybe a little diagram too, just to be extra thorough." he smiled.

"Like we used to do to figure out what video game you should buy, and what books and CDs for me?" She had the sweetest memories of those times.

"Yeah just, like that, we thought we were rich but, that summer job money ran out fast. Pro and cons always helped, didn't they? I can't say I'm not disappointed to hear you are thinking of moving," he shrugged, "but I hope no matter what happens, we stay talking. I'll help you get the landscape ready."

A wave of gratefulness washed over her. Finally, someone that respected her decision. Of course, it had to be Gabo.

"Thanks. I have forgotten who I am a bit," she breathed. "After Daddy passed, my life became more difficult. Mom moved back to Panama and...it's been hard, that's all."

His hand, warm and large, squeezed hers. Gabo understood how larger than life her daddy had been for her. The loss of him had been devastating.

"I came to see your mother after the funeral."

"My mom told be about your visit. Thank you for that." She nodded.

"It is ok. I wanted to come to the funeral but, I didn't know if I was welcome." he said.

"So you wrote me that beautiful message and sent me all those books. They kept me sane," she said. His hand was warm on top of hers. For a fanciful instant, she imagined him in her life after the funeral. Having him as the wall to lean on to keep from crumbling. Even that small gesture had been an oasis to her when everything seemed dry.

"Why didn't you reply then? I just wanted to make sure you were ok."

"I know, I'm sorry, I was just too lost at that time. I read them all, though. Sweet stories about redemption and second chances..." she trailed off. She hadn't missed the underlying message of the books, but at that time she'd not been ready to reach out. Everything surrounding her father's death reminded her of the past and how hurt she'd been with him, and why they'd grown apart. It had all been too raw.

"It was the least I could do. I told you with those books what I couldn't tell you back then."

There was a hollowness that never left her now. But the

warmth he managed to fill with his mere presence was a welcome change.

WHENEVER SHE HAD A NEW OUTFIT ON, IT MEANT SHE WAS SET to have a fantastic day. She was wearing a gray jumpsuit with structured oversized sleeves with a hint of cleavage and wide legs, and the ensemble was giving her all she needed. She was power walking down the hall to her office after having lunch with her coworkers in a nearby café when she got a message.

Gabo: Hello, old friend.

Alicia and Gabo had chilled together for the past two weeks as if they hadn't been separated for fifteen years. Trusting her instinct had paid off, and they settled into groove of calls, texts and hang outs at each other's place. To be with him again, not having to say much and still be on the same wavelength? It was a heady sensation. The other thing that was heady? Her response to him. She was acting like she hadn't had any in a while. Thank Goddess for her vibrators and steamy romance books because she was in a state since having Gabo back in her life.

Alicia: Old? You have the wrong number, sir.

She turned the last corner and came into her office with a few minutes to spare before meeting with her boss and the director of a non-for-profit organization.

Gabo: after we work on your landscape on Saturday morning, Mason wants us to co-host a bbq and pool party.
Alicia: Work on my landscape, huh?

Gabo: Oh, whenever you want me to, I'll come and fertilize your bush

Alicia: Oh, Gahd. 1 out 10.

Gabo: Ouch

Alicia: tell Mason I said why can't he host his own party? pls quote me

Gabo: what are we 12?

Gabo: never mind don't answer.

Gabo: He knows I'm great with my grill, so he wants us to host.

She checked for new emails, scrolling through to see if Jack had sent any pertinent information before this meeting. Of course, he had sent her no hint of who she was meeting nor the name of the non-for-profit organization.

Alicia: what do I have to contribute to this co-hosting then?

Gabo: your fantastic personality and witty conversation skills. Per Mason. I agree.

Alicia: ok, I'm convinced. Flattery will get you everywhere. I'll make an invite later today.

Gabo: ok, hey can I call you later?

Alicia: sure, everything ok?

Gabo: yeah, let me call you right after this meeting.

She walked in with a perma-smile to the conference room and stopped cold when none other than Gabriel Miller Garcia rose to greet her next to her boss. She couldn't continue to revert to a fifteen-year-old every time she saw this man. The textbook definition of butterflies fluttered in her belly. She also felt some butterflies in other places down south.

It didn't take much to connect that Gabo was the son of a

family friend Jack mentioned as starting a non-for-profit. The world was small.

She noticed Gabo was taken aback, but he found his composure very quickly. He looked scrumptious in a gray suit with a white starched shirt, open at the collar. His hair was freshly cut, fade on point, and for a moment, she wished she could run her hands over his soft hair. *Stop it, Alicia Marie, he is your friend. Only your friend.*

"Gabo, allow me to introduce you to my amazing colleague and the head of finance at Sentinel Hospitality Inc., Alicia Powell Torres. Alicia, this is Gabriel Miller Garcia, his father and my father go way back. Both general managers in their heyday."

Of fucking course, Mr. Miller was Mr. Hospitality himself, and had been the one to get her a foot in for this interview many years ago. She should've put two and two together. Gabo raised one eyebrow, a message that he would follow her lead.

"Actually, Jack, I've known Gabo for many years. We were childhood neighbors." Gabo frowned at her words. "And good friends." she finished, and Gabo's brow relaxed. If Jack thought her answer was odd, he didn't let it show.

"Fantastic! If you both know each other, this should go even smoother, unless you think it would be an issue working together?"

Again, Gabo nodded imperceptibly just for her to know he would be good with whatever she wanted. She took a deep breath, she said, "Why don't we sit down and talk about the project, and then we can decide how we are going to move forward?"

"IF YOU THINK THIS IS TOO WEIRD, I CAN TELL JACK I CAN FIND funds elsewhere." Gabo followed her into her office. The meeting with Jack was short and succinct, laying out how the partnership would work and the starting funds that would be transferred to Gabo's organization to get the center up and running.

She sat down on her desk and fired up her laptop. After a beat, she realized she left him standing and gestured to the chair across her desk.

"Please sit down. This is my office, you can be at ease here," she smiled, hoping the turmoil of spending even more time with Gabo wasn't apparent on her face.

"You sure? Because if I remember well, the looks you've given me today mean you are not too pleased."

"That's not true. But why'd you say things like, 'If I remember well' and 'The Alicia I knew'," she said with a passing imitation of his baritone voice.

"I'm trying to reconcile who you were and who you are now. I miss knowing everything about you. The things that made you vibe. You at thirteen, at sixteen, at nineteen, I knew them all. I could have graduated summa cum laude with a Ph.D. about Alicia Marie Powell Torres. Now, I'm a student that took a few semesters off and is a bit off his game."

She grumbled, secretly flattered at his words. Because she understood, because it was the same for her. Gabo had been her person. The one she could trust the most.

"Well, you're not wrong about my face today. Chilling with you these past two weeks, it has been wonderful, but..."

"Overwhelming?" he said with gentleness. His elbows were on her desk, his body leaning towards her across the space, and damn, he looked fine.

"Yes, Gabo, it's like you came back like a hurricane into my life, and you wanted us to go back to a hundred right away. Now, we have one more thing throwing us together." She pushed back her ergonomic chair. She'd been enjoying their time together, but this? This was an additional thing to pull them together, and she was leery about the whole situation. At the same time, she could not lie to herself, she wanted to help him and she wanted to work with him. But was it fair to either one of them to deepen their friendship when she was planning to leave? She glanced at Gabo and saw he was starting to sweat, she stared at him wondering why he was so hot when she kept her office at seventy degrees.

"Are you alright?" she asked. Gabo took a deep breath, then felt as if steel replaced his backbone.

"Yeah, look, remember how I'd ask you to talk right? Well, I had asked Pops to get me in some doors to secure funding and last night he told me about this meeting...after I had asked him about Jack and his company, I realized it was at your job, but I thought my involvement with you would be minimal. I swear I was going to tell you after the meeting, I didn't think Jack was going to pull you into the project.

I'm not going to sit down here and lie and tell you I'm not glad you are part of the project, because Alicia, now that you are back in my life, I am making moves to ensure you understand I want to be around you. Whatever it takes. Your friendship is that important to me." Gabo finished his speech with an air of a man about to get his ass chewed up. She sensed he realized he was pushing it with this move, but she also understood her personal feelings should not interfere with the good work he and Mason were doing. Still, to commit to this was one more thing pulling her to him, and she had her own plans and dreams to fulfill. A potential job in New York that would shift her focus to giving to her community and, most important, a fresh start away from Florida and all the memories that were suffocating her.

"Is this about you leaving?"

"You know me too well," she mumbled.

"I heard that."

"Yes and no. Look, if we've established a strong enough friendship, we should be able to be friends across states. I realize the last time we tried the long-distance friendship thing, we effed things up a bit. But we aren't children anymore; we can be friends. But committing to The Gifted Athlete's program then bailing out..." she shook her head.

"Let us worry about that if you leave, but for now, we could really use your help."

She could not miss the large "if" he placed in that sentence and couldn't decide if to be relieved or disappointed about his lack of concern in her leaving. She stayed silent, taking him in.

"Don't make me beg Powell, I will, if I have to. Based on the partnerships Jack laid out, we could work together real well. I could use your help on some of the event sponsorship and planning. I'd be lost doing all of that without you." His voice was deep and compelling, and he managed to warm something in her long gone cold. He was leaning all the way on her desk now, so close. It would only take her to stretch a bit to reach across to him. She saw the second he realized, and his eyes flashed with a promise. She sat back, heat enveloping her. She tried to put some distance, now she understood why he was sweating, she was heated herself.

She glanced at him and his earnest, nervous face was what did it for her. She could never refuse him when he deployed those eyes at her, her instinct to help out won out her desire to run for cover.

Ya ok, ok, no need to grovel, Gabo, I'd do anything for you... And Mason." Was that her voice, all breathy? God. She needed to pull herself together. She couldn't not let her conflicting feelings and desires mess her up right now.

Right when she thought they would move on for the conversation, he answered in a low voice that resonated deep inside of her.

"Oh, I don't think you are ready for me to test that 'any-thing'. "But maybe one day I'll take you up on that."

CHAPTER 9

ALICIA

"**B**uenas!" She stood outside of Gabo's gate with some grocery bags for the party later today.

"Alicia, why are you waiting by the gate? My house is your house. I left my side of the gate opened since I came over that night we saw each other."

She smiled at the knowledge. The Florida sun was bearing down on them, heating her skin and masking the flush that grew as she heard Gabo's words. She'd also left her side open but didn't think it was wise to say anything right now. He reached out and grabbed the bags from her, and she followed his fine ass inside of his terrace.

"This is going to be a good day! I brought my wit and great conversation skills," she said cheerily trying to move on from the topic. Hopefully he missed how flustered she got.

"And all this food. I told you not to worry about getting anything. I got a bunch of food."

"Well, yes, but my Mami raised me right. I can't be a co-host, and not bring food, you know I love baking." she answered.

She attempted to act normal but Gabo was tempting her restraint today. His broad back flexed as he put the bags on the kitchen counter. Oh Goddess, if only she could tackle all of that. She was doing her best not to pay attention to her inconvenient attraction for him, but her attraction did not give a shit about her feelings. It had a mind of its own, but now wasn't the time to catch any feelings, physical or otherwise.

"Here, let me put these bags away, I have some empanaditas in the oven, and I'm going to make a ceviche. I also made some cupcakes for dessert. I have to run back to the house to finish getting ready." She stood beside him, and together they worked on unpacking all the stuff she had bought for the party.

"Slow down, Alicia, we have time. People won't be here for few hours."

"I know, but I haven't entertained in a while."

"Why not? Your parents and you used to have people over all the time. What changed?"

"Nothing really, just Daddy..."

"Yes, things haven't been the same in the block after his passing." As two magnets attract each other, her body leaned towards him, and she rested herself for a bit against Gabo. His magnetic field was wreaking havoc on her. Sparks travelled through her as she met his solid body. It was delicious to let go and let him hold her weight.

"I missed you. I'm also looking forward to today," he said into her hair. They stood together, basking on each other's contact, enjoying the silence that could only be comfortable between two people that knew each other beyond words.

OH GOD, HER BELLY WAS GOING TO HURT TOMORROW. THEIR friends had arrived a while ago, and were all hanging out around the pool. Drinks were poured, snacks were passed around, and music helped set the mood for a warm summer day full of good vibes.

"I swear, I keep turning around and wondering, is she talking to me? She thinks I'm in charge? For fuck sakes, who made me the most adult of the adults here?" Mariana had them screaming as she told the story of a stylist that was just learning the ropes and looking for Mariana to guide her through everything.

"Girl, tell me about it. When did we become the ones to call the shots? I'm still not ready to adult. At the same time, I feel I've been one since I was fifteen," said Janina, her coworker and single mother of twin boys.

"That's how it is for most of us. We've had to learn very early to act like adults, but still, it hits a little different at thirty," Mason chuckled, a beer on his hand as he sat next to Mari.

"Thirty? Speak for yourself, Mason. I'm forever twenty-five," Mari's best friend Migue said.

This was the most fun she had in a long time. She hadn't realize how much she'd missed spending time with her friends, letting her guard down and embracing the moment. Gabo sat next to her, her body moved as his shook with laughter as they joked about their thirty and grown stories. To sit this near to him made her very aware... of his presence, to say the least.

Gabo got up from the chaise they were sharing and grabbed fresh drinks from the cooler. When he bent over, her eyes couldn't help but stray. Thank God for sunglasses. Her libido had come raring back to life since Gabo returned to her life at the most inconvenient of times. She glanced back at her friends and spotted Mason smirking at her. She lowered her glasses, stared straight at her friend, and shrugged. Mason laughed out loud.

Gabo strolled back, his steps assured and his posture easy. He delivered her beer and a bottle of water as he sat back down. He'd noticed, without her saying anything, that she had finished her beer.

This man. These were the details that made her melt. The ease they felt with each other was captivating. To have someone that understood her that way he did, and to know him. It made her happy— such a simple word, but so hard to attain. Moments of authentic happiness were as ethereal to her as catching a shooting star these days.

"Thanks, you didn't need to," she said only for his ears.

"Of course I did, gotta take care of my co-host, keep you hydrated." His hand held hers, and that playful warmth became something more. Her treacherous body kept betraying her, responding to Gabo and his nearness. She shifted a little back from the chaise, then decided she needed a cool down. Her hormones needed to get in check and with the program. She couldn't keep lusting after her friend. If she kept up at this pace, she would end up jumping his fine ass.

She stood and stretched, then glanced at her friends. "Who wants to get into the water?" And without further thought, she took off her summer dress and jumped into the pool.

GABO

"If I'd known you were going to burn the ribs, I wouldn't have let you anywhere near my baby backs." Mason's voice startled him out of his daze. Gabo was by the grill getting ribs, burgers, and chorizos ready. His backyard and pool deck were filled with laughter, music, and the scent of suntan lotion, with a hint of smoked BBQ. Gabo couldn't ask for more. A mix of Mason's coworkers, Mariana's friends, and a few of Alicia's coworkers—she called them the melanated army— were all chilling together.

"Bruh, do you need a bib or something? You cannot stop looking at her." Mason said none too quiet. Gabo flipped the burgers. They were indeed on the darker side. Oh well, nothing that a bit of mayoketchup couldn't cure.

He decided to act oblivious. Maybe that would get Mason off his case. "I don't know what you're talking about." At the same time, he tried hard not to look over at where Alicia was laughing with one of her coworkers, Mariana, and Mariana's best friend, the four of them were sitting on the pool ledge. Alicia's laughter had him breathless.

"Oh, so we're playing that game today?" Mason said, looking like that GIF of Charlamagne Tha God where he lifts his glasses in astonishment.

"Are you gonna tell me what's happening with Mariana?" He countered, trying to shift the subject by all means necessary. It was becoming more difficult to pretend he wasn't lusting after his friend, with her riot of curls all around her face, her sunglasses hiding her vision but only making him want to figure out what they would say to him if he had access to them right now. Her dimples were in full display, her joy contagious. She was wearing a pink bathing suit that did her curves fantastic justice and he wished he could tug it down and...best not to go there.

He couldn't help but look once more at the dip of her cleavage, which displayed her breasts to the best advantage. He definitely did not need to be thinking about her titties. At this rate, he would need to jump in the cold pool to avoid any tightness being visible through his swim trunks.

"Ok, that was a great faint, and I'll give you credit for it, but I'll say that if I were you and had an amazing friend like that...'that' in all capital letters, I would have already tried to make a move," Mason said, smirking as he strolled away.

He grabbed a cold beer on the opposite side of the terrace, greeting people as he walked, and came back to the grill. He kept gazing at Alicia as he finished the meats, flipping them absently...oh shit, she was coming towards him. She plunged into the pool while he had been admiring her. She swam towards his end of the pool and climbed the pool ladder.

There are situations one shouldn't have to go through, without having unfettered access to his fist and complete privacy, and this was one of them. Water cascaded from her shoulders down to her body as she pushed up with the momentum, gravity making her curves bounce and move with a buoyancy he wished he could see without the damn bathing suit. Water glistened on her hips and thighs as she grabbed her towel and he got a glimpse of her ass. Ten piedad. The beach towel perfectly hugged her curves as she sauntered over him.

"Gabo, I came over so I could put everything you need on the buns."

"You...are...what?" He must have heard her wrong —surely.

"For the burgers, The toppings? I was thinking of just putting it over the buns so it would be easier for people to assemble their burgers. We are doing them Colombian style, right?"Her head was cocked to the side, a Cheshire smile on her face.

He cleared his throat. "Yeah, that should work." He put the food on an aluminum pan and followed her inside the kitchen, the ever-present pull he always felt when she was around leading him.

Her towel-covered ass wasn't less heart race-inducing than the bathing suite glimpse he got earlier, which was why he lost his mind and all sense of clarity once he walked into the house. He slid the door closed, and most of the loud music quieted down to a murmur.

"Mariana had me dying with her Mero's impersonation from the last episode, the one you were telling me about earlier in the morning."

He leaned against the kitchen counter, seeing how completely at ease she was in his parents' kitchen. Not much had changed since he lived here, and she remember the location of everything.

"I love seeing you here. It reminds me of the good days," he said. She turned around and dipped her face down. She hid her eyes, but her smile and dimples told him he was on the right track.

"Sí? That's nice, y tú qué? Are you just going to stand there gawking at me while I do all the work?" Whenever he made these comments to her, she found a way to deflect and push the attention away. But he didn't have it today.

"You know, our mothers always thought we were going to end up together..." He walked closer and stood next to her, leaning against the counter to face her as she worked. He didn't touch her, but his body was now a breath away from hers. He could smell the sunscreen and the lemon and coconut oil of her lotion. She took deep breaths as she crushed some potato chips for the toppings.

"Ahh, yes, the Miller Powell dream. We sure showed them, didn't we?" The potato chips were now pulverized.

"Did you ever imagine that same fairy tale ending?" His voice dropped low. His eyes were trained on hers. She stopped the massacre of the potatoes chips and looked right at him, her eyes shining, lips parted.

"Once upon a time I did...but we know how that story ends." Her husky voice traveled all the way down to his dick, and the semi became a full hard-on. God, he had it bad for this woman. Her voice could make him hard in seconds.

She licked her bottom lip, and he desperately wished he could lick the same spot. She moved a little closer to him, erasing the distance between them. "How about you Gabo, did you ever dream?"

"Whatever I answer, you won't believe me, will you, Alicia Marie?" The two were circling topics they promised not to circle anymore for the sake of a clean start. But the intimacy of the kitchen, the heat of her body, and her voice, were all conspiring to make him lose his mind and loosen his tongue in the process.

He leaned in closer, bending to ensure his mouth was close to her ear. Her profile was flush against his, her softness against his side. Her body was utterly relaxed against his, and it felt so right.

"What if I told you I always dreamed..." he whispered.

One minute her body was soft and yielding against him, damp, seeking his. Then, nothing. She stood straight, looking flustered, and turned towards the counter to finish putting the toppings together. She got ahold of herself like the moment between them was all a fantasy.

"You play too much. I'm going to take these things outside. I wouldn't want them to get too cold." And out she walked. Towel still in place.

ALICIA SIXTEEN YEARS OLD

"Hello, good afternoon!" She greeted the empty house. It was the first day in weeks that her parents weren't home when she arrived. A few weeks ago, her dad had gotten what he liked to call "extreme exhaustion from teaching those ungrateful fifteen-year-olds" and took a leave of absence from teaching high school math. She couldn't remember the last time her dad had taken one sick day off, so she found it odd. When she questioned her mother about it, Mami had said, "Your dad has been teaching nonstop since I met him, full school years and tutoring in the summer. He just needs a break."

She took off her shoes, placing them in the shoe closet, and dropped her backpack in there as well, and went straight to the kitchen. PE had been brutal today, and she was extra hungry. Mami left a plate of pollo guisado with rice, black beans, and a lettuce and tomato salad in the fridge with a post-it on the top: **Eat the salad, please... We'll be back a little late tonight, after 7 pm.**

After eating her food in the quiet house, she made her way to her room, changing to lounge wear. Her current read was Still Waters by Juliana Rivero. It surprised her that Mami had let her buy it on their last excursion to the bookstore, but her mom had been distracted lately.

She grabbed her book and walked down the stairs and into the family room, the odd quiet of the house disconcerting. Having Daddy as a teacher meant that they were home around the same time. They would hang out and talk about each other's day.

She immersed herself in the book, the current scene took place in a car after the main characters had a date. That tingle she sometimes felt deep inside of her had transformed to a full-blown tremble.

"Alicia! Alicia, can you hear me?"

She dropped the book, startled by Gabo's smiling face pressed against the sliding door glass.

She got up and opened it for him. "Hey, Gabo, Hey, what's up? What you up to?" She didn't think she could stand any longer without him noticing something was odd, so she sat back down. Every sensation was on display for Gabo to see.

"Why are you acting all weird on me, Powell?" There he was, not reading the room. He plopped right next to her on the sectional, his legs and arms sprawled, his lanky frame long and lean. Gabo was wearing a black t-shirt, jeans, and was barefoot. He often had lunch and walked right over, like this was an extension of his house. His eyes were fixated on her face, and she sincerely hoped she wasn't blushing right now.

"I thought I had closed the gate."

"Oh, it's like that? You didn't want me to come to see you today? Did I do something at school?" he asked curiously.

"Of course you didn't. We cool. No drama this week." She shook her head and laughed at herself.

It was amazing being the only girl in a group of all guy friends, but it was also exhausting. Thank God she had her cousins Mariana and Aayala to talk girl stuff, but at school, it could be lonely to not have a lot of girlfriends. It didn't help that half the sophomore year girls and some guys had a crush on Gabo, Mason, or Malik. Whenever Gabo had a new girl he was talking to, it always created problems for Alicia.

"Good, because Rocio and I aren't talking anymore. She was a little too intense this weekend with all the calling. She even left a message in my backpack."

"That explains all the evil eyes she was throwing my way this week. Why do you always do this?" She relaxed enough that she could be normal around him again. She curled her feet under her and played with one of her two cornrow braids.

"Sorry, I might have told her we were hanging out this weekend." He shrugged with a sheepish look. He was oblivious to what that meant to Rocio, who already thought Alicia and Gabo had a secret thing going on. No one ever believed they were just friends.

"Well, that was stupid. I swear I don't know how many times I have to tell you. You make things challenging with girls at school."

"Come on, Powell, it can't be all that bad. You are my best friend. If I'm talking to a girl, and she doesn't understand that," he shook his head, "then she doesn't get me at all. I can't date someone that doesn't get me. You are very important to me." Every time he said things like that, she couldn't help imagine what it would be if they dated. But she realized that wasn't how he felt about her.

"Enough about me. How about you and knucklehead? Did you talk to him today?"

"Stop calling him 'knucklehead'. Tariq called me today, and we talked a bit, but I'm not super into him. It's nice to have someone to talk to, though," she said. Tariq was their same age and attended the same high school as Mariana and Aayala. They had met in one of the quince's Mariana had invited her to last year.

"He is probably a knucklehead, and you know it," Gabo grumbled. He was super adorable in his protective best friend's role.

"Oh, stop it!" she scolded.

"Hey, what were you reading when I was calling you? I kept knocking and calling you, but you were super lost in it." He picked up the book, and her eyes almost jumped out of her head.

"Nothing, just one of my books." She attempted nonchalance while trying to take the book from Gabo, but he read her too well.

"Aja, whatever it is, you obviously don't want me to see it, so I have to read it now!"

"Gabo, don't be an ass!"

Gabo stood up to avoid her reaching for the book, and to try to wrestle him would be a lost cause. Her skin tingled all over and touching him right now felt odd. Gabo stood up tall and cleared his throat, making a show of preparing himself to recite from the book; with an annoying, pompous voice, he said:

"Desiree responded to Joe's advances with eager acceptance. He was aching for her, and had wanted her for the longest time, since they were freshmen in college. She touched his hardness with confidence and his dick jumped in his pants. He didn't think he was going to last long if she kept touching him like that." His eyes widened, and he flushed darkly. He stayed quiet, reading in silence. He sat down without a word.

She had not read this passage yet, so she moved close to read over his shoulder, and her breath caught in her throat. She couldn't help but read the scene where Joseph pleasured

Desiree with his hands in the car. A pin could drop in her house, and it would cause a commotion, things were so quiet.

"Powell, I didn't know you were reading sexy books." Gabo's growled.

"I don't? I mostly read young adult novels, but I got permission to get this one, and I, well..."

"What, Alicia, were you curious?" His head turned to her, looking at her with a mix of surprise and longing.

"Of course I'm curious! You and the boys talk about what you have and have not done with girls. Mariana and Aayala, both virgins, are still a little ahead of me, so I hate asking dumb questions. I thought, why not read it for myself?" She shrugged, nervous, warm, and jittery all at the same time.

"I don't even know what the curve looks like for you and what you have and have not done." He closed his eyes like he was in pain, sprawling again in her sectional.

"First base stuff, some second base..."

"Who did you let into second base with you, Alicia?" Gabo's voice almost growled.

"Trevor." He had been her only boyfriend so far, and they had dated for six months beginning of the school year.

A harsh sigh escaped Gabo's lips, and he sat up.

"Look, we are best friends, right?" He asked her, his eyes almost pleading. He took her hand while speaking to her, and the contact made her shiver inside.

"Yes, we are."

"So, we should be able to talk about these things, no?" His hands, big and warm, held her smaller one, and he rubbed the top of the thumb with his own one.

"Should we? I don't know Gabo. That is the one thing that seems to be hard for me to open up with you about." He moved his body closer to her, so close she could see brown flecks in his eyes. His breath smelled like mint and the lunch his mom must have made for him.

"You should be able to tell me anything, Alicia Marie. I hope you know that," he scoffed.

"Ok then, have you touched a girl like that?"

Gabo groaned. "Of course, you would ask that first."

She laughed a little at seeing his distress, then mumbled. "See, not that easy."

Instead of answering back, he stared at her, then his lips cracked, and he leaned over her. She froze, equal parts of excitement and fear.

"What are you doing, Gabo?" She said against his mouth, and he startled back as if he hadn't realized he had gotten so close to her.

"Shit, sorry Ali, sorry I just, I got carried away with the moment." Ali, he only called her that when he was being extra sweet to her. He pushed back away and sat, quiet for a second. "I have." He said.

She did not understand what he meant, the last five minutes had her all confused. "What do you mean?"

He sighed. "I have, touched a girl, like that."

"Oh, I figured. How was it? I mean did you like it?" she asked.

"I did, it was…" He got up and started pacing the room. "It was exciting. I, yeah…sorry, I don't know how to talk to you about this. I guess you might have been right, it is weird."

A sense of disappointment she didn't want to inspect too close filled her chest, making her cold.

"It's ok. I think the book has us both a little off." She went back to the corner of the sectional, putting more space between them, wondering how it would be to have Gabo touch her.

CHAPTER 10

"Mamita, how are you? I missed your call earlier! So sorry." Her mom's voice came through her car while she drove home from work. It had been a long week, and she was glad she had taken tomorrow off to decompress and get things done in the house.

"It is ok Mami, I'm on my way home, and today is my Friday! So I get to sleep in a bit tomorrow and keep working on moving all your plants to the front of the house."

"Ay, mis plantitas, how is that going so far? You are still stuck with selling the house?"

"Sí Mami, nothing has changed much. Work is the same old same old. Gabo has been a dream. He has helped me replant most of them to the front and some to his own house. We also donated the ferns to a wildlife sanctuary."

"I'm glad to hear you are treating my plants well!" She could hear her mom was in the kitchen, the sounds of pots and pans like music to her ears. She could picture her in her

Panama apartment, windows open and a smile on her face while she moved around.

"Tienes that project with the organization de Gabo and Mason, that is an excellent opportunity y un cambiecito, no?" She loved how her mom couldn't help but weave Spanish into her sentences. It made her homesick.

"Well, yes, that's true, but the bulk of my day is still the same. I want to make a difference, and although I love Gifted Athletes of Broward, that is just a side project in the eyes of my boss. I have to make sure they stick to all they have promised the guys because my boss is not anything but profit-driven."

"Ay bendito, are you saying he would pull out of the project and take away the funds?"

"No, I don't think so. It seems Jack's dad is tight with Mr. M, but you never know." She navigated her car to the far right lane to get ready to exit the highway.

"I have a real shot with the opening I told you about in New York. They actually called me for the third round of interviews."

Silence. The pots and pans stopped their clanking.

"Alicia. I thought you were giving Florida another chance, Mi vida?" her mom asked tentatively.

"No se Mami, I guess I'm leaving it all to the cosmos. But I can't tell you how excited I am about this organization. They do really good work, and—"

"What does that mean, Alicia Marie Powell Torres, 'leaving it to the cosmos', you mean to Jesus Christ, right? When are you going to church?"

"Church? Mami, you should know better by now. Organized religion is not the solution to our problems."

Another sigh, this one of defeat.

"Ok, we raised you to be your own woman and to question everything, so it should not surprise me you did just that. Your daddy would be proud," her mom said. Her dad had encouraged her to understand her mother's religion but to question it all, to investigate about different beliefs and to find her truth on her own. By college, Alicia knew she that whatever she believed in, it wasn't what came from organized religion. She was still figuring it out to this day.

"It would have delighted him to have another ally to stay home with him on Sundays."

"The man was a heathen, but I loved him just as he was," her mom said, voice raw with emotion, and a knot grew in Alicia's throat. They rarely spoke about Daddy anymore. It brought too many painful memories.

"He was a heathen and proud of it," she smiled, her eyes tearing, and the memory of her father kept them both company for the rest of the ride home.

Mariana: Do you hoes want to go to a new bar tonight?
Alicia: No se bebita, I'm supposed to get together with Gabo to go over some of these donor events.
Aayala: Since you've been hanging out with Gabo, you've gone domestic. I strangely approve.
Alicia: Yo? You should come thru. We can have some drinks.
Mariana: I'm not ruining your romantic night
Alicia: What romance? Nvmd, there's no romantic anything happening. I'll tell Gabo to bring Mason.
Mariana: K. I'll consider
Aayala: I can't come thru. I have two shoots in the studio tonight.
Alicia: Boooo.

DINNER WAS GOING TO BE SIMPLE TONIGHT. SHE PULLED SOME spinach, cucumbers, radicchio, and a salad dressing. Her green plantains were already peeled and waiting to be fried for the first round. Her brown stew chicken simmered in the pot. She'd made enough food for a small army just in case the crew stopped by for drinks and hadn't had dinner. A few months ago, outside of hanging out with Mari and Aayala, she'd had scoffed at inviting people into her home. Now, something was shifting, the actual fact that she was putting herself out there, spending time with her friends was improving her mood. She'd also invited Gabo and he'd accepted immediately.

Things with Gabo were promising. After that fraught encounter last Saturday, she'd opened a new vibrator and had a Sunday of pure relief. She fanned herself, thinking about all she fantasized about while using her new toy. Gabo dicking her down against the window in her room, giving him head while they were in the pool, him eating her out against the kitchen counter. Her fantasy Gabo liked it dirty, and she wondered if she was right about him.

Was it that bad to take a risk and just let him have his way with her? She chopped the cucumber a little too aggressively, squashing some of the last slices. Of course, it was bad. Alicia wanted to heal their friendship, not introduce one more messy twist. She was allergic to mess in her old age. She placed the cucumbers on top of the lettuce and started slicing the radicchio.

Alicia realized he wanted her, too. That was the problem. How was she supposed to keep her hands to herself with that knowledge, how was she supposed to stop crossing the line with him? She hadn't missed the drool fest he had going on Saturday before she came to him to get the food ready. She hoped her self-control stayed with her today, as it had the last time she had been tempted by him.

Drogba by Afro B came up next on her playlist, and as it always happened when she heard the song, she started dancing, letting herself go with the music. She turned the volume up, put her hands up, and let the rhythm take over.

GABO

The Powells gate door stood open, which meant Alicia expected him to let himself in. He walked across her pool terrace and checked for the sliding door. He opened it quietly, expecting to find Alicia in her kitchen cooking. She was dancing instead.

God preserve him. Grown-up Alicia was going to kill him. He had strategically taken a shower right before coming over and busted a nut at the memory of her body against his, last Saturday in his kitchen. It took that little to get him going. He was acting like the punk teenager he used to be.

Now here she was, back turned to him, standing in her kitchen, her ass and hips moving to a sweet yet filthy whine that had him rooted on the spot, body tense with anticipation. She was utterly oblivious to his presence, her arms bent on the elbows, open to her chest and hands in fists that dared him to approach. She turned around, and his heart skipped a beat, the blood pumping in his vein so fast, the speed was creating instantaneous heat through his body. Her eyes were closed, and one hand pressed against the top of her breast as if she couldn't help herself but touch. He could not in good conscience continue staring without letting her know he was there, but he did not want to startle her either. In the end, he called her name softly, "Alicia."

Her eyes shot wide open, and a bright smile illuminated her face. If finding her dancing heated his blood, that smile melted his heart. She wan't hiding any of her thoughts right now. And what he saw had him hoping against hope.

"Come, don't stand there. Help me fry the patacones. I just finished the salad. I press, you fry." She pointed to the pan with hot oil, waiting for the second round of frying. Was he supposed to act like she hadn't wrecked him minutes ago?

"I made stew chicken to go with it. I realize you'll be disappointed I didn't make my daddy's rice an' peas, but I couldn't help myself. This is still my favorite combo of Mami and Daddy's food."

He guessed he had to go on. Arousal was still coursing through him, a semi making him tight in the crotch area, but he would survive.

"That is ok, you cooked it the other day, we straight." He went straight to the bowl of smashed plantains she already started and placed them gently in the sizzling oil.

"What is your go-to meal now that you have to adult and feed yourself?" Alicia asked him while opening the fridge to get him a Guinness, his favorite beer. He remembered she didn't like it, so the fact that it was in her fridge... "Old family recipes don't count," she continued.

He gave her a soft kiss on her cheek as a thank you and kept working on the plantains. He checked them once every other minute, knowing Alicia would kill him if he burned the patacones.

"I make a mean pork belly ramen. I'll make you some this weekend if you like." He watched her toss the salad and place it on a serving bowl.

"Oh, I love ramen. I'll take you up on that invitation. Living next to each other makes cooking much easier. I feed you. You feed me." If he could only do more than feed her. She clearly wasn't feeling him the way he was feeling her.

"I made entirely too much food. I thought the crew would stop by for some drinks, but it seems Mari has changed plans."

"I told Mason to stop by if he wanted, but he said he had a date tonight." He followed her to the dining table and placed the bowl in the middle, and they sat down.

"Really... I wonder if that is why Mariana flaked on me too..." she wondered and dug in.

He took a bite of her stew chicken, and a burst of flavor came into his mouth. She'd kept some of the chicken's crunchiness from its fried skin underneath the brown sauce full of spices and vegetables. "This is—wow."

"Right? Oh, I forgot the ketchup. I'll be right back!"

He laughed and called out to her while she ran to the kitchen, "What would you do in a world without ketchup?"

"Calla Gabo! Why do you speak of such blasphemy!" She plopped back down on the chair and laughed at his skeptical face.

"You cannot tell me you eat patacones without ketchup?"

"Why use ketchup when you have this delicious brown stew?" He demonstrated by soaking some of the savory goodness with his plantain.

"Ok, you eat it that way and miss out on this pairing made from heaven." She dipped her patacon in ketchup, then bit on the crunchy goodness and closed her eyes in satisfaction. "Delicious."

This is how it could be with them. He reminded himself that he just got her back in his life. It was meant to take a while. He should take things slow, see where the friendship took them, but dammit, he had waited for years to be here. His concerns about mixing friendship with lust hadn't faded. But they dulled with every minute he spent with Alicia. He had to ask where her head was at the moment, what she wanted from all of this. Make life happen.

"About last week. We didn't talk about what happened." Gabo took a big bite of the plantain to stop himself from revealing how essential her answer was to him. Alicia took a sip of her beer, putting it down, taking her time to answer.

"I thought we were good."

"I thought so too, but I walked in today and saw you

dancing, and if I were a braver man, I would have asked to join you, just to have you move that way against me." That plantain was no help—failed strategy for anyone who was wondering.

Alicia flushed, and she looked down. Her dimples were the only sign he was on the right track.

"I don't know if this is right. But I cannot help that I want all of you, all the time. I want to do things to you I've fantasized about for a long ass time."

"Damn, what did I put in that stew chicken?" she chuckled, "You are in a sharing mood today."

He looked at her, eyebrow raised, and willed her to look up. Slowly her eyes moved up, and he was confronted with reluctance, but what captivated him was the longing and tenderness that told him he was not in this alone.

"You want me too, Alicia. I don't think this is one-sided."

A scoff, then she popped a plantain in her mouth, trying the same failed strategy he'd tried before. He could have told her it wouldn't work. After she swallowed, she looked at him with amusement. "So, we are doing this today?"

He nodded.

"Ok, our friendship is what's most important to me. We don't have the best track record of mixing anything else." She looked at him earnestly.

"That is not exactly accurate..." Memory served him, showing him quick snapshots of theirs last interactions together.

"Not exactly accurate, but promises are promises."

Frustration laced his tone. "Maybe we should talk about everything that happened then,"

"No, I don't think we should. I don't see how any of it would change where we are today, and today is us trying to be us again."

"What if 'us' is bigger than this, more than what we

currently give each other? Because I'm ready to give you more," he said straight faced.

Her face betrayed surprise, then she smiled. She took another sip of her beer. Then she got up and walked over to him, and took his hand.

He stood and followed her, incapable of denying her anything. She had her phone in her hand, and after a couple of touches, the song "Tu Amor me hace bien." from Marc Anthony came up in her sound system. Her warm hand in his took him to her family room.

She dimmed the lights, and their bodies acted like magnets. He let go of her hand and charted a path with his fingertips from her hands up to her shoulder and back down through the middle of her back, ending right above her ass. His hand tingled along the way, his body welcoming to the soft touch of her curves against his.

Alicia sighed against him, then placed one arm over his shoulder and the other hand hanging next to her, and he took the opportunity to intertwine their fingers and felt her body give all of her tension to him. Her body melted to his like honey dissolving in hot tea, both of them changing to become one substance together.

The song was so familiar to him, reminding him of times past. The familiar lyrics told her what he couldn't yet say with words. "Your love does me good. Your love disarms me." He moved her at the four-time beat of the salsa song, bypassing the usual turns and twirls and just enjoying their two bodies moving in unison.

He didn't know anymore if this was just pure lust. He had cared for her for so long that the feelings were all one in his heart. Friendship, love, passion. He did not know where one began, and the other ended.

"Do you remember dancing to this song during our prom?" she asked. Her voice was tentative, so unlike her, made him involuntarily squeeze her. The yield of all of her soft parts against his was chaos to his senses. He looked down seeing the shadow of her cleavage and the unforgettable view of her against him.

"Yes, I do. I wished I had invited you to go with me," he answered softly. Her head rested on his shoulder, and he could smell the lemon and coconut oil, and that something that was all her, all woman. It made him hungry, the yearning for her growing by each touch, each word.

"I wish that too. I thought for a minute that you were going to ask me to prom. But then... we know how that story ended." Her body moved languidly with him, her pure sensuality speaking to his filthy mind. She was enticing him to get lost in the possibility of her being his and him being hers.

"I missed you," she whispered.

His heart broke into pieces, and in a frozen moment, his jagged edges all coalesced and reformed again at her words. There was so much hurt, longing, and confusion in her words, and deep down, he realized this woman had the power to destroy him if he gave her his full heart.

"I cannot go back in time, but I can show you now everything that you make me feel. Will you let me show you?"

She moved and he was mesmerized. At that moment, time stood still as she raised her body to his, the scrape of her shirt dragging the movement, all of it creating warmth and current in her wake. Every part of his touched by hers was a live wire ready to spark. She stopped right when their mouths were just inches away from each other.

"Kiss me, Gabo."

He was powerless to the lure of her and triumphant all at the same time. He forgot everything from before, any of his worries about what was to come, and lowered his lips to her lush softness.

Their kiss was tentative at first. He kissed the corner of

her lip, knowing that the full impact would be something to brace for. Her breath hitched, and he couldn't help but claim the gift she was giving him. He let himself be swept by the current, sparking him alive. This kiss was everything that had led them to this place in time. A totality. The sum of all their past in one carnal gesture of passion and need. He'd never be the same after this kiss. This kiss marked the beginning for him. He felt it everywhere.

She moaned when his tongue licked inside her mouth, and his hands grew restless. He couldn't keep this as a kiss only. The two of them together, after all they'd been through. He should have known it would be explosive.

He touched the sides of her lush breasts, moving down the valleys and shadows of her side all the way to her hips. Her other arm moved to his shoulder and her titties. God, her titties so full and soft, pressed against his hard chest.

His hands searched, and soon he had a healthy handful of her fine, fine ass in his hands. He heard her gasp when she felt his dick against her belly, and he chased that gasp to deepen the kiss. He was desperate, almost feral, for her. "I knew it would be like this," he groaned. One kiss followed another, and soon desperation drove them both. The longing of *what if* turned into the answer of right now.

Her tongue, so sweet and bold, nudged inside his mouth. She was hungry and needy, and a growl escaped his lips when she nipped his bottom lip. "Fuck, Alicia, you taste so sweet." His voice was raw and rasp, all his strength gone to other places in his anatomy.. "Ali, I want you so much, but I'll take anything you give me. I want you to know that."

He had to slow down. The heat enveloping them both was threatening to sweep him away. He pressed quick kisses to her soft mouth, her cheek was damp from the heat between their two bodies, between her eyes as she closed them in stillness. A kiss to her temple, the slight beat of her blood coursing through her to match his. She whimpered in the silence. The song had ended while they were enveloped in each other.

"Gabo," His name spoken by her, more of a moan than anything else, made his dick jump inside his jeans. But he knew if he pushed more, she would bolt, so he just held her close until they'd calmed down.

"I'm just going to hold you a little longer. Then I'm going to step away and go to my house before I lay you on this floor and fuck you till the sun comes up." He heard her breath skip and then her body tensed.

"I won't do that because I know you aren't ready. I have time. I'm not going anywhere."

She relaxed against him, and snuggled closer to his embrace, and for now, that is all he needed.

GABO EIGHTEEN YEARS OLD

He plopped on his Pop's recliner and smacked his face with his hand. On his way home today, he had planned to ask Alicia to the prom. First, she made fun of him about the messages appearing in his locker room and backpack from the girls letting him know they wanted to go with him. Then, she told him how Tariq had asked her to his prom and her conundrum about not wanting to invite him to theirs. Afterwards, somehow, he ended up suggesting they all go as friends, including Mason and Malik. The fuck? Alicia had given him an obvious chance to ask, and he blew it like an idiot.

"What's up with you son, what is wrong?" His pop's voice startled him out of his misery, and he sat up, knowing the old man like him to be composed—a man.

"Hey, Pops, I was just..." His dad was on the strict side of the spectrum of fathers, but he meant well. It was his odd way to show him, love. The guy had made his mom fall in love with him, and let's face it. His mom was the most brilliant woman he knew aside from Alicia and Alicia's mom, so Gabo was a bit out of his league.

Girls came to him; he very rarely had to ask. His game was rusty. Maybe his pops had some words of wisdom about Alicia.

"Pops, I want to ask Alicia to go with me to the prom, but not as friends, like an actual date."

His dad was by the kitchen island, drinking water, and paused in his movements. A frown crystalized in his face, and dread snaked through Gabo's spine.

"I don't think that is a good idea, son."

"I like her Pops. No other girl makes me feel the way Alicia makes me feel."

"But she is your best friend."

"I understand, but I can't help my feelings for her," he shrugged. He couldn't find a better way to explain how Alicia's wit, joy, intelligence, and fake bravado all called to him. He definitely couldn't tell him she was the main star of most of his jack-off sessions.

"Son, I can't tell you what to do. You're eighteen, going on nineteen by the end of this year. What I can say is that what you have with Alicia, that type of friendship is hard to find." His dad paused and put his bottle of water down.

"Romantic love can sometimes complicate things. I would hate to see you fuck things up with her. You both are too young, going to different schools, and it could mean the end of things with you. And you know she needs you." The fact that his pops use the word "fuck" made him realize how serious this conversation was. He talked to him like a man, giving him advice as if he saw him as an equal.

"If you were older," his dad continued, "I might see things differently, but, no, I don't think it is a good idea. Your Mother and I found each other when she was twenty-three, and I was twenty-eight. Nineteen-year-old me knew nothing of life. You keep getting with these girls and lasting less than a few months with them. I'm telling you, it's not the right time, and you also have to be at peace that it might never be the right time." Pop's face was grim. He understood what he was telling him hurt. Gabo just stared at his dad.

Pops walked over to him where he was sitting up in the sectional and pulled him up with one hand, he embraced him, and at that moment, he realized his dad had given him his first grown man advice. And it utterly sucked.

CHAPTER 11

GABO

"I kissed Alicia."

"We have been here for hours, working side by side, and you decided to keep that in all this time? Damn."

It was the weekend. Mason and Gabo had been hard at work painting The Gifted Athletes Center of Broward. The building they had been able to rent through the initial funds donated by Alicia's company was a large hall with benches around the room's perimeter. There was a large counter by the entrance where a receptionist would eventually sit, and four different additional smaller rooms for one-on-one academic advisory sessions and tutoring. Behind the building, there was plenty of open space that they planned to convert into a small picnic area and a multipurpose court for the athletes to practice.

Mason stopped painting and put his roller down, turning to Gabo.

"We were working." Was all he answered to Mason.

If Mason and Gabo were fifteen-year-old teenagers, he was certain Mason would have rolled his eyes next. Instead, he went over to the fridge behind the little snack nook in the hall and pulled out two bottles of water.

"Tell me more." Mason sat on one of the benches, and he sat on top of one of the tables with his legs propped up.

"I kissed her. It was last night, and I haven't heard from her at all today. She is probably freaking the fuck out."

"Why would she be freaking out?" Mason drank his water.

"She's been cautious with me since we reconnected. Before, when we were young, she was so open and upfront with all her feelings. But now, it is hard for me to have a read of her. What she has outwardly told me, though, is that she does not want to ruin our friendship."

"So basically, she is keeping you at arm's length, same way you used to do when we were teenagers?" Mason smirked, the asshole.

"Yes, I haven't failed to see the irony there."

"Everything that happened in the past, you gotta let it go —this opportunity you have with her now, it's golden. But you have to let her work her things out, man. You both have your war scars from before."

"Yeah, you are right." He took a swig of his water, relieved by the cold liquid. The work of painting such an ample space was a welcome strain on his muscles and had worked for a while to keep his thoughts at bay. He took off his shirt and wiped his face with his t-shirt.

"Yeah, I'm right. But also, don't do your turtle thing, please." Mason insisted.

"What do you mean?"

"You know what I mean. What's that Spanish saying your ma says, it's all you? You've translated it to me before…"

Recognition sparked, and Gabo realized exactly what Mason was talking about, "Tranquilo pero seguro."

Mason continued, "Quiet but sure? That's it, right? Don't do all of that. Don't take forever to figure your shit out. Be sure what you want and once Alicia is ready, go for it."

ALICIA

Her eyes were trained on the black and white wall. She was back in her sanctuary. Mari was behind parting her hair to start braiding her Senegalese twists.

"I asked Gabo to kiss me." Mari stopped and turned her around on the salon chair to face her.

"Chiquita, I'm gonna need for you to speak up because I did not just hear what I think I heard." Mari's eyes were wide.

"And he did. He kissed me, and I kissed him back."

"Ok, normally, I would say this is not the ninth grade. But," Mari put up her finger, "kissing Gabo, that's a whole other situation altogether. Ya'll took twenty-three years to work up the courage to kiss. I need reinforcements." Mari grabbed her phone off her table and video called Aayala.

"Cos! Wha gwaan?"

"Aayala, I'm here with Alicia, and she just told me that Gabo and she kissed."

"Waaaaaaa, about damn time!" Her cousin Aayala screamed all the way from New York. Aayala had just returned after her photoshoot sessions in Miami.

Alicia huffed, a combination of a laugh and a groan coming out of her mouth.

"No, I didn't want this to happen. Actually I did, not gonna lie. But I shouldn't want it to happen." Another groan, and she covered her face. The decision to kiss Gabo had been an impulsive one, but it had been so right. She decided to trust her gut, and she hadn't done that in a long time. Her instinct had yet to steer her wrong with him, but all the baggage from the past kept coming back to her. She was a rational woman, and letting instinct drive her decision-making process with Gabo was not coming easy for her.

"Alicia, that is wild. That man wants you so bad. I've been around you when we are all hanging out, and he cannot take his eyes away from you. When you aren't paying attention, he looks at you with these doe eyes..." Mari said with an earnest look, then burst out laughing.

"I hate you," Alicia said to her smile.

"You lie! You love me," Mari volleyed back.

"Why are you hesitating, Alicia?" Aayala asked the real question.

"Because he is my friend, and we've fucked it up before. On top of that, I'm moving to New York as soon as I can sell the house and get a job."

"Whoa, calm down, chiquita, it's going to be ok, what do you want?" Mari's voice grounded her a little.

"I want to understand why all of a sudden everything is upside down. When I finally start getting my shit together to move, Gabo comes back, making a whole mess of my emotions... Old me would have leapt at this chance with him, but that is not me anymore. My grown woman brain is telling me that putting all of my plans on the line for him is reckless."

"But It doesn't need to be a life-altering decision. Why can't you accept what he is offering without putting any labels on it?" Aayala asked.

"Agree a hundred percent. If this were me, I would be riding that train all the way home, and by that train, I mean his dick in case you were all confused," Mari offered, even though no one wanted all that information.

"I think you both may have a point. I'm not gonna lie. If I was horny before that kiss, now I'm straight up thirsty. The man knows how to kiss," Alicia fanned herself, remembering the heated encounters she had with Gabo.

"Now that's what I'm talking about. This is the conversation I'm here for," Mari chimed in.

"I have to figure out what I want before I see him again. Whatever it is, I know he'll respect it, but he has left the proverbial ball in my court."

"Ok, then just do the friends with benefits for now. I mean is not an answer to all of your questions. But it gets Gabo fucking you on the regular," Aayala said, holding her laugh.

Mari cackled, and that got Alicia laughing too.

"You both are *the* worst. I cannot with you two. We accomplished nothing today," she said, gasping for air as she laughed again.

"Baby girl, you need to do what feels right. I asked you to consider going with the flow when he came back, and it has been working so far. Don't let your inner doubts stop you now." Aayala, always the voice of reason.

CHAPTER 12

Gabo: cooking ramen tonight, want some?
Alicia: You don't play fair, Miller. What time should I come thru?
Gabo: Five, I want to get you in bed nice and early.
Alicia: I'm gonna ignore that last text message.
Gabo: Sure you will... ;)

He realized the best way to approach things with Alicia was to let her make the next move. That didn't mean he was going to let her just retreat into her corner. No, he was going to be nice while playing a little dirty. He was going to keep making the moves to make his life happen the way he wanted it to happen. Deciding to move out of his court side seats to his own life and being on the court, was a heady rush. There were moments where he'd surprised himself, how forward he was with her compared to how he was in relationships.

His ex-girlfriend would not recognize him, April had been the one to push everything forward with them, she invited him to their first date, she planned all their outings, the only thing he held firm was their sexual relationship. The fact he wanted to wait to have sex with her had fascinated her. They got to know each other but after a year and a half, nothing had changed for him. She saw it all as romantic and old-school but in the best of ways, she'd had terrible experiences in her previous relationships and Gabo had been kind and present. She built castles in the air, and he didn't have the heart to correct her. He managed to fuck things up to the point she had been hoping he was going to propose, when he announced to her he had plans to move within the year. It was then he moved out of the sidelines and took charge of his life. It was something he worked on every day.

"Hello, good evening, I'm here for the ramen and the ramen only." Alicia came in through his sliding door, dressed in baggy pants and an oversized t-shirt. Wash day must have been today, as her hair was in twists all the way down to that ass. She looked beautiful, and it was funny to him she thought all of those clothes would stop him from wanting her. Delusional.

"You're just in time, come get the drinks and the spoons for the table." She walked towards him and came close. He stood still, letting her body and her scent filled his senses. Was he sniffing her right now? He was down bad.

She stood on tiptoe and reached for him. Her soft, lush lips grazed the side of his mouth, and a current ran through his spine, straight to his dick. She lingered a little enjoying the contact, and his hand moved to the small of her back, where it belonged. She pulled back softly, and he let his hand linger until he had no choice but to let go. When she stepped away, he could see her eyes were heavily lidded, and she was breathing a little faster. Good.

"We can skip the ramen and go right into dessert if you prefer." His voice was low.

She smiled, mischievous and lovely, "No, I want what you promised me. Feed me, Gabriel Ernesto."

"Ok, be like that," he smiled back. There was plenty of time later. "You know where's everything. There is beer, wine, and lemonade in the fridge. Pick your poison."

"What do you want to drink?" She asked as she moved around collecting spoons, forks with one hand then opening his fridge with the other.

"I'm having whiskey tonight."

"Oh, ok. I see you. If you are having, I'll join."

"Oh Gabo, that ramen," Alicia groaned in ecstasy, "was the best ramen I have tasted in a while. Thanks for making dinner for me."

He needed to figure out how to make her moan like that without food as soon as humanly possible.

She sat on his parents' patio, the night air heavy with humidity and the sounds of the water lulling her. Gabo had just returned from inside with two fresh glasses of whiskey and gave her a drink. His hands lingered a little longer than necessary, her face flushing in reaction. He had done this throughout the night. Passed her the spoon she'd reached for, a lingering caress to her arms as he walked to the kitchen, his hand on the small of her back as he passed her a dish to dry.

"I'm glad you like it. I've come a long way. From making you grilled cheese sandwiches to ramen."

"Oh God, your infamous grilled cheese," she laughed. Alicia, in repose, relaxed in his parents' outdoor sectional, hair all over, eyes shining in the dim light, feet bared, was one of the sexiest things he had seen in his life. Her relaxation, the fact that she was letting go and just being here with him, was more of a lure to him than her beauty could ever be. At this moment, he realized no matter what she decided, friends or lovers, he was already falling, and there was nothing to hold on to avoid the fall.

"That was the time where my mom and dad were not around much, and you made it your mission to keep me fed at all times. You kept texting me to get my sandwich or packed extra for me for school. It was sweet," she said. These were turbulent waters.

"I figured out that all those times they were gone in the afternoon, and that time he was home because of exhaustion was the first time he had treatment for his prostate cancer? And they kept it a whole secret." Alicia her shook her head and brought her knees up to her body, hugging herself as she continued talking. "I'm not certain why that was a good idea at the time, but well, we know your thoughts on it. The second time it came back was right after sophomore year in college. The year you and I stopped talking. Sometimes I wonder how I would have coped with it all if you were around."

He inhaled deeply, knowing how painful it must have been for her to go through that. Her Dad was larger than life for her. It must have been awful to see him go through therapy, radiation, and surgery and not know if he would come out of it well. And he understood his part in all of it.

"I wish I'd tried harder to get you to listen, to talk to me. I didn't know how to be there for you, for you to trust me again." The regret still lingered deep inside of him, remembering the days after their fall out. Calls to her cellphone, then her house phone for Mr. Powell of all people to ask him to stop calling—'*Not because we don't welcome you here but because Alicia needs space for a while, there is a lot she is going through right now son, with my diagnosis and all. I promise once things get better with my health, she will be in a better place to talk.*'

So he waited, and the waiting had been brutal. Then, once his parents told him Mr. Powell was better, he waited for her call. But she never reached back. By then, his feelings were hurt, and his pride took over any reasoning, and he could not find his way back to her.

"You can't blame yourself. I wasn't ready, and I needed to be there for my Daddy. And he got better. We had him for many more years before things got bad. I miss him so much it aches. It's taken me time to deal with it all."

He couldn't sit there and not be close to her. Her pain and grief were an additional occupant in the space where he thought he was reaching her at last. That pull that always tugged at him had him standing up to go to her corner of the sectional. He gathered her in his arms, and she just sighed and let him hold her. Her hair smelled of some herbal oil he could not recognize, she rested her head on his shoulder. She was a balm to the simmering anger taking over inside. Anger at himself and the world, and at their youth for allowing their separation to happen. He should have been there for her. All these years, he should have swallowed his pride and come back to her.

"I missed you, and I said it before, but I don't know if you understand what it truly means," she said, her voice low and filled with so much depth of emotion he could not untangle it all.

"You've told me, and I know how it felt to be away from you all these years. I would have been there for you if you had just..."

"If I had let you. You can say it. It is our truth. My circle is small, but I think you never left it. Even though I pretended you weren't in it anymore, the reality is you were always essential to me."

Her words broke him and gave him the absolution he wasn't sure he deserved. He held her tight and let the silence fill the space, not confident if he could ever be able to tell her the amount of regret that filled him, for the opportunities missed, for the chance to take a risk for her, with her.

ALICIA

The silence was a gift. Gabo held her close and gave her the space she needed to air out the grief that she realized she had never breathed out. She snuggled close to him and closed her eyes, the moment of heaviness passing by like a dandelion in the sky, each particle a second of pain and remembrance. She realized it would return, it never went far these days, but for now, she let go of the burden.

"I'm so sorry for bringing the mood down, we had such a good dinner, and I didn't mean to be such a downer."

She heard him scoff and hold her tighter, his arms were surrounding her underneath her chest, and his body had become her cushion. She could stay like this forever. Gabo had always been an affectionate friend, and the way he held her was no different from how he had held her in the past when they would hang out and watch movies or with other friends, but what lay now between them made the fact he was holding fraught with tension.

"You could never ruin my night...Ok, there was that time you were puking after we all went out because you drank too much. I was scared shitless. I had to bring you back to Mr. And Mrs. Powell and face imminent death," he said in mock horror.

She chuckled at the memory of that night. "Yeah, I don't remember much of that night, especially the end, but somehow you got me home safe. And my parents didn't realize what had happened, so, for me, you are a total hero."

"I wish. A hero would have noticed you drinking a little bit too much. Here I thought you had stamina with a Panamanian mother and a Jamaican father, but it turns out you were a lightweight."

"How dare you, I'm no lightweight. I'd skipped lunch and dinner that day! I'd been in the salon all day."

"Speaking about the salon. Your hair is beautiful. Mari's killing it." His hand ran through her hair, causing her body to shiver in delight. Only this man could touch her hair and get away with that.

Gabo's plans to seduce her, with his proximity, caresses, and unexpected touches, had been working. But like it sometimes happened, an innocent memory would trigger another, and suddenly she was trapped in another moment and time. She wanted a rewind to the beginning of the night.

"Tell me something to get my mind off of sad thoughts, something shocking," she asked.

"Mhm, that is putting me on the spot," he said. She could see his wheels turning.

"Remember the day I found you, reading that book?"

"You've found me many a time reading a book," she smiled.

"You know what I'm talking about, but you are going to make me spell it out."

"It is only fair. Bringing that up is embarrassing to this day," she chuckled.

"So you do remember, you devil woman. Well, after that day, I looked online for the book and read it top to bottom."

"What?" She turned her head to looked at him and saw his eyes sparkling brown in the dim light.

"Yeah, and it was eye-opening. I mean, I was already doing some things. I was seventeen being a year older than you and all."

"Ohh yeah. You'n old man," she snorted.

He ignored her and continued, "But reading it was eye-opening. So, I kept buying romance books. My parents had no idea. Once I moved out, there was no turning back. To this day, I read them."

She sat up and left his embrace, turning her body in the seat so she could face him fully. She squealed and reached out and touched his arm. "Oh, it's on! For real?"

"I think I may have lost my hearing on one ear. Yes, I do. But that was not the shocking part."

"There's more. Hold on. I'm not ready."

He snorted. "One of my number one fantasies is being with you curled up together in that sectional of yours reading to each other. In my fantasy, things inevitably get hot and heavy, and we end up masturbating in front of each other."

PEOPLE DESCRIBE MOMENTS WHERE ONE MAKES A LIFE-altering decision. This was not one of those moments. There was no rational thought process after Gabo told her his fantasy. Only a direct hit to her center, arousal capturing her immediately, her body a kaleidoscope of reactions. From the tingling of her spine, cruising to the dampening of her pussy. Ending at the irregular heartbeat in her chest.

She stood from the sectional and offered him her hand, same as she had the night they danced together. She did not care if this was the right decision to make, but for the time being, she was letting adrenaline drive her movements, and her want for him to dictate the next moves.

He took her hand in his, looked up at her with one eyebrow raised and squeezed, the action a question. Her response was to squeeze back and nod, an answer given. He understood this was not a full yes to what he wanted, but for tonight it would do.

"Are you making my fantasy come true tonight?" His

voice was almost a rumble, it made her spine tingle and her underwear wet in response. She rubbed her legs together and small mercies that she had picked these oversized sweatpants because they hid her movements from him.

He stood up with economy of movement, graceful and powerful, and the things she tried not to notice too much when they were hanging out together, all stood in evident relief today. His t-shirt fitted to his body, his torso wide in the shoulder tapering down in his waist, and his jeans a comfortable fit that hid his powerful legs, strong from his swimming. And that ass. She knew he had a thing for her ass. But what he did not realize is that she had a full-on crush on his.

"If you keep looking at me like that, there will be no book reading, just you, screaming my name as I make you come with my mouth." His impatience was apparent in the roughness of his voice, and she trembled from how turned on she was for him.

She jumped a little when he took control, and soon they were walking across their two patios into her house. They could have stayed in his house, but she wanted the whole experience of this fantasy of his.

"Sit down, Alicia. And take off those pants," he said, voice clipped, he was at the end of something, and she wondered if she could push a little.

"I shouldn't take them off. If we were hanging out in your fantasy, I would have them on, no?"

"Ali...can I take off your pants? In my fantasy, you are in boy shorts and a t-shirt, no bra, nothing else."

Fuck, this man was going to kill her. She could have never imagined he was this forward in bed. For all she had hoped for when she was a teenager, they'd never even kissed as friends. Secretly, this was a fulfillment of her fantasy as well.

She dragged her oversized pants down, and the cold of

the room hit her for a second, but Gabo's eyes zeroed on her legs all the way up to her face, and she was hot again. He reached out to her, then paused, "Can I touch you?"

"Yes."

He raised her t-shirt to confirm she was wearing her boy shorts. The man knew her too well and too long. Her underwear for comfy days was boy shorts. He saw the navy-blue underwear and gave a low deep groan that connected directly with her pussy.

She sat down, her shirt covering her for the most part, and she folded her legs underneath her body, hot, sensual, and hungry for him. She stared at him for a beat with heavy-lidded eyes. He gave her a matching look of hunger that told her he wanted to consume her. Then he shook his head, breathed in and out, and sat down close to her. His body turned towards hers.

He took off his shirt and left his jeans on. His chest was right in front of her, and she wanted to touch, kiss, bite, and claim it all as hers. His arms were thick with the type of muscles definition from an active man. His chest had some hair at the top that tapered down to a line leading straight to the promised land.

"You can't be looking at me like that and not touch." The basic need of his voice made her clench inside.

She ran her finger from his corded shoulder down his pectoral muscle, circled one nipple, and was rewarded with another groan. She looked down and smiled, reckless, alive, and so powerful right now. He made her feel cherished, hot as fuck, and she just wanted whatever they could get from each other tonight.

"Ali, what do you want to read?" Her nickname only he called her sounded not only sweet but filthy right now.

"What were you reading last?" she asked, her voice almost unrecognizable to her.

"I guess in my horniness, I didn't think of the details, but I can read you one from my kindle. It's straight-up smut, though. I'll gift it to you."

"I don't care if it's smut. I care that it's with you, Gabo."

Her shallow breathing was loud in the room, he sent her the book, and she opened her reading app right way. The scene he referred to was...explicit. The book was a novella about a traveling executive that fucks her driver. Alicia was already superheated but knowing that Gabo had read a book she'd also read, and came to, was too much.

"I have this one too, for my sessions with my vibrator," she told him while he read the same passage. Gabo's hand was resting on top of his zipper, his dick's outline showing on the jeans, and she was desperate to see more. Her attention was barely on the book on her phone. Hands large and calloused rubbed the denim-covered bulk that promised to be of epic proportions. What she had in front of her was all she needed. She could have masturbated to this view alone, but he started reading out loud, and his low voice held her mesmerized.

"Don't you dare close that partition now," his voice gravely. His eyes looking at me through the rearview mirror, making my pussy clench in need.

"Well, Orlando," I purr, "I thought you were a professional."

"I'm indeed Ms. Smith. Ask me for what you want, and you shall get it."

She paused, trying to understand what Orlando was trying to say.

"I pride myself in giving our hotel guests everything they desire. It is our hotel's motto. Votre désir est mon ordre. Ask me, Ms. Smith," he clarified.

With that last statement, I'm left hungry for him and lose all my very limited inhibitions. "Fuck me, Orlando."

"Your wish is my command."

He looked up to her to see what she was doing. Listening to him read the filthy book had her reaching down inside her soaked underwear. She played with herself, teasing and prolonging the pleasure. If she moved too fast, she would shatter in front of him.

"Ali, te quiero ver." "Alzate el t-shirt." Hearing him tell her in Spanish ruined her. She lost herself to the moment and him, her legs were weak, and a stream was traveling through her body down, where her pussy was crying out for attention.

She lifted her t-shirt and kept touching herself, teasing him and herself in the process.

"I want to see you too, Gabo."

He stood in front of her, unbuckled his jeans, and in one swift motion dropped his pants. His boxer briefs were tented, and she closed her eyes for a minute to take all of that greatness in. It deserved a moment.

Thank you, Goddess, you must love me indeed for sending me this gift.

Gabo's dick jumped once inside his boxers as he stroked himself slowly, all for her viewing pleasure.

"More," she said breathy and low, her hands circling her pussy with desperate need.

"More what, Ali?"

"Read more for me."

He grabbed the phone again and read in that voice suited only for her and her fantasies.

"God, I knew they would be magnificent." he pushes my lace bra down with both hands and no gentleness. He is hungry for me as I am for him, and the air that soon hits my tits has my nipples hardening to attention.

"Such suckable nipples you have, Ms. Smith, do you need me to lick them for you?"

"Yes, Orlando, I need you to lick them, please," see, I can play nice too...*when I know I am getting something I want.*

She was desperate now. His words conjured a spell on her where she lost all sense of inhibition. She opened up her legs, still clad in her underwear, and her hands moved in tandem with his hand. The fact that his boxers shielded her from what she wanted to see made it kinky and forbidden, but that bulge to the side was...

His hands rubbed down his bulky length above the boxers while his eyes told her all he wanted to do to her.

"I need to touch you," he said, almost all growl.

"Yes, please, touch me." She was frantic for him.

He dropped his phone on the floor and came to her, dick in hand. He bent over, and their lips met, open and hungry, the kiss a frenzy of need and pent-up enthusiasm. This need of theirs had grown through the years to evolve to a yearning that touch could not simply quell. It needed surrender. For each of them to bare themselves to each other.

She was clawing at his shoulders, and he parted her legs under him, her cotton underwear wet, around his hips. He pressed her down until she was lying flat on the couch and he started raining kisses all over her face, neck, and chest. He tried to leave his weight off hers, but as she searched back for his lips and sucked his tongue into her mouth, he gave this noise that was a mix of a growl and a moan and pressed down on her, his dick meeting her cotton-covered wetness, and they both gasped at the contact.

She grounded her hips against his, and he responded to the call. "Fuck Alicia, I didn't even get to see you bared to me. I don't know if I'm going to last much longer." His voice was deep and full of longing.

The fact that he was so far gone by just masturbating in front of her and seeing her do the same was one of the most erotic encounters of her life. And they still had most of their clothes on.

His hips were moving fast on each slide, the friction of his clad dick hitting her pussy and making her cry out. Alicia was gasping for breath now, so close to her the pinnacle. She could almost taste it. She surrounded him with her thighs again, chasing that moment where he would set her free while he pressed open-mouth kisses on her neck, telling her filthy promises of what he would do next to her and what other fantasies he had, making her body shiver.

"Fuck, you taste so good." Then he bit her right between her neck and shoulder, and the fantasy he'd woven crystallized around him and her, closing in from within and bursting in a show of lights behind her eyes. She shuddered her release and Gabo moved, the friction now fire between them. He gave a deep low groan. His release added to the liquid heat they had created together.

His body slumped on top of hers, the quickness of the experience seeping into her, now that she was more clear-minded. She took time to enjoy the hardness of his bare chest against her clad top. She held her thighs open for him, and he rolled off her into the back of the couch, then gathered her and spooned her.

His breath was still harsh against her ear, and she closed her eyes, relishing the feel of him. "I cannot fucking believe I just came in my boxers on my first time with you. Scratch that. I believe it." His body rumbled with amusement behind her.

"Are you ok Ali, did you enjoy yourself?" He asked. *Ali*, to hear him call her that again, melted her heart. His large hand ran from her shoulder softly down to her arm, giving her goosebumps along the way.

"You know the answer to that question," she answered with a self-satisfied smile.

"I wanted it to be special for you too. This was my wet dream fantasy. I have many more with you as the protagonist. Come to think of it, all my fantasies have you as the main character."

Her heart skipped a beat, then resumed its normal programming. They remained in silence for a minute, then he spoke again. "I want to stay here with you like this, but I need to change my underwear and shower."

She chuckled and got up, her legs loose, her body languid from the orgasm. "Ok, I'll leave the sliding door open. I'm going up to do the same and get in bed."

"You are ok with me coming back?"

"Yes, but to sleep only, we have shit to figure out, or at least I do. For tonight I just want my friend to hold me tight until I fall asleep."

He stood up and hugged her tight to him, kissing the top of her head.

"You think and do all your mental gymnastics, and I'll be right here waiting. Next time, I need to see all of these curves, no clothes on, ok?" He squeezed her ass for extra emphasis.

She burrowed into him and pressed his semi-hardon against her belly. She pulled back. "Again? Ok, young blood."

"With you, Alicia, always, but I'll behave tonight."

She went upstairs in a daze, showered, brushed her teeth, and wrapped her hair, all movements purely mechanical, things her body knew what to do through muscle memory. She refused to freak out or overanalyze what this meant for her, for him, for them. Tomorrow would be a new day... She got in bed and fell asleep right away, and when she woke up around 2:00 a.m., the press of Gabo's body in his PJs behind her, and she fell right back asleep, satisfied.

CHAPTER 13

GABO

Waking up besides Alicia Powell Torres wasn't a first-time occurrence, but it was the first time he'd held her to sleep after dry humping her like a horny teenager. He nutted in his boxers, for fuck's sake. The wildest part is he would do it all over for the opportunity to touch her again.

She laid on her side, her face cradled on his hand and body curled around his arm. Her ass, plump, lush, and perfect, was pushed up against his crotch and his dick lay hard against it in blissful abandon. Her legs were tangled up with his and his other arm laid on her soft belly underneath her shirt. It seems all his limbs had found a refuge in her. Her long lashes created a shadow over her smooth brown skin and cheeks, her mouth open, making his dick ask for seconds.

To feel her body vibrate against his, to hear her cries of abandon, it had been so much and not nearly enough. He was a greedy bastard, hard at the thought of exploring each and every inch of her lush curves, but more than anything, getting to know her when she let her guard down, her inhibitions out of the window.

His heart thumped in his chest. He understood that last night something had changed for him. He hoped for the sake of his sanity that she was on board.

"I can hear you think, Gabriel Ernesto." Her voice took him out of his thoughts and had him focusing the armful of luscious woman he had next to him. "I can also feel you warm, hard, and ready. But you have to wait." His dick pressed deeper into her soft ass in an involuntary response. She chuckled, rolled over to the other side of her king bed, then turned around to look at him. Her hair laid under a satin hair wrap that framed her face and gave her a virtuous look, which had him thinking of making her come while fucking her with it on.

"Whoa, what just crossed your mind? Do I even want to know?"

"You're talking too much."

He pulled her against him and kissed her good morning. She sighed in surrender, and his dick rejoiced at the contact of her belly against him. He took his time, languid kisses that explored her thoroughly until she was gasping for breath, pressing her breasts against him and rolling her hips, making him grind into her.

"Mmmm, Good Morning, Gabo."

"Good morning Ali. This is how I want to wake you up every morning."

Alicia stiffened slightly, and he a rock dropped in his stomach. "Gabo..."

"Alicia, don't tell me you don't feel what I feel." He pulled back to see her face clearly; her eyes were soft and pleading.

"I don't know. I just want us to take it slow. I think for

now being friends, with - fuck, I hate the cliche of it all - but friends with benefits is probably the best idea for us."

There was a monster inside of him screaming, kicking, and raging at hearing her ask to be friends with benefits, when for him this was the start of something bigger. He'd always been afraid of letting his imagination run wild with the possibilities of being with Alicia. Now that he wanted that, she was pulling back.

"I've so much to decide still. I don't want to commit to something to you then fall through. I know there is something here, but my life was already in motion before you moved. You know what I mean?" She spoke fast, voice low and urgent, her hands were holding him, and he could feel the dampness in hers.

"I don't want to hurt you," she finished.

The beast inside howled and cried out that she was already hurting him. By closing the door to all possibilities, she was effectively stomping all his hopes down.

"What's between us is real, and I want us to stay close while I'm still here if you are good with that?" The hesitation in her tone was another dagger.

"Ali, whatever you want to do, I'll take. I hope we can trust each other enough to raise the flag if things get too deep. But you have to promise me you won't just pull away without talking to me first. Not this time."

Her breath hitched, and her eyes closed as if in pain.

He shook her hands, "Mírame a los ojos y prométeme que no me vas a dejar atrás."

"Gabo—" her voice was anguished, conflict clear on her face.

"I'm not saying don't move. If that's what works for you," he squeezed her hands, "I can only wish you the best. I realize we came to each other at crossroads. And it is too much, too soon to ask you to stay. But I'm asking for you not to shut me out. We can be friends, Alicia y Gabo, no matter where we are. Even if in different continents."

She nodded silently; her eyes full of all the words she couldn't say. He wanted to compel her, to make her talk, spill all that was inside of her. To tell him what stopped her from just saying "fuck it all" and having her stay and figure shit out together.

But he couldn't. Plain old preservation stopped him from pressing her further for putting it all in the line.

"Come here. There is no need to be so far. If you want me to be your fuck boy, then your fuck boy I'll be." He held her close to him, her body rigid with tension beginning to relax until she was softening in his arms. This woman had him acting like a fool.

"Not a fuck boy, I want a fuck man, please and thank you," she said, face buried against his chest.

"Alicia, not too long ago, you said you would do anything for me, but the reality between us, is you've always known you just have to ask."

CHAPTER 14

GABO

You learn a lot from a person when you see them in their element. The trick is to understand what their element is. He sat across Ms. Powell-Torres. He couldn't think of her in any other way as he studied her under his lashes while the staccato sound of her nails against the keyboard continued in the quiet office.

"So, I think we can pull a list of our top leisure clients for the luxury hotels in our portfolio and give them an invitation to the Madison, which is the crown beauty of our hotels."

"Which one is the Madison again? Is that the one that opened a few years ago by Hollywood beach?" he asked.

"Have you been there?"

"Yeah, my dad took us to dinner once when my Mom and I were visiting. Fancy digs. Do you think it's too pretentious to do a reception there?" His thoughts swirled as he considered all the optics of this event.

"I see what you mean, but, no, I don't think so. Sadly, some people you want to donate are attracted by the location of the event itself. In this capitalist world, money attracts money."

"Yeah, you're right..."

"Are you going to ask Mr. M to help with invites?" She stopped typing, and all her focus was on him. Eyes attentive and soft, a slight smile on her face that told him she was interested in everything that would come out of his mouth.

She had a way of doing that. She was a great multitasker. He'd seen her study for an exam while cooking dinner for her parents and watch TV at the same time, so whenever she focused all her attention on something, it was... intense. Not intense in that "you are in front of the classroom and your pants dropped, and everyone is watching" intense. But the "this person is mystic and can read all your thoughts and desires" intense.

"Nah, I don't think I should ask Pops."

"Why not? He is very well connected in my industry. Everyone that is everyone knows Mr. Miller, the general manager of the iconic Five Winds resort."

Those eyes, dark brown and knowing. She asked what she already knew the answers for, so why was she pushing?

"I know, but he already connected me with your company. It's enough."

"Is it enough?"

Is it enough? That answer had many layers, and he had no mental capacity to tackle them at the moment. He guessed they would play the stare game then.

Awareness crackled between the two of them. This was and would always be why Alicia would be one of his people. No matter what, even while they were supposedly not friends, he always counted as someone that was his. Someone that he would jump off a plane and rescue them from jail type of people. His body sat basking in the pure knowledge of being known.

"Ok, Gabriel Ernesto, I won't stay in your business." She looked down to her desk, the connection snapped, as her intense scrutiny ended, and he had his thoughts to himself again.

"I want you to stay in my business, though," he said.

Alicia's eyes widened in awareness, then soften imperceptibly.

"Now?" She leaned imperceptibly as if she couldn't quite hear across the desk.

"Alicia Maria, do you have a a few minutes…" A white woman walked into Alicia's office looking as if the office was hers. "Oh, who do we have here? Will you introduce us, Alicia?" the woman said.

He stood up as the woman settled herself in Alicia's office with no care for Alicia's privacy or agenda. He looked at Alicia, awaiting the introduction, and saw when Alicia's body language made a metamorphosis. Her shirt-clad shoulders went up, eyebrows set in a rigid line, and her mouth set in a subtle, toothless smile. Oh shit. She must not like this woman.

"Jenny…how are you today? We missed you in the executive morning lineup this morning." A head tilt from Alicia. A visible flinch from Jenny. A direct hit.

"Sorry, where are my manners? Jennifer, this is Gabriel Miller. He is the co-founder of Gifted Athletes of Broward. Gabo, this is my colleague and VP of Operations, Jennifer Winters."

"Nice to meet you, Jennifer." He shook hands with her, and tried to ignore the smirk on her face.

"So sorry to interrupt your meeting," said Jennifer.

"Jennifer, you aren't sorry, and you know it. How can I be of assistance today?" countered Alicia.

"I wanted to review the documents for the next board meeting." Jenny kept her eyes between the two of them. He sat back down and held his stance relaxed, but he felt Alicia's tension like it was his own.

"I have them already. If you like, please take a look at my calendar, and we can set a time for us to review formally."

"Oh, of course, of course. I see here that you are very busy with the little philanthropic project Jack allowed you to work on. So I'll get back to my office to do some actual work, and when you are ready, you let me know, ok?"

There were so many daggers being thrown left and right he was in danger in the middle of the battlefield. He realized, though, that he should not interject, no matter how much he wanted to say something to defend Alicia. She was a professional, and he wasn't about to undermine her with some white knight bullshit.

"Absolutely, Jenny. Go ahead and set the meeting to review the work I did and present each time in these meetings. On my own." That smile. That said, she didn't give a flying fuck about Jenny, and her innuendo was it for him. To see her not take a shit at work made him want to ensure he was up to the task of being with her. To be hers.

"Well, ok then," Jenny scoffed, outmaneuvered. "See you, Mr. Miller. Alicia Maria."

After that tense exchange, Jenny left, having the grace not to continue goading Alicia into any more ugliness.

"That was..." he trailed off.

"That was why I can't stay in this job anymore. Reason 1,567."

A frisson of unease ran through him at the bleakness of her tone.

ALICIA

The Gifted Athlete Center of Broward was officially in service. The wall was painted in vibrant colors, which the students had already promised to adorn with some art of their own.

Twenty students were sitting around the benches in different poses of relaxation and repose. It was heartening to see faces from the different students nodding as they listened to what the center was planning to offer. Mason and Gabo explained the goals they wanted to accomplish with them if they agreed to be part of the program in the middle of the hall.

Mason was always a people person, and seeing him in action showed her how much he was a natural for this, but what surprised her was Gabo. He was poised and measured. He took his time to listen to the teenagers as they laid their goals and concerns and gave them answers with the thoughtful attention of their intellect. Some people treat children and teenagers as subordinates, to be seen but not heard. Gabo treated them as people worthy of attention and respect.

Her cellphone rang, and at first, she thought it was the office. Technically, she was still on her workday, having come after lunch to work on some plans for the first donor reception they were planning to host.

She saw the caller was Angela Garcia from the job in New York and stepped away from the hall to take the call. Her hands were damp, and she walked outside to take the call.

"Hello Alicia, how are you? This is Angela Garcia."

"Hello, Angela! I'm well, thank you, and you?"

"I'm doing well, thank you, I'm calling to set up the last round of interviews. I wanted to congratulate you on making it to the last round. We have had a rigorous process, and the road has not been easy. We have an excellent and qualified candidate in you, and one of our internal managers also has applied for the promotion. Now I don't want you to think that you are at a disadvantage. Both of you bring unique qualities to the position that has made the decision very hard to make. This is why we have added one final round of interviews that our Board of Trustees Chairwoman will perform. Do you have any availability next week, Thursday or Friday?"

"Either day works for me, Angela. I'll rearrange my schedule accordingly. Thank you so much for the opportunity and for moving me forward." There was a momentary sense of joy for making it through this last round, and for a minute, she had the urge to go share with Gabo. Then reality settled in.

"Absolutely dear, how is the search for a buyer going?" Alicia had mentioned in passing on her first interview that she was doing work to her home to sell it and move to New York.

"It is paused, the work that needs to be done will be happening in December, but not to worry, worst-case scenario, I'll move before the house selling." Her stomach twisted to knots, and a sense of unease crept up through her.

"Ok, no rush, dear. The process on our side is stalling as well, as both of you have made it mighty hard for us. So if we need to push the start date, if the position goes to you, that is certainly something we can take a look at, don't worry! Take care, and I will send you all the details to your email."

"Thanks, Angela! Have a great day."

Alicia stood outside of the center, her stomach full of knots at the thought of sharing this news with Gabo. He was the first person she thought to tell. After a few years in the same role, it was satisfying to know she could move out of the corporate world and move to an organization working for their community.

She walked in, still in her thoughts, and bumped into Mason.

"All good there, Powell?"

"Yes," she answered, air rushing out of her lungs.

"Damn. Whatever it is, it sounds heavy." He held her by her upper arms and looked at her.

"All good?" he asked softly. "My brother treating you well?"

"Yes, Gabo is a prince. I'm the messy one."

He nodded thoughtfully. "Yeah, it runs in the family."

Alicia burst out laughing. "I don't know how you and Gabo put up with us Torres girls."

"We do so because we can't help but be tugged by your gravitational pull, I thought you understood?"

Mason walked back to the hall after that statement, leaving her standing staring after him in wonder.

GABO

The smell of Juan Valdez lured his senses enough to have him open his eyes. He hadn't heard his alarm, but he could see he had snoozed. Again. Mornings were not the best time to interact with him. He didn't like early wake-ups. Anything after eight was fair business, but ask him to wake up before that and…well, he could act like a veritable beast. He did not like mornings, never had.

He walked down the stairs, wondering where that coffee smell was coming from; he hadn't set up his automatic coffee maker. And there was Alicia, making two cups of coffee and placing some muffins on his countertop.

"Alicia, what you doing here so early?"

"I know you mentioned you were trying to wake up earlier to make sure you got in all our consulting work done before switching gears to Gifted Athletes. I thought to help. I wake up early so I can beat the traffic to my office, so instead of making my breakfast in my kitchen, I'll just make it here."

She pointed to the coffee and the muffins. She looked like a vision, ready for her workday and smile on her face. "That way, the lure of Colombian coffee will be your wakeup motivation."

He walked down the stairs, and the pull that always had him gravitating towards her brought him in front of her, with a goofy smile on his face.

"You know the motivation won't be the coffee nor the muffins, right? It'll be you. Thank you, Ali."

He pressed a soft kiss on her cheek and wished her a good day at work. He could start all his days like this; he could see her in his life, just like this.

***

THE PERK OF BEING HIS OWN BOSS WAS THAT HE DECIDED WHEN to take a mother fucking break. The prospectus in front of him was making his head pound and his eyes swim.

Financial security meant that while Mason and he were working on their non-for-profit full throttle, he was still burning two ends of the candle. He worked consulting jobs with various colleges and private schools, providing his expertise in creating new academic programs. He'd planned ahead for this moment in his life but having savings didn't offer him a foolproof safety net.

Then there was Alicia, if his work and responsibilities were big rocks in the container that was his mind, then Alicia was the sand that filled all the crevices, finding any empty spot to saturate his mind with thoughts of her.

Her offer of "friends with benefits" was as unsurprising as it was painful. For a moment Saturday night, he thought he was penetrating the barriers she had erected between them, but somehow at the end of the night, he ended up taking what she was willing to give. He blamed his dick and the want that was consuming him. After all, he was willing to take a risk on Alicia. She, in turn, no longer was ready to take a chance on him. Turnabout was a kick in the nuts.

He closed his laptop, rubbing his eyes and looking outside of his window. It was that time of the year when the sun started setting by six. A swim would do him and his aches, internal and external, some good right now.

In no time, he was downstairs and outside getting in his pool. The water was warm after a sunny day, his arms and legs powered through the water, the weightless feel of his body gliding through was allowing him to clear his mind free of all thoughts.

He had his water headphones on and was immersed in the moment. Stroke after stroke, he glided, finally relaxing. After losing count of his laps, he slowed down enough to approach the end of the pool and rest for a minute.

Alicia sat on one of the day beds directly in his line of sight, a look of naked need in her eyes. She sat with her legs together folded under her, her favorite way and his favorite as well. Today she was wearing one of those maxi dresses, with thin straps on her shoulders. Its neckline showed him her heaving full breasts as she breathed in and out, the rest of her body hidden behind vibrant reds and oranges of the fabric.

Time stood still while they each took in their fill. She broke the spell first and looked down, dimples showing, and shook her head slightly.

"I texted you several times. It's my turn to cook. I wanted to know if you wanted to eat with me." Her rich voice was quiet in the darkening night. The automatic lights of the terrace illuminated her with an ethereal glow. There was a question in her statement and underlying current he could not miss.

"I could eat." Was his response. His body, which had

relaxed after the swim, was tensing up again but for a very different reason.

"What do you want to eat?" Her response was sultry, and they both recognized they were not speaking about food right now.

"I've been hungry, so hungry for a long time." He propelled out of the pool in one powerful push of his arms. Alicia's eyes traveled away from his face down his body, following the water cascading down to his tented swim trunks.

"Is there anything that I can give you?" She asked. He reached for the towel he had left on this side of the pool and dried himself enough, and threw the towel back on the floor. If this was what she wanted, he was more than able and willing to give it to her good. Forget his feelings. Forget the underlying hurt right now. He was burning by the way she was looking at him.

"Stand up, Alicia." His voice was firm. None of the gentleness remained, only the primal need to have her.

She looked up and took her time to unfold herself and stand, her luminous brown skin of her arms and chest a beacon calling him to touch. Her hair was down to the small of her back in her golden-brown twists; her eyes were sultry and heavy lidded. He stepped into her and pressed her softness to his hard hot body.

"Do you think you can satisfy my hunger?" he spoke to her, breaths mingling in the warm night. He leaned into her lush mouth and sank into her, welcomed by her embrace. He was home.

This was not a leisurely kiss. He worshipped her with his mouth, pushing her to her limits; he wanted her with a relentless passion that took his breath away. She was giving as much back, her tongue twined with him, meshing together in ragged breaths.

She must have just showered after work because she tasted like peppermint and smelled of citrus. His hands were full of her. He didn't know where to touch first, so he tried everything. Her smooth, bare arms, her neck, her cool cheeks down to her glorious plump titties, her curved belly, and her magnificent ass. He decided this was where his hands needed to be the most and took two overflowing handfuls and pressed her to him.

She gasped, and her body rolled into him, her belly cradling his dick with sweet contact.

"Who owns this ass?" he growled. He was losing all sense of civility, losing his mind to her scent and heat and the mewling sounds she was making. He wanted to plunge into her right now, but he knew he needed to make it good for her too. He kneaded her ass, and she rolled her hips and waist again.

"It is yours, Papi." His dick hardened even more, if that was a possibility, he could drill a wall he was so hard. Her husky voice calling him Papi was too much, and for a second, his brain short-circuited as he imagined fucking her, slow and steady, with her bent over, taking all of him.

He lowered his head to her ear, "Are you going to let me fuck you there one day?"

"Mmm maybe, one day if you are good," she responded. He nipped her ear. "Oh, I'll be good, good."

"Less talk, more action." She pulled him to her and kissed him, sucking his tongue to hers, and he let himself enjoy her. She bit his bottom lip, and he groaned into her mouth. They were explosive together. The night in her living room was but a quick taste of how it could be for the two of them.

He needed to slow things down. He was too close to losing it all and slaking his undying hunger in her. He wanted this to be good for her. He needed that. His hand coasted over her shoulder, and he took her strap between his fingers. His finger trailed softly down her neckline, her body shivered, and a sigh escaped her mouth. He took the other strap and let her dress fall off her shoulder. Her dress crumpled around her and pulled around her hips.

"Why aren't you wearing a bra?" he moaned. She was trying to torture him.

"Are you complaining?"

"Fuck no," he assured her. Her breasts were large, more than a handful for his big hands. She had thick brown nipples that were begging to be touched. He closed his eyes, her luxurious body something to savor instead of taking a shot to the head.

She raised her eyebrow when he opened his eyes again and dropped her dress down her hips. It whooshed down her body and draped around her on the floor. The night was still, the occasional noise of cars driving around the neighborhood accompanied their jagged breaths. "Alicia, you are magnificent."

She raised her head high and stood proud in front of him, such a contrast to any other time he had paid her a compliment. Her desire made her confident and so fucking sexy because of it. "Your turn," she said.

He unlaced his pants with practiced movements and peeled his swim trunks off. You would think the damp fabric would be a detriment to his dick, but to the contrary, his length bobbed out of the pants bounced hard against his stomach.

Her eyes widened, then a smile of pure mischief came to her face. She erased the space between them, and her hand touched him, sure and firm. Somehow, she knew just how to handle him. His hips moved in their own volition, seeking her hand and the release that was building in his spine. He closed his eyes, reduced to panting while she jacked him off. The pressure began to gather, and he knew he had to stop her. "Oh no, you're not gonna make me cum before I get to taste you."

He laid her on the day bed, and she relaxed for him, a queen awaiting her subject to pleasure her. He braced himself on his arms and hovered over her; his mouth traveled down from her neck, his nips making her shake a little. His mouth landed on her breasts, and using his tongue, he kissed around the fat curve of them and around her areola, everywhere but her nipples, until she was panting under him.

By the time he took her left nipple in his mouth and sucked, she cried out loud. "You liked that, Ali?" He couldn't help the smug tone of his question whispered against her nipple.

"Fucker, you know I do, do it again," she sighed and pushed his head back to her. He sucked and licked and even suckled, until she became desperate, her hips seeking him in movements that had him wanting to sink into her.

He kept dragging kisses down her body, and soon he found himself looking at her pussy. Her lips were thick and the lushness of it almost hid her clit from his view. He opened her up and kissed her reverently. "I've wanted to taste you for so long. So many years." Her scent was earthy and rich, and he lost himself to her taste.

His only need right now was to make her scream. He wanted to be an expert in Alicia. To know her every hidden place. He learned her needs through his senses. How the touch of her thighs hugged his face when he hit a particularly good spot; the sound when she gasped, mewled, and moaned his name; the sight of her seeing her body ripple in pleasure and the sweet taste as she came all over his mouth, drenching him in her juices.

She was now languid, laying down her hand gently caressing his shoulder in circular motions, and he wanted to be the better person and leave her like this satisfied and at peace, but his dick was not about to let him walk away from her.

"You laying there satisfied and smug in your pleasure is going to be one of my new fantasies of you. I've pictured you here, fucking you hard over one of the day beds, my dick deep inside you while you milked me with your warm tightness."

"My God, Gabo, all along you had this filthy mouth and mind full of fantasies of me, and I had no idea," she said with wonder. "Where else?"

"I have fucked you all over this house, your house, in your room, on your pool deck, on your desk at work, you name it, I have imagined it and most likely came screaming your name."

She spread her legs and said, "What are you waiting for?"

He raised himself over her body and moved to align his dick to her warmth. She welcomed him, and then he froze. "Shit, I don't have a condom here. I have to go to my room."

She stayed quiet for a beat. "I wouldn't do this with anyone else, but it is you. I was tested not too long ago, and I am free of any concerns. I'm also on the pill."

She dropped that bit of knowledge for him to decide, giving him the space to make the final call. "I trust you, Alicia. I tested right after I got here. And I haven't been with anyone for more than two years give or take."

"Two years?" she said incredulously.

"Yeah, I haven't connected with anyone like that for a while," he shrugged.

"Ok then," she said.

"Ok then," he answered back.

He kissed her long and languid, not wanting to talk anymore or even imagine that this might not feel as meaningful to her as it did to him.

Soon they were back to panting and grinding, their

bodies seeking each other in the moonlight. She dragged her hands down his back and grabbed his ass with a possessive moan that had him bucking into her. He couldn't wait any longer and pulled back to ensure he was lined up with her. She was warm, and wet, and perfect. He slid in slowly, giving her time to adjust, but she pulled him with her hands on his ass, and he lost the little control he had left and plunged into her slick sex.

What came next, he couldn't describe in detail because his mind went into overdrive, and he was filled with a sense of complete unrestraint: her body, her smell of earth, and the woman around him. The tight hold of her and the way her body undulated to meet every hard thrust would be sensations he would remember in the sort of way that one remembers how to breathe. The way that muscle memory is essential to life she was essential to him, and his body showed her in a thousand ways even if he could not bare his heart to her.

When he heard her scream his name just as he had fantasized, she bucked and squeezed his dick to the point he saw stars, the little rational thought he had, left his body. He was pure sensual pleasure, and when he reached his orgasm, he spilled in her all of the love in his heart, using the only language he could at the moment.

CHAPTER 15

Five days as friends with benefits. Five incredible days where normally her vibrators would have gotten used at least once a day and instead had not been touched. It was a new record.

Alicia sat on her dining room table the first night she had not eaten dinner with Gabo since the night of the pool terrace. A pile of documents sat on each side of her, and two screens showed spreadsheets that had her full attention. It was budget season, and that meant bringing work home.

The problem was her heart was not in it anymore. She kept getting sidetracked, looking at videos of travel experiences and adding places to her never ending list of locations she wanted to visit. The new twist was that she'd started picturing Gabo alongside her adventures. It was distracting to say the least.

Alicia stopped enjoying her work, not because of her duties, but because she was tired of working for the benefit of the few versus the benefit of all. Being with Gabo dulled the sense of urgency she felt, the utter sense of lost and pending doom that if she did not do something soon, to change her the path she was in, she would be lost.

She sat back staring at the wall in the dining room table, looking at a picture of her daddy, her mami, and her, all laughing coming out of church one Sunday. One of the few times she remembered her dad going to church with them had been Easter Sunday, and her mother had promised him to do a big fish fry at the house if he just attended with them. It had worked.

The house that surrounded her still had all the hard memories of the past. She looked around. And she remembered. She remembered the hard days when her daddy had barely any energy to stand, the arguments with her mother in low voices to avoid disturbing her father all because they had thought keeping her in the dark about her father's sickness had been the right thing.

Prostate cancer. He had an early onset of it, and then it had come back a few years later. She had found out the second time, in the most unexpected way. If she had not arrived a day early as a surprise to her parents, who knew if they would have ever told her?

The lull of years of cautious success of remission and then the last diagnosis, a different cancer now in attacking his lungs, his tobacco habit was coming to wreak havoc with his body, and with the last of her sanity and sense of wholeness.

"I'm not part of this family, I always thought it was you and Daddy and me, but all along, it was just the two of you. Who else knows Mami? Who else was in on the secret?" The weight of the prescription bottle in her hand, incensed her further. She shook the bottle at her mother, who sat in the couch crying.

"Why would you not tell me Daddy was sick, Mami? If I had not arrived a day early to surprise you both, how would I have

known of this? Were you planning to keep me in the dark?" She had never spoken to her mother like that, never screamed in rage and desperation at her. Her throat was raw, and her heart was broken, her daddy, her hero, was sick, and she had not been by his side. She hadn't even known.

"Yes, Alicia, I was. Because you are young and your life is starting, and I know you if you found out would cancel school and come and live here by his side and just bury yourself under the worry of his health. I cannot do that to you, mamita. You deserve to live your life." Her mom looked at her with fierce conviction in her wet eyes, still justifying her stupid decision.

"And if he had died, what then, Mami? What would you have told me? This makes no sense, I get to choose how I spend my life, and you and Daddy are my everything. My friends, they are important, Gabo he is my rock, but the two of you..." Her voice broke, and she let all the anguish come out of her, she cried herself until she could not take it anymore, her father was sick with stage three cancer, and they did not know what would happen next.

She shook herself of the hard memories and focused back on work, letting the clock tick by. For the first time, it felt wrong not to share what was happening with anyone else. After the interview, she had the impulse to call Gabo and tell him everything, but a frisson of foreboding had changed her mind

Gabo: Are you sure you don't need any help with those reports?

Alicia: Even if I did. Last I heard, you're in Higher Education, not Finance

Gabo: I could help with motivation and encouragement. And we could work on the last invitations for the reception next month.

Alicia: Tomorrow. Promise. I just want to get through this pile of work today, ok?

> Gabo: I miss you. My dick misses you too.
> Alicia: You nasty. I love it. Go to sleep. Or better yet, go and jack off thinking of me.
> Gabo: Too late, I did that already.

She laughed and put down the phone. One of the best things about fucking Gabo was how nasty and filthy he could be. During the day with his text messages, or when they were hanging out and he was aroused. So, essentially all the time. It was like now that he had permission to tell her how he felt, he couldn't stop telling her. And he had shown her already some of those ways. Her kitchen, her room, his kitchen, her pool terrace, his office, and her living room had all seen some of his fantasies come to life. Maybe she could wrap things up early and give him a call. The night still had hours to go, and a quickie never hurt anyone...

GABO

> Alicia: Good morning. I miss you, and I surprised my vibrators by using them again. When are you coming by today? PS: Thank you for moving the last of the plants to the front. You are too good to me.
> Gabo: I am taking a shower, and I will be there right after.

He had woken up to a text from Alicia that had him hard the second he read it. Fuck. This woman had him making a castle in his head. He accepted that she was more focused on the physical side of the relationship, and for now, it worked for him as well. He thought Alicia needed space. She had gone through so much with her family these past years, and their friendship was still on the mend.

Just because he wanted to wife her up and give her the

world didn't mean it needed to be on his schedule. She should take her time. He'd taken his sweet ass time to realize she was it for him. He had always loved Alicia, so no lightning bolt had to strike him to make him realized he loved her.

The in-love part, he suspected, had been there for a long time as well, but he had never let it have a name, have a place more than a small compartment in his heart. Now that he had given it air, it bounced around, taking space and time, and it all overwhelmed him. He also was bursting at the seams wanting her to see it in his face, but dreading what she would say if it somehow came to light.

So he would wait. He would wait for her because she was worth it and because she did it for him. That was what friends did for each other.

He went into the bathroom and had a long hot shower. He avoided jacking off to the thought of how she screamed his name when he hit that spot with his dick she so loved. Gabo hadn't seen Alicia for three days. What had been one day of a break had morphed into one more and another as she became more and more buried in work. He felt guilty of her extra work. She had been putting a lot of hours into working with him and Mason to plan this sponsor's reception that was fast approaching, as well as the grant applications.

Yesterday, he found out that the two of the grants had been approved, which came just at the right time as they needed to get supplies, and still had more work to do in the center to make it functional and comfortable for the athletes. So today they were all going out to celebrate. Mason, Marina, a few of Mason's friends, Alicia and Gabo, were all going to go to a burlesque show (Mariana's idea) and have some drinks to celebrate.

But before that, he was going to hang out with his girl.

No work, no landscaping, just the two of them, zero plans but to enjoy each other's company.

HE CHECKED THE GATE. IT STOOD OPEN, SO HE LET HIMSELF IN through the house sliding door. Alicia wasn't downstairs. He could hear the shower in the upstairs bedroom and decided that one could never be too clean.

He knocked on the door of her bathroom, and when she said to come in, he opened the door to find her gloriously wet skin glistening with bubbles and soap.

"Buenos dias Gabo."

He stripped naked faster than he could say hello and opened the shower door and stepped inside. He pressed himself behind her and she shuddered in satisfaction.

"I missed you so much." He kissed her neck. Her hair was piled up in a complicated tower wrapped in satin and a clear shower cap. Having easy access to her neck, he licked and kissed until she was undulating against his dick.

"I missed you too, and my pussy also missed you."

This was going to be over real soon. But he'd make sure she got hers first.

He turned her around and shut off the water kissing her with all the pent-up passion of the last few days. He stayed addicted to her kisses and her presence. Even if they hadn't been having sex, it was her company he had missed the most.

She moaned and palmed his dick, and he couldn't think straight.

"If you keep that up, I'm going to fuck you fast and hard."

"Promises, promises."

He pinched her nipple to make her behave, and she laughed and gasped in a mixture of sounds that had his dick thrusting seeking her warm haven. He turned her around again, pushing her body against the shower wall, and she purred, she fucking purred, and he lost his mind. He touched her ass reverently, hands open sliding from the bottom to the top, and promised her, "Soon, soon I will be in here, and I'll make sure you love it."

Then he spanked her hard.

She moaned in response and arched the small of her back, pushing her ass out to give him better access. He had discovered through their time together that Alicia loved to get her ass tapped. And he loved doing it. So it was a win-win situation.

He slid in to his homecoming. "Fuck," he rasped. "I don't want to wait to see you so many days again, ok?"

"I know it sucked. I missed you too."

They kissed slow, drugging kisses that communicated better what they could not say with words. The pace was relentless. There was a contrast in the way he was pounding into her hard and fast versus the kisses she was giving, slow and languorous, that was a mirror of where their hearts were.

"Gabo, I'm coming," she moaned, arching back her head on his shoulder.

"Dale, don't hold back." His voice was deep and husky.

When she came, she shuddered in ecstasy, taking him with her. Always with her.

***

They laid in a tangle of legs on her couch, eating her platanitos and reading a new book. It had been her turn to pick, and they were both deep into the story.

"I cannot believe this negro left her high and dry without talking to her first." He was upset.

"Awww, baby, you sound genuinely distraught. I agree, though. He's trippin'."

She turned, placed her bookmark, and closed her book.

"You are so careful with your books, bookmarks and everything." he said.

"Yeah, I'm not a barbarian, folding the pages of my precious babies like you do." she playfully scoffed.

"So neat and careful. I noticed in your room, all the things are perfectly in order, the bookcase color ordinated, the bed always made. It makes me want to rumple you a bit." he said.

"Ok don't start with all of that, I don't want us to be late for tonight and the way you are looking at me we'll end up missing the outing all together." she said and he laughed at her clutching her neck in mock horror.

"Ok, I have to go upstairs and start getting dressed, but you are free to hang out here. My tablet controls the TV. Here it is. The password is 1986. I'll be ready in an hour, and we can head to your house for you to get ready. Does that work?"

From previous experience, Alicia had learned that he disliked waiting for her while getting dressed. She liked to take her time to get dressed until she deemed herself perfectly ready, and there were many house parties, school events, and more where he'd been forced to wait for her. Before, she'd given zero cares in the world that he disliked waiting, so her considerate way of planning warmed him.

He kissed her short and sweet. "Ok, I'll head over in about a half-hour or so and will get ready to. I'll be back here waiting."

He used the tablet to browse the TV and settled in to watch some Desus and Mero episodes. He woke up realizing he'd dozed off for fifteen minutes. The day had been a marathon of laughter and some fantastic fucking, and he was relaxed and in a great mood.

The tablet locked while he was sleeping, and there was a notification of an email on the top. He pressed the password and tried swiping the email away; instead, the device took him to the message.

He was about to close the messaging app when his eyes were drawn to the email's subject. Last round of interviews. As anyone in this situation can attest, knowing the right thing to do versus what one ends up doing is very different.

He read the email, a chill settled across his body. In very succinct terms, the email stated that Alicia was a top candidate for a position as a finance executive in New York for a non-for-profit organization. It seems she had been in the interview process for at least a month.

The subject of her moving was one they navigated with a lot of careful words and deliberate sentences. She had never bluntly said she was not moving. Still, in conversations, she'd mentioned she was "letting things happened as they needed to happen." Come to find out, the vagueness in her words was not about considering staying, but about not letting him know how advanced she was in the process of moving.

That she had not told him was proof that she was not trusting him completely, and that stung. And he wanted more from her.

The more he thought about it, the more his anger simmered at the bottom of his thoughts, volcanic and inevitable. He went to his house and got ready, the conversation of this email wasn't going to be easy to approach.

———

ALICIA LOOKED LIKE A DREAM IN AN ELECTRIC BLUE JUMPSUIT that hugged her curves in all the right places and a neckline that was deep and enticed him to look.

His body stood in high alert, its usual sate when she was

around, but his anger and overall hurt blunted the overall effect. He'd debated saying something, but tonight was a night of celebration, and deep down, he was concerned and afraid that he would say some shit that would just push her away. She was not ready for this conversation, but damned it. He deserved better than being left in the dark.

They arrived at the location of the show and parked.

"Ok, I don't know what is happening, but I recognize that you are upset. Your vein in your temple seems about to burst," she said.

"You are interviewing for a job in New York." He dropped the words like boulders. He was pissed, and her disregard for his state of mind was the last straw.

She hesitated at first, then she set her shoulders and jaw, and he realized this would not go well.

"Yes, I am. I'm in the last set of interviews. Now tell me, Gabo, how do you know that?" She turned in her seat to face him. Everything in her posture screamed annoyance. He looked at her, took two deep breaths, then turned his face back to the front of the car.

"It wasn't intentional. The email came up on your tablet, and I pressed the notification by mistake. It was a quick email, so I had essentially read it before I realized what I was looking at. It's not right, and that's my bad. But damn it, Alicia, when were you going to say something? When it was too late, and you had packed your bags and were ready to board the plane?"

"I told you I was in a weird place in my life. I am selling the house and planning to move. I told you. Don't act surprised, Gabo." She raised her voice.

"I'm not acting surprised! I'm saying you should have said something! Even before we were fucking, you should have said something. Because we are supposed to be fixing shit between us. How can we do that when you are keeping things from me that are important in your life?" He realized that the anger inside morphed to unfulfilled hurt, but he had no way to express the turmoil of emotions running through him.

"So you are upset, not because I may leave, but because I didn't tell you?" Her voice sounded confused, and when he looked at her, he saw an underlining vulnerability and hurt. He could not be seeing that. Alicia had pushed these friends with benefits things intentionally and with eyes open.

"Yes, I should have known. I can't dictate your life, Alicia; your comings and goings. You are your own person, but I thought I meant more than that, at least a 'hey I'm interviewing, and I am in the last round.'"

Alicia's shoulders slumped, and sadness suffused her face.

"No one knows I'm that ahead in the interviews....you are the only one, now." He suspected Mari would give her hell for it, and her mom seemed to be hoping for something different for her. Her family in New York might be happy, though, specially Aayala. He could only imagine the position she was in, that her decision was not something anyone else supported. How could he hold on to his anger when she was hurting, too? He knew he was right in being mad but his need to support her outweighed his need to stay mad. He held her hands across the car and squeezed them tight.

"Alicia, you can do anything you put your mind and your heart to. I..." *I wish you would give us a chance, that you would slow down, or even tell me to come.* What he ended up saying was, "I support you. I'm going to miss you when you are gone. I wish we had more time in the meanwhile, and I'm here."

She looked at him, tears in her eyes, her hands in his, and nodded. He didn't know what the nod meant, and, seeing her cry was fucking him up, so he tugged her gently, and she came, hugging him across the console.

A knock on his window startled them apart.

"Yo, come on, let's see some titties!" Mariana hollered at them while Mason stood behind her, cheering.

They looked at each other, and the silence spoke to all the things they'd left unsaid.

ALICIA

They sat in a large booth. The place assaulted the senses, with red, deep-cushioned booths, chairs and black tables, undressed cocktail servers, handing drinks, and mingling with the crowd. The place meant to replicate the cabaret bars of the past. With an air of mystery and sensuality, it was the perfect establishment for a burlesque show.

Too bad she couldn't enjoy it. Her friends on the other hand were having a great time. They laughed and drank while they waited for the show to start. Mariana kept giving her glances, knowing something was wrong but not wanting to bring attention to her and dampening everyone else's fun.

Gabo sat next to Mason and Mariana, and Mason's coworker Jason sat between her and Gabo. Jennifer, the tipsy lady, and another coworker, Mario, were there too. Migue and his husband sat on the opposite end of the table to round things up.

Gabo looked tired and withdrawn though he kept up with the conversation with Mason and Jason, but she could tell his wasn't into it. Whatever that conversation was in his car before coming in, she understood she hurt him with her silence and omission of the truth. Somehow he had hurt her too, she worried and expected him to ask her to stay, to try to live here for him, and she had been prepared to turn him down, but when the opportunity came, nothing was offered. He'd given up the race before standing on the start line.

It was unfair to be mad, to expect something different

when she was not prepared to give one inch of her original plan to move away, but for a moment, she thought she could maybe take that leap with him. The impulse had been short-lived, and it was better they had talked and got on the same page.

She jolted out of her thoughts, a kick under the table startling her. Her head swiveled back and forth to find the culprit. When she saw Mason's innocent face, and slightly narrowed eyes, she made a 'what the fuck' face. He smiled kindly and nodded towards the bathroom.

"Hey Jason, sorry, so sorry, I need to go to the ladies' room." She squeezed out of the booth, and she heard Mason say, "I'll walk with you. I was on my way there myself."

They left the table behind, and Mason guided her through a corridor that led to a smaller empty room that seemed to be room for events. A drape separated the two spaces and kept the room secluded.

"What the fuck happened to the two of you? You both look horrible," Mason said. He sat down at a cocktail table by the corner.

"I can't do this, Mason, please."

"He is all clammed up, so it's up to you to tell me why my bruh, who seemed to be very happy last I saw him, is sulking with a drink in his hand."

"Did he tell you I'm moving to New York?" She asked curiously.

"He's told me he was hoping the move wasn't a done deal, yes." Mason pushed back in his chair and crossed his arms.

"Well, I'm interviewing for a job there. I'm in the top two." She could see his face changing, disappointment creeping in. "Mason, Gabo hasn't seen me in years. He hasn't seen what the years did to me, what the loss of my father did to my family. But you have. You've been around."

He nodded, solemn, compassion filling his gaze.

"I need change. Big change, know what I mean? Gabo being here is...is a novelty. I love him dearly. He is my friend, same as I love you, and I love Mariana."

Mason raised his palm and stopped her.

"I was with you until you said that bullshit at the end. Gabo is special to you. You don't just feel fraternal love for him."

"It doesn't matter. I have to go. I can't sit in that house anymore and be surrounded by memories. Even at the old apartment I saw my dad everywhere. My job is suffocating me, and now that Gabo is here, I'm getting out and doing more, but I haven't been able to shake this feeling that this is all for now, that I'll slide back to the same ol'. I think I am doing the right thing."

"Powell. I've not said much besides answer your questions for the most part. You just told me a lot of nothing to convince me you need to move to New York. Are you trying to convince me, or are you trying to convince yourself?"

Right at the moment of that troubling question, Gabo walked in. His face appeared clouded and still upset.

"Mason, can you give us a minute?" he asked, crossing his arms over his chest.

"Sure thing. Treat her well or else." Mason pointed his finger at Gabo then walked out.

"Are you ok?" Gabo asked.

God, this man. He was worried about her.

"I'll be alright. You?" she asked.

"I don't know, but I'll try." That statement broke her a little. "I'm still a little pissed at you, to be honest," he said.

"I know." She couldn't just stand there and see him like this. She stood up and walked towards where he was standing.

"I'm a little pissed at you too," she said. "It makes no sense," she whispered.

He shook his head then pulled her into him.

"We can be pissed at each other together," he whispered.

"That sounds...dangerous," she said, voice husky.

He caught her mouth and showed her what he meant. His mouth punished her, and she fought him with all her might. Soon they were pulling at each other's clothes. He managed to unzip her jumpsuit, and it dropped on the floor. His shirt fell open, and his dick was out and hard.

"Bend over that table," he told her roughly. She braced herself against the high-top table he pointed at and stepped out of the jumpsuit—the noise of the crowd outside filtering through the drapes bringing an illicit feeling to the moment. "Wouldn't want anyone to know how desperate you are for my dick," he said. She moaned at his filthy words and when his hard dick went in with one hard thrust. She had to hold on tight to the table, though the table struggled to hold her up, too.

He pounded into her, his breath ragged as he found a rhythm that had her begging for forgiveness. "Fuck, fuck Gabo right there." She transformed into pure vibrations, her body trembling as Gabo hit her spot over and over again. "You better be quiet, or they'll hear you outside," he said. She didn't care. She was long gone. She tried to push back, meet his thrusts, but he kept his relentless pace. She could only hold on and take that dick he promised.

He touched her clit, and just the touch and she exploded in a full body orgasm that left her legs weak. Her pussy gripped him hard, and she heard him curse, "Fuck, fuck, fuck."

Gabo slowed down to let her catch her breath. "You ok?" he asked.

"Yeah," she replied, still dazed.

"Good, because I'm not done with you."

Fuck.

He had her coming again in minutes, his pace slow and hard. He'd caught a second wind and held her in place, making sure she took it all.

"Papi, please."

"Please, what?"

"Please, have mercy," she cried, her pussy tightening around his dick while he kept on fucking her with slow hard thrusts.

He pulled out of her and sat on a sofa next to the tall table. He held her against him and somehow got her to sit on his dick with very little help from her.

She spread her legs and bounced on him, chasing her next orgasm, but he was having none of it. "No, tonight, you are going to take what I have to give." He held her tight and, with short staccato thrusts, proceeded to fuck her to oblivion. She heard his veiled message, and took what he had to give, because the rest, she didn't know if she was ready to receive.

She started screaming his name at the same time the crowd burst into applause. He groaned her name, and his hotness filled her up. She was going to feel this one for days.

Gabo lifted her and set her to rights, all the while his hurt stood up like a third occupant in the room.

"Wa gwaan baby girl?" Aayala's voice sounded thick with sleep.

"So sorry for waking you up. I need to talk to someone, and Mari will rip me one if I tell her how confused I am." Alicia could hear Aayala's sheet rustling on the other side of the phone then her phone gave the alert for Aayala's video call. She answered.

"Oh damn Licy, what's wrong? Why are you crying?" Aayala asked as soon as she saw her face.

Gabo had dropped her off after their night with their friends, and had not even attempted to stay over as usual. She'd set parameters to their friends with benefits arrangements to avoid catching too many feelings but that hope had dissolved like a tower of salt in the rain. She was catching feelings for Gabo, all the ones she had before, now with the strength of maturity, experience, and reason.

No matter how much she tried to hold on to her plans to stay, she found herself imagining a life with Gabo. A life where they worked on figuring out their baggage and moving into the sunset together, no matter how corny that sounded.

Tonight she'd realize that her brain and her heart were in two different places, and the battle for what to do next paralyzed her to a complete standstill.

"I don't know what to do about Gabo." Was all she could manage to say, the knot in her throat threatening to cut her breathing.

"What do you want to do?" Aayala asked, as if it was that easy.

"It's not that easy!" she replied back, tears falling down her eyes. Why was she crying? She'd managed to hold back tears through so much heartache through the years.

"Licy…" The tenderness in Aayala threatened to overwhelm her. "It is that easy. You are making it harder than it needs to be. What do you want?"

The knot in her throat got harder as she fought her way through all the baggage that sat on top of her, but at the end of it, she found clarity she had not felt before. She held on to that. It was a small flame, fighting dampness and lack of air, it struggled to stay on, and instinctively she knew what it required. The only way it was going to stay on, was by giving it air and care, by stopping the spiral down to nothingness and start acknowledging she was living in the past.

"I want him, I want to try."

Aayala smiled. "There you go then. That was easy, wasn't it? The hard part will be sticking to it. But that's why you have Mari and me. You are not alone, Licy." Aayala's last words dissolved the knot in her throat and she took a deep breath of acceptance.

CHAPTER 16

GABO

A knock on his front door at 7:00 a.m.

Who the fuck was waking him up on a Sunday at 7:00 a.m.? He was sore, hurt, tired, and couldn't deal with any bullshit this early.

He jogged down the stairs, forgoing putting a t-shirt on. Whoever was outside had to deal with the fact that he had been sleeping. He realized it was his sliding door where he heard the knock, and there she stood. Alicia. Her hair was still in her silk wrap, eyes red-rimmed, and her cheeks were red. He took a deep breath, a weight lifting from his chest. She walked in and threw her arms around his neck and clung to him, her body pressed to him so dear and familiar.

"I'm sorry I shut you out, I don't even realize when I do it anymore, but I don't want to do it to you," she spoke to his shoulder, body trembling, and he could only close his eyes and stand strong for her.

"Shhh, it is ok Alicia, I'm here."

"I know you are, you annoyingly fine man. Why are you here? You came to just mess up all my plans." she laughed.

She pulled back, and his heart squeezed when he saw how tired she looked.

"I have a ton of things I need to figure out, but I don't want one of them to be you. I have no idea what the future brings, and I cannot promise to stay here forever. But I can promise to try. I want to try with you, I want to see where this goes, I'm not sure if you are into long-distance or I don't know, but I wanna give it a try, whatever this is, or becomes," she paused. "I can't believe I'm rambling."

He pulled her close and kissed her. Desperate in his need of her, her body melting into him. After the initial frenzy of contact, the kiss slowed down, not so much sexual, but full of comfort.

"Have you slept at all?"

"No, I haven't after you dropped me off, I just..." Her yawn cut off the rest of her sentence.

"Ok, up with you, let me take you to bed...to sleep." After he saw her eyebrows raised at his comment.

"You need to rest, Alicia, and I need to hold you tight."

7:00 a.m. Sunday wake-ups were worth it after all.

ALICIA

"Are you whining while looking at yourself in the mirror?"

Sun was coming in through her window while Beenie Man's voice singing "Who Am I" streamed through her Bluetooth speakers. She was lifted today, lightness suspending her in air, a kite in the sky. To let go was good for the soul. She had a date with Gabo. Their first date. The music had her mellow, the morning vibes making her sway her hips to the music as she finalized getting ready.

"Yes, I am. What do you think of this fit?" Aayala was on her tablet on a video call, her official outfit judge for the day.

"You look hot mama. I tried snatching that purple romper from you last time I was in Florida."

She did one last check of everything. Eyebrows, flawless. Light mascara. Check. Body moisturized. Triple check. Red matte lip. On point. Body deodorant to avoid thigh shafting. A must. Her anticipation for today's date with Gabo. Off the charts.

"So this is a date? On a weekday?"

"Yep, Gabo invited me on a whole day date. We have a million memories of hangouts, but he wanted to take me out officially. And he wanted me to play hooky."

"And you played hooky?" Alicia could not mistake the skepticism in Aayala's voice.

"Whatever. Why are you judging me?" she laughed in mock outrage. "I took a paid day off but still..."

"I knew it. You are the worst! So where is this romantic date happening?"

"I don't know. It's a surprise. But he told me to dress for somewhere outdoors, that we would be under the sun. And to wear a bathing suit underneath."

"Bathing suit? Gabo thinks he slick. Please make sure to take some extra underwear and a change of clothes, in case things get too hot, and your pussy juices are flowing."

"Stop." Laughter bubbled up in her, effervescent and inevitable. She sat on her bed and faced her cousin. She couldn't help the smile on her face. "I'm a little nervous, and to be honest, I don't know what I am doing. But I like that. Am I reckless?"

"Nooo, Girl. This is what I wanted for you. Zero worries, even if just for a little while. You were taking life too seriously. You deserve to do self-care and for Gabo, do some of that care for you."

The doorbell rang. Her heart skipped a beat.

"I think he is here."

"Ok, baby girl! Have fun, and have some sexy, sweaty sex for me, ok? I am living vicariously through you and Mari these days," Aayala said before hanging up.

She skipped down the stairs as if she was a teenager. She truly was excited for what he had planned today.

Alicia opened the door and saw him standing by the door, sunglasses on, hands in his pink summer shorts, fresh fade, and a cute smile on his full lips.

"Hi, Alicia. Preciosa como siempre."And just like that, her heart skipped a beat again. This man could get it any day. Any time.

"You flatterer, where are you taking me today?"

"Here, give me your bag. After you." He took her beach bag where she had put a change of clothes, towels, and a few personal items, not knowing what to expect and wanting to be prepared.

"For real? You aren't going to tell me?"

"Do you understand how surprises work?"

"Fine," she said, disgruntled, and he laughed at her tone. He opened the car door and waited for her to get in, then went to the driver's seat and drove out of her parking lot.

"You understand I'm going to bug you for the whole car ride, right?" He looked at her while he focused on driving out of their neighborhood.

"Do your worst," he said with a wide grin.

***

"A YACHT! REALLY?"

A white yacht was anchored on the sparkling waters of the marina. The boat was all sleek lines and flowy shapes. She could see from the dock that it had open access in the back with cozy cream-colored seats, and it looked like it also had an indoor portion. The yacht's front had a cushioned surface with mats and pillows to lounge in luxury and bask in the sun. She turned to Gabo with a giant smile on her face, her excitement mirrored in his open expression.

"Yes, Alicia Marie, just for the two of us, for the day."

He opened his trunk and brought out a large cooler bag he swung in front of him, along with her bag and his tote.

"The boat is fully stocked with snacks and drinks, but I brought you a special treat."

Childlike excitement coursed through her. She could not remember the last time someone had thoroughly surprise her, especially not on an ordinary day. This was no typical day, though. It has been a while since she had taken the time to relax and enjoy a day of leisure.

"That's not your dick in a box, right?"

He burst out laughing, not expecting her question. She was secretly pleased to have surprised him, even if it was just with humor.

"You're something Ali, and I love it. It's not my dick, though. I'll give that to you later." He winked. "I made you arepas with carne demechada and some with cheese."

"Ohh yes, you clearly know the way to my heart."

THE SMELL OF THE SEA AND PENT-UP EMOTIONS FILLED HER senses. To be here today, lounging in luxury comfort with her best friend, was something she would not have imagined a few months ago. Now the only smell missing was...sunscreen.

"Gabo, come over here so I can put some sunscreen on you."

Gabo was shirtless, sitting across her facing the boat's

interior, looking like a spread in a magazine. She had the view of the sea and the foam that followed them in their trajectory.

"Nah, I'm good." He was looking decidedly good indeed. It still was surprising to realize Gabo, her best friend, was such a fine-looking man. She wasn't one to be wild about muscles and sculpt. She preferred men that were physically imposing in other ways. Presence and sense of self were decidedly sexier than any six-pack she had ever seen. It did not hurt that Gabo had broad shoulders and was large in such a delicious way, especially on his thighs and arms, that made her think he could carry her non-dainty behind if he wanted.

"Really? Are you still in denial about what sunscreen does for you? Come here. You need sunscreen." she said.

"I don't burn. And I'm Black."

"No matter how much you look like your mom, that half-white is why you need that 90 SPF. I mean, you'd need it anyways. Thank God you have your mom's stamp on your lips and ass. I'd have to cut you loose if not."

"Oh, but you love these lips and this ass." His smirk told her he was trying to rile her up on this peaceful day.

"Stop trying to distract me!" she smiled and put some sunscreen on her hands. "Come," she purred, "I'll give you a nice rub."

That was enough incentive. He sauntered to her and sat still for her hands. Touching him like this, with all her noble intentions non withstanding, still gave her a frisson of awareness, his broad shoulders, his shifting muscles as she massaged his back, all on the right side of innocent, with a little bit of spice. She could absolutely get used to doing this —all the time.

"There, you are good to go." She patted his back.

"What about you? I can help you." He took the sunscreen

from her and turned around to face her, bracketing her with his powerful legs.

"I'm straight. I applied right before you came to get me. You know, like a responsible adult."

Just like the cloud currently blocking the sunlight, his face grew contemplative.

"You're very responsible now, aren't you? You always were, but now sometimes I see you, and there is this weight on your shoulders. A myriad of invisible bags around and on you."

His astute observation was no surprise to her. Here was a man who always had a true sense of her well-being even as a young adult and most oblivious—a sense of her internal compass. She shrugged, uncomfortable with the intensity of his gaze. Since they started having sex, Gabo had seen her naked and explored her to his heart content. This was an exploration she was not comfortable enduring.

"You seem all grown up, too, Gabo. I am so glad you and Mason pushed and started this non-for-profit. You took a risk, and I think you will be so surprised to see it pay off."

"So you are still trying to deflect by focusing on me? And who said I was speaking about work?" He removed her sunglasses with a gentle hand that made her heart constrict then took his off.

"I used to let you do that a lot before. Not sure I'll let you do it now that we are friends again. Who do you talk to now, Alicia? Who do you confide in when you're confused or conflicted? When you need to speak what's in your heart and know that someone holds your secrets with care and lack of judgment?"

The bravery of asking someone to jump with you with no cord was something she couldn't relate to, at least not anymore. Who was keen to do that type of jumping? There's a sense of security in the known, in the tried and true, in having your feet on earth and not aspiring to heights inaccessible or inconceivable. There was an audacity to his question that made her pause. She simply existed every day, knowing exactly what to expect. She couldn't imagine a world where she had what he offered.

He looked at her for a long time. Many unspoken words were exchanged as the breeze of the afternoon sang in her ears accompanied by the yacht's motor and the music while Gabo looked at her with startling understanding.

"I want to be that person for you if you let me, Ali. I want you to be unapologetically you. I miss being your person, you have become my person in this short amount of time. I cannot help it. The instant we were on speaking terms again, I remembered all the ways that caring for you felt right."

"I miss being that person from before. I'm not certain that's who I am today." Standing fast was as important right now as breathing. Her hands were damp, and her heart was tight on her chest. She looked down at him expectantly, hoping he got the message she was sending without words. *Leave it alone. I'm not ready.*

"Enough of all of this deep talk. It's meant to be a fun day! I want to go to the front and lay there for a while. You coming?"

He sighed, his eyes still on her. He stood up and pulled her to him, giving her a sweet short kiss. A kiss to calm, a kiss to answer her request. He heard it. He got it. "Come, Alicia Marie, let's lay on the front and enjoy the day."

GABO

He wanted this day to last. He wanted to pause time and have Alicia all to himself, for more than a day, all her attention on the two of them.

After the captain had taken them around the waterways,

they anchored in an inlet with blue waters close to a tall lighthouse in the north. The crystalline water had been inviting, and he was able to coax her into enjoying a swim together.

He told her about his relationship with his dad. How his dad's expectations still weighed heavily on him even as an adult. How this non-for-profit was a cause of concern for his dad because of the lack of stability it could bring.

She told him about her mother, how moving away strained their relationship, and how she found ways to stay close and in contact with her even while being disappointed in her mom's decision to move.

They spoke about their dreams for the future. Alicia still focused on the move to New York, which she expressed was a way to reset her life and refocus it with purpose. He told her how he saw the non-for-profit becoming an organization that helped athletes and other marginalized students beyond their county and the many ways they could help the community they served with access to education and meals.

They used the inside cabin, which had a comfortable bed that Alicia invited him to visit with a mischievous smile that had him hard just seeing her intention. She gave him head with such enthusiasm, using not only her lips and tongue but her hands and even her luscious breasts. The tension on his body built so fast; the speed of his orgasm blindsided him. In an embarrassingly short time, she had him coming while he bit his lips to stop from screaming her name without restrain.

Now they were back outside in the back of the boat while they watched the sun start to lower on the horizon. He had his girl snuggled up in his arms, her back resting on his front while he surrounded her with his arms and legs.

"You know, I think that was a record for us," she said. He

took a swig of his beer then offered her the bottle. She took a sip and gave it back to him.

"What do you mean?"

"Fastest time to come. If we had not fucked before, I would have been concerned about your stamina." She couldn't finish the words before she laughed.

"Oh, so you want to make this a competition? Because now that I know how you like me to finger you while I lick that beautiful pussy of yours, I'm certain I can make you come in a few minutes."

"I'd like to see you try."

"Are you still ticklish?" He brushed his hands along her sides, the synthetic texture of her bathing suit under his fingers.

"Don't you dare Gabriel Ernesto!" Her body tensed up on him, and she started pulling away, his body growing cold once away from the lush weight of her. He pulled her back to him, wrapping his hands and resting them on her belly with a gesture of peace.

"Ok, then, you better take me seriously when I say I'm taking the gauntlet you just put out. I will make you come faster than I came today."

"I look forward to that." She reached back and kissed him on his mouth. He returned it with a short one of his own, then as it happened with them, it grew bigger, their want always there right beneath the surface, ready to crest at the smallest incentive.

They broke apart; who knew how much time had passed though he sure as fuck didn't care. One of his hands was inside of her bathing suit, holding her breast, while the other held her hip. His head was full of all the ways he wanted to lay her down and fulfill his earlier promise. She took a deep breath that he felt through his body; the yacht's motor and lapping of the water lulling them as they started their return to the dock.

"I love this song. It has always reminded me of you."

"Tierra del Olvido" by Carlos Vives played in the sound system connected to his playlist. It was a song about longing for a lover. He dared not to dream.

"This song Alicia?"

She stiffened in his arms for a second, as he glided his hands across her body, out of her bathing suit, grazing her nipple. He charted his path down to cradle her belly again, wishing against wishes that holding her like this would make her open up fully to him.

"I mean, you used to play this song all the time. This is one of the songs you played to me that first night in your house."

Her hesitation was annoying and frustrating. For a minute, he thought...

"But yes, the words also make me think of you. Of us before everything. La Tierra del Olvido...I guess that is a mythical place in my mind now, the place you and I existed when everything was perfect."

He kissed the side of her neck, momentarily at a loss to say more than showing her how touched he was by her words.

"I must confess I also think of you when I hear this song. I see a thousand pictures of you. In my backroom listening to it for the first time with me when you were twelve, as a fifteen-year-old dancing to it at your quince, in my pool when you asked me to play it at one of our many pool parties. You, lying down on my couch with your eyes closed while telling me about one of your admirers—so many memories. The song makes me ache every time I listen to it; it's connected to you. As so many songs from that first day are connected to you."

Her body relaxed against him, in a sigh of complete surrender. His chest was full, and the words that he should say were all stuck in his throat. He found solace in her lips then, inevitably searching her for what he knew he felt for her.

With kisses and caresses, he soon had her lying down on the soft floor pillows. Her loveliness spread in front of him like a feast for him to enjoy. He wanted to worship every lush part of her. Her eyes were heavy-lidded, and her breasts were rising and falling with each of her deep breaths. The bathing suit had nothing on her lovely breasts, which seemed to be trying to escape through the top and the sides in recklessness.

He ran a finger down the line of the suit, finding her nipple stiff and ready for his hand.

He carried his body over hers, reverently lowering the strap of her bathing suit to show her breast, golden and glistening on the light of the sunset. He took his time to savor her, to elicit her gasps and her moans, until she begged him for more. He wanted her to be as desperate as he was. Every time he touched her, it got better than the last time.

He left her like that, one breast bared in the twilight, the need for her making him forget they weren't alone. The captain could come to the back to check on them at any time but in this moment, he only had the mind to worship her body, to make her feel as intensely as he was feeling right now.

One swipe of her bathing suit to the side, and he uncovered her pussy to his eyes and his tongue. He took his time, her taste making him hard and her scent of ocean and earth urging him forward, causing him to lose some of the composure of his slow exploration.

Her sweet cries reverberated through her, and soon he had her panting, desperate for her orgasm. God, he loved to hear her like this. It was the only time he brought them close together in mind and body.

He raised his head for a second to see how glorious she looked. Her face flushed, and her eyes dilated with her passion. She looked disheveled with her tit and lips bared, her black bathing suit otherwise in place.

The vision of her like this had him adjusting himself and hoping he could make this good for her before he lost all sense of composure. She had that type of power over him. She was so desperate she didn't even say a word about the houses and mansions they were passing by the intracoastal waterway.

"Gabo, if you don't go back to eating me out, I'm going to make you pay tonight."

"Your wishes are my command, baby. I'll make it better."

And he meant it. When she came a few minutes later with her body convulsing in unadulterated pleasure against his mouth, he was glad he had not taken the gauntlet to make her come fast. Even though his body was hard as a rock and tense with pent up arousal, there was always time for more once they got home. He planned to have her the entire night and show what her words meant to him.

CHAPTER 17

GABO

"I don't think I've expressed how much I hate hardware stores," Alicia said.

They were once more walking the aisles of Home Depot, looking for some additional planters for Alicia's front yard. She'd been complaining nonstop since they arrived, even though she had been the one to say the plants they'd moved would have more "character" if they were in new planters. He pushed the cart while she browsed the aisles in search of the perfect pots for her plants.

She was lucky he liked her.

"You express it every time we have to come here," He responded.

"Yet here we are again." Alicia turned around with a ceramic pot and looked at him like he was torturing her.

"Yes, because I want to be close to you, and you need to finalize this project of yours so that when your uncle is ready, the pool terrace work goes quick." He pulled her close to him and nuzzled her neck, hand traveling down to her backside. Since their argument last week, they were back to tentative normalcy. She seemed to be more open to sharing, and they were definitely having a lot of sex, but he still had his doubts.

"You know I can't stand you when you try to be rational, right?" She reached up and gave him a quick kiss that left him wanting more. "Sure, I'll remind you next time you are screaming 'all of this is yours, Gabo' while I'm fucking you hard." He massaged her ass, then reached down and stole one more kiss while she giggled.

"You're nasty," she said. He went back to her neck and whispered in her ear how truly nasty he was. If anyone were to walk up the aisle at right this instant, they would get an eyeful.

"Ok, ok, let's move fast so we can get—oh. Tariq, hi," she said. He pulled back from where he'd been buried in her neck, and looked up to see Tariq. It had been years since he'd seen him. He knew she'd had some type of relationship with him and for some reason, he'd never liked the guy. His muscles tightened, and a burning sensation started in his stomach.

"Alicia, how are you?" Tariq stood across from them in the aisle, pushing a shopping cart full of paint.

Tariq was first-generation Jamaican American like her father, and they always connected because of that. He'd resented that this man had known a side of Alicia Gabo hadn't seen after they'd parted ways in college. Tariq had been there for her through her father's sickness and consequent passing.

He knew his irrational response came from a place of lack of security, if he knew where he stood with Alicia, he would not care as much.

He paid attention to how Alicia looked at Tariq; she inspected Tariq's face with slight concern in her eyes. Tariq looked surprised to see her; there was affection and a naked need in his eyes that had Gabo pulling Alicia into him, a possessive move he was helpless to stop.

"I'm good, and you? Back so soon?" she asked.

"Yeah, I try to come often. I'm here visiting my mother." Tariq pointed to the paint in his cart. "I'm working on home improvement for her while I'm here, I'm staying thru for Thanksgiving," Tariq responded with a gentle smile on his face. He was so focused on Alicia, Gabo doubted he registered that Alicia was with someone.

"That's what's up. I'm glad Ms. T won't be alone for the holidays. I went by her house the other day after work to visit with her." Tariq was looking between Alicia and him, a quizzical look on his face.

"You remember Gabo, right? My best friend?" *Best friend...*

"Yeah, of course. Hey, how are you?" Tariq reached out to dab him up, and he had no choice but to let go of Alicia to reciprocate. He left his hand in the small of her back, though. If he thought he could get away with it, he would put it on her ass, but Gabo was certain she would drop kick him if he did that.

"I'm alright. Good, to see you man," Gabo said reluctantly.

"Well, I don't want to keep you from your mom. Say hello to her from me, please," Alicia said.

"I will. It was good seeing you Alicia, you look good." Tariq looked at him, a slight painful expression crossing his face momentarily, and then he reached out and shook his hand.

"Good to see you, Gabo. Take care of her."

There was silence while Tariq turned the corner, then a sharp blow to his side.

"Fuck, Alicia, what was that for?" He touched his side and looked at her with an annoyed frown.

"What was that for? What was wrong with you?"

"Sorry. You know I have an irrational dislike for him."

"You never liked him because he and I dated off and on, but we know that back then, you just wanted friendship, so this toxic masculinity thing you have going on has to go."

"I'm not toxic. I was just taken by surprise, that's all." He softened his tone, knowing she was getting upset now.

"It was just… he still has feelings for you. You know that, right? I don't know much about your romantic life, so to be confronted with that while you and I are in this weird place…"

"If you want to know, you can just ask." He did not miss the exasperated tone of her words as she walked away from him to keep browsing the aisle.

"Did you date him again after high school?" He held his breath, already having an inkling of this answer.

"Yes, I did, off and on for about five years. We were that couple. The one everyone thought was going to end up together." She shrugged and shook her head.

It hurt to hear that. For a while, their families had thought it would be the two of them, Gabo and Alicia. But he fucked it up.

"We parted ways for a long time, but remained close. Then after my Daddy died…he was there." Her eyes gentled in remembrance. "Things got complicated, and we got back together for a little while about three years ago. We did the casual dating thing for a while again." She paused, pursing her lips, her eyes looking away from him, cloudy with recollections "I found out he was talking to a friend of his that he had slept with, and I didn't take it very well. I didn't appreciate being out of the loop, more than anything, to be honest." She kept walking, a reflective look on her face while he walked beside her taking it all in. All this history she had with another man…

"I broke things off with him without giving him a lot of

space to explain." She shook her head again, in embarrassment now. "Once, I was ready to talk, he tried hard, but I completely shut down. He moved to New York a year ago. I found out from his mom, he had been planning to propose." Alicia grimaced at those last words.

"Would you have said yes?" He did not know how he had the strength to ask the question.

"I've thought about it now after it all passed, and I think I would have. But I don't think I'd have said yes for the right reasons or if we would have lasted." She shrugged, a look of uncomfortable truths realized.

Every word was a gut punch. His mom had kept him abreast of things through the years, all the little details she could pick up about Alicia's life, but it seems she had left out a very considerable detail. He wondered if his mom had purposely done that, knowing it would have hurt him to hear Alicia had someone so important in her life that had basically taken his place. Was that the real reason she had wanted to move to New York?

They finished shopping and returned to her house to work on the planting in the front. Through the afternoon, while they joked and worked, the unease in his stomach turned to dull pain and stayed with him.

ALICIA TWENTY YEARS OLD

"Hey gorgeous, did you get in well last night?"

"Hi Tariq, I did. How are you?" She was lying down in her childhood bed, the morning sun peeking through her window. The house was quiet, her Mom and Dad had not woken up yet, and she was enjoying the period of calm before hanging out with her parents and seeing her friends for the day.

This semester had been intense, schoolwork had taken a lot of her time, and when she hadn't been working on school things, she had tried her best to keep an active social life, going to parties and dorm hangouts.

She had also tried to wean herself from her unrequited crush on Gabo. After years of solid friendship interspersed with moments of tension, she was ready to give up that dream, which is why she was on the phone with Tariq.

"I'm good. I wanted to come through a little later. Maybe we can hang out in your pool?" His voice was gravelly and mellow through her phone, and she couldn't deny it was doing it for her. She rubbed her legs slowly, the bedsheets tangling around her.

"Sure, Mariana was coming through as well, so we can all hang out."

"Ok, I'll bring a friend or two; see you later."

THE AIR SMELLED OF GRASS, CHLORAMINES, AND SUMMER excitement. Alicia glided on a blue pool float while Tariq stood close to her, the two reconnecting with each other.

"So, are you planning to go out tonight?"

"Yeah, there's that fish fry Tony sent a flyer for online. I thought we could go see some of the old crew," Mariana chimed in, floating by in her pink float. She was being pushed by Tariq's friend Joe.

"I guess we are going tonight, I'd planned to see what my school friends were up to, but I haven't heard from them since I arrived last night," she tried to hide the hurt in her voice.

She had texted both Gabo and Mason to invite them to the pool hangout, but Mason had replied, explaining he had gone to the keys with some of the old basketball crew, and Gabo had not responded.

She had been disappointed but not surprised. These past months, Gabo had misinterpreted her attempt to get over her crush as distance and had been insistent something was wrong. He had grown sullen, even sometimes short. Things somewhat tense between them.

"I guess that would be Gabo and his boys, right?"

"Yes, those are my ride or die." Or at least they used to be. Everything changed after high school, and she knew that, but still, she hoped that their connection would stand the test of time.

"Sometimes, I think I have no chance with you," he breathed.

"Why do you say that?"

"Because whenever Gabo is around, or you mention his name, there is this look on your face, it's not the same for the other guys. Just him."

Her face flushed, and she was glad for her shades. At least he did not see how right he was.

"And speaking of the devil…"

Tariq looked towards the back part of the terrace, and she turned her head and saw Gabo there. He was wearing a Dolphins jersey and black cargo shorts. His hair was a little different. He had let his top part grow longer than usual with a fade on the sides.

Every time she saw Gabo again during one of their college breaks, she was surprised to see how handsome he was. His full lips and brown bedroom eyes were hypnotizing. Finally, he had grown a little into his ears, but they were still prominent, the one feature that made him quirky and helped bring down some of the heat that his otherwise model looks brought on. His square jaw had a little of a stubble which worked for her well.

And then there was his body. Well, swimming was paying off. That's all she would say about that. The girls at NYU were probably doing the grown-up equivalent of sticking messages in his backpack. But how could she blame them? He was so fine and so dear.

Gabo scowled while he looked around, then something made his face soften. She realized she had been smiling at him without realizing it. He smiled back.

"That is what I mean, right there…" She heard Tariq say under his breath.

"Alicia Marie."

"Gabriel Ernesto."

"Hello everyone, Mariana. I see you stay wild and free."

"And you, Miller, stay loose and allusive." Mariana splashed water at him as he walked by, then looked at Alicia and winked. She always had her back, but sometimes she said and saw too much.

Gabo walked over to her, and Tariq looked at her with intensity, then murmured, "I'll leave you two to connect. I know you haven't seen each other for a minute." He dabbed Gabo's hands, he said louder, "Gabo, how are you."

"I'm better now that I've seen my best friend, and you?"

Small talk finished, Tariq went over to the other side of the pool to join Mariana and Joe and left Gabo and her to some privacy. He was barefoot as always.

He sat down and dangled his legs in the water.

"Party without me?" He took her shades off her face and raised his eyebrow. His touch, so familiar to her, had her melting.

"I texted you earlier, Gabo." She tried to snatch the glasses from his hands. But he pulled back.

"Be careful, or you'll get your hair wet and my bad. My cellphone was in my Pop's car. I was out with the boys last night and left it there."

"I thought you had resorted to ignoring me," she said.

"Why would you say that?" he said, insulted.

"Well, you have been acting weird these past months."

"Oh Alicia, you know that out of the two of us, I have not been the one acting weird." He shook his head and reached out and pulled her float closer to him. She bristled at his comment, somehow he'd managed to be the hurt party.

"You've been the one freezing me out these past months, so when you ignored my text..." she shrugged. His face of utter outraged took the sting off that assumption.

"Fuck that. I'd never freeze you out. Would you do that to me?" His voice had an urgency she could not understand.

"No, of course not. We are too close for that," she answered sincerely. No matter what her romantic feelings for him, he was still her best friend. He was confusing her with how intense he was right now.

"Promise me, Alicia, promise me you won't do it."

"Woa, porque tan intenso?" she asked, alarmed by his intensity.

"Alicia," he growled. She would not examine why it made her tingle a little bit.

"I. Won't. Do. It. Satisfied?"

"I wish I were," he mumbled. *What did that mean?* He looked at her deeply, and when she thought he would say more, she felt a sudden push as Mariana came barreling through the water and bumped her off the float. She pushed back up sputtering water while she heard Mariana cackling and saw Gabo received similar treatment and was now fully clothed in the water. His bright smile told her they were ok for now.

WHEN THE SUN STARTED SETTING, TARIQ AND HIS FRIEND LEFT with promises to meet at the fish fry. Mariana lingered for a bit and then bluntly asked if she was still planning to go out tonight, but she knew the answer.

After seeing Gabo today and their weird interlude, they'd had a good time. They stayed close to each other through the hangout. Tariq tried a few times to get some one-on-one time with her, but inevitably Gabo found a way to insert himself into each conversation. It made for an awkward afternoon.

After Mariana left, Gabo helped her pick up the remaining cups and napkins around the pool, and together, they arranged all the furniture back to its original place. Her parents were home but, after saying hello, had sequestered themselves in their room upstairs. She sat down in one of the day beds and stretched out, still in her bathing suit and shorts. Gabo relaxed on the lounge chair next to her shirtless, a beer in his hand keeping him cool from the hot summer evening.

"What made you stay behind and not go to the fish fry?" His voice low and alert.

"I'm tired. By the time we would have made a fashionable entrance, it would be around 10 p.m. I'll go for the next one. They do it every other week." The fish fry was an all-out party a Jamaican friend of Mariana's organized with their parents twice a month. Their entire backyard was set up for the fish fry with a built-in bar and DJ booth.

"I was hoping your answer was going to be to stay with me."

"That too, but you don't deserve it. You were an ass to Tariq today." She closed her eyes and laid on her back, one arm on top of her face, all the exam work and the drive from yesterday catching up to her. She tried to block her feelings as she had this conversation with Gabo.

"I wish I had it in me to apologize, but I don't. He has always had a thing for you," he said and a frisson of annoyance went through her.

"Yes, you're right, he does. He asked me out today." She raised her arms and peeked at him on the lounge chair. If he wanted to push her buttons, she would test his as well. He was also lying down facing up, but his eyes were open.

"And what did you answer, Alicia?" She could barely hear him. His voice was velvet in the darkening night.

"I said I wasn't sure…."

"Why?"

"Are you going to make me say it?" This had been going on for a year, the pull and tug the maybe yes, maybe no. And he always pulled back. She was tired of it and just wanted to go back to seeing him as a friend only.

"What do you mean?" he replied.

"Fine, let's keep pretending then." She was exasperated and wanted him to leave. "You should go home. I'm going to head upstairs, wash and dry my hair to the best of my ability and go to bed."

"I can help you with your hair if you like." In the past, he had helped her detangle or section her hair after she'd wash it. He had learned from helping his mother since he was a preteen. She loved when he'd offered before, now she just wanted him gone.

"No, it's ok." She stood up and waited for him to stand as well. Her hands were crossed, and her jaw, stiff.

He looked at her for a long time then stood up slowly, he sauntered to her and crowded her, his height had him looking down to meet her eyes.

His hand took hers, and with soft fingers, he caressed from her hand to her wrist and up her inner elbow, until he landed on her shoulder. He was always affectionate but in a brother and sister kind of way...with a few exceptions through the years. This was one of those exceptions.

She shivered, and he pulled her into him and hugged her, still quiet. She could feel his heartbeat and wished for a moment he felt the same as she did. All these mixed signals, especially these last couple of years as they became woman and man, had been exhausting. The innocence of their friendship chipped away to leave a tangle of friendship, dedication, and a ball of sexual tension that was threatening to take over everything else.

Alicia shifted side to side, and when she stood still again, she felt him. Her spine arched, and a sensation of cold and warmth spread from there to the rest of her body. He was hardening against her, and she wanted to hoot in triumph. Here was the physical manifestation of what he felt for her.

Making a move, she pushed closer into him and moaned when she felt his hard-on pressed up against her belly. The moan triggered something in him, and he bent down and rained kisses over her eyes, her brow, her temple, and then down to her neck, collar bone, his hands everywhere.

Then they were nowhere again. He separated from her and took a big gulp of air. She felt as if a bucket of iced water had been dumped on her head.

"I should leave. I know you have things to do." His voice was deeper than usual.

"What just happened? Why are you leaving now?" She sounded upset, but what he'd just snatched away yet again left her feeling uncharitable.

"Fuck, Alicia, I don't. I am s—"

"Don't you dare apologize, Gabriel Ernesto," she threatened. She could not handle it if he decided to apologize.

"Ok, then I won't, but I don't want to mess things up. We are friends. Friends! Just this afternoon, you promised me you would not freeze me out after thinking I had ignored you. And things have been weird between you and me. You are right. I just miss the simplicity of our friendship, of who we are together."

The simplicity of our friendship. For some reason, that phrase stuck left her to her spot. The realization that, once again, she'd allowed Gabo to mess with her emotions. She didn't know how much she had to give, but her tank was running low. She loved him. He was her best friend, but this was not fun anymore.

"Ok, go, Gabo."

He sighed in exasperation. "Don't be mad at me, Alicia. I didn't mean to."

"Oh, but you did, again you did. You let me feel these feelings. You let me feel you! Hard against me, in my parents' backyard. Then you tell me you want the simplicity of our friendship. You need to make up your mind. I don't think I have it in me to keep playing this game much longer."

With that parting shot, she went into her house and slid the door closed.

He stayed on the other side, looking at her with eyes full of panic. She turned around and left him there.

ALICIA

An army of men swarmed towards her parents' home. She stood in her front door, in sweatpants and a t-shirt looking at the crew that had arrived with Tío Toño this morning.

Three pickup trucks lined up the front of the driveway. There were six men in total unloading toolboxes, ladders, and materials. She stood braced against the frame of the door, looking casual to the quick eye, but if anyone were to look closer, they would see her leg tapping rapidly as a restlessness filled her body.

"Buenos Dias chiquita! What do you have there for your Tío Toño?"

"How do you know this was for you?" she asked, handing him the thermal mug of coffee and an hojaldra, a Panamanian breakfast flour-based fried good, wrapped in a paper towel.

"I know what you like, Tío. That is why I'm your favorite

niece." She turned around and walked into the house. Her uncle followed behind.

"So if you start today, how does it look for completion?" she asked as she walked to her kitchen.

"Bueno, I checked the back, and it looks pretty clear. We're going to start with that work today. That should take a couple of days, weather permitting, then we will swap the windows. That will take como tres días. Last will be the roof. My guys will be working on it starting on Monday. If all goes well, we should be done in dos weeks max."

She stopped and held herself to the counter. Her chest tightened, and the restlessness increased.

"That is quick," she said, measured. Maybe he wouldn't pick up on her unease.

"Oh! Ahora, you're shocked it's quick. I thought you wanted to get away from all of us and go to your Nueva York?"

"Possibly, yes. I have some things to consider now before making a final decision." Of course, he picked up on it.

"Mija, you are confused, and you have been for years. I'm guessing ese pelao, Gabo is to blame."

"I'm not confused Tío, I'm homesick for a home that is no longer here. I have memories that suffocate me just by breathing this air. I can't convince Mami to return." She gestured around her and dropped her hand. "This house is full of Daddy, and there are some nights I cannot sleep for hearing his phantom laughter or a smelling a whiff of his cologne."

"Bueno Chiquita, but make fresh memories. Sell the house. We agree on that. Do new things, Be your age. When I was thirty-five, I was living life! Don't run. You have family here that love you, and that pelao who I always thought was head over heels for you."

"Ay Tío, you want me to hold my breath for Gabo." She

shook her head. "He and I bumped into Tariq the other day, and it was like he'd seen a ghost. And seeing Tariq…."

"Come sit down with me, mija."

He held her hand, and they sat down in the breakfast nook.

"Go ahead. You seem to need to talk," he said gently.

She told him how she thought she missed telling Gabo that she did not love Tariq. Even though she thought she explained herself. How Gabo had been a little distant since that day. Once she shared with him that the work was starting in the house, he had become even quieter. It was so close to what happened to them before, but she didn't want to compare. In this instance, he was the one trying to have a genuine go at a relationship with her. Alicia had all her walls up. Now that they were crumbling around her, he was retreating yet again.

She had her future life on the line for Gabo, and he could not even vocalize what he needed. She couldn't find the words to explain to him what she was inside of her either. Time was running out for them and all their half-said declarations. The hurts from the past were starting to catch up to them.

"Why do you avoid speaking about the things that matter to you the most?" her uncle asked. That was his takeaway.

"I'm not keeping anything from him anymore. He knows I don't know if I'm staying, but I'm trying to give us a real chance!"

"Are you truly?" He sat back, finishing the coffee in one last gulp. Honestly, he had a throat of steel because that coffee was piping hot.

She dropped her head to the table, despair running through her.

"Sometimes, I think that our time has passed, and we are forcing this to happen. Sometimes I think it might be better to move to New York, as I had always planned. Sometimes, I'm mad at him for coming so late into my life and expecting me to stop everything for one more chance."

Tío placed a reassuring hand on her shoulder. "That is what you two need to talk about."

She shook her head. "No, this is not on me. I don't need to clarify anything. I'm trying Tío. I have tried for the two of us many times before. This time I can only live for myself, do what is best for me. If it is meant to work out, then Gabo needs to step up."

Her uncle looked at her with concerned eyes, and she resisted the fact that he could see deep down the hurt and confusion driving her. He could read her too well. He got up and dusted his hands. There was nothing to dust off.

"Call your Mama. I can only help so much, I'm an old man, and old men don't know how to finesse these conversations. If I say more, I'll hurt your feelings. Call your Mama. You need to talk this through chiquita, ok?"

Gabo: I should be there by 8 pm. I had a late night at the center.

Alicia: Take your time. The crew worked till late today, and I had dinner with my uncle. I have some company.

Gabo: I haven't been able to check the RSVPs; it was hectic today

Alicia: don't you worry about the reception. I'll take care of all of that. Focus on the center and the students. That's the important thing.

Gabo: You are too good to me.

Alicia: And don't you forget it.

SHE PUT DOWN HER PHONE AND SAT ON HER BED, THINKING about the conversation with her uncle this morning. Everything that he said, and did not say, stayed with her throughout the day. She knew staying in silence with her thoughts could be detrimental today, so she called her mother.

"Alicia Marie, I spoke with your uncle, qué pasa mamita? I thought all was well with Gabo?" Her mom answered the phone like they were in the middle of a conversation.

"It is not, *not* well," she chuckled. "I don't know what to do, Ma. He is in my head and my heart all the time, but I can't seem to stay."

"I don't think you should make any decisions until you sell the house, Alicia. I think being there is not good for you."

"You're probably right, I've tried to stay afloat while staying here, but it wasn't a good idea."

"Why don't you move in with Gabo until the work is done?"

"No, I couldn't ask, and he hasn't offered."

"Pero, you two are in a relationship. You should be able to ask mamita?"

"That is the thing. He's never asked to be in a relationship, not really. He just asked me to try. And I sometimes feel that I'm trying, and he is in his head and fears, and I can't do this for him right now. I can't be the person who waits for him again."

"Alicia…"

"No, Mami, don't worry. Thank you, I needed this." she said, hit by a burst of clarity. She needed some assurances from Gabo that he hadn't fully given.

"No. Alicia, I didn't mean to imply that he is not supportive."

"You didn't, Mami. It's ok. I did."

She went to sleep with more questions in her head. But

one thing she knew was true, she was going to continue going with the flow, but she was betting on herself only. She was the only person she could trust one hundred percent.

GABO

The smell of baked bread greeted him when he opened Alicia's sliding door Sunday morning.

Oh Shit. She was baking.

Plantain tarts were resting on the counter. He spied some type of cupcakes on the breakfast nook, and she was mixing what seemed to be pound cake. Gabo walked toward the kitchen, seeing the tension on her shoulders and the pinched looked on her face. It seemed that all the baking hadn't erased whatever had caused her to go into stress baking. He stood behind her, kissed the top of her head, and wrapped his arms around her.

"Ali, how are you?"

"Good morning. I'm good. You?" she said sweetly.

Ok, it seems it was not him stressing her out, but he wouldn't jump to premature conclusions. He knew Alicia in this state meant that whatever was stressing her out, she couldn't work out through logic and pros and cons. She needed the manual work to clear her mind. Always did. Since he had known her, she was prone to put all her worries into baking. He'd been the recipient of many baked goods in the past.

"I'm good, but you are worrying me. I haven't seen you this stressed out since that time you thought Mr. Pollock was going to give you a B minus," she looked up and smirked, then brought her eyes back to the mixer.

"They offered me the job in New York."

The sentence dropped like a flat rock on a lake, and she stood back to see how far the ripple would go.

She looked back up to his face again, the yellow batter in the mixer rotating over and over, the smooth thickness a sharp contrast to the spike in his pressure. The news was expected but shocking nonetheless.

He'd navigated their time together with the expectation that there would be a time where Alicia would make a final decision about them. The shocking part was that he wasn't sure what her decision would be.

"What are you—" His cellphone went off, and he looked at Alicia.

"Go ahead. You should answer." He wanted to reach out and touch her brow, have her relax even if for a minute. Maybe he should just take her on a drive, go to an old music store, like they used to. His ringtone brought him back to reality, and he picked up.

"Hello?" he said, annoyed at the interruption.

"Gabo, love. How are you? I just read your email! I want to walk you through your options. I was a little excited to see you are considering moving back." It was his ex, April, now his realtor, who could speak a thousand words a second.

She was calling about the email he sent her last night. He'd asked in blunt terms where he was on his closing procedure and what would happen if he pulled out.

It had been an impulsive email, entirely out of the norm for him, but he needed to exhaust all possibilities with Alicia. If that meant moving back to New York to be with her, then he wanted to understand what that meant. He'd had to figure out how to work on the center virtually, and Mason would kill him, but he wanted to explore it all at least. It was perhaps all a pipe dream anyway. Who said Alicia wanted him in New York City?

He muted the call and told Alicia he would take it upstairs. She waved him away, already back into her flow. He sighed. Had he missed an opportunity?

GABO

Thirty-Six.

The number of years that he had been on this earth. Today he was to spend it with the people that loved him the most and that he could not live without. If someone had told him a year ago that he would spend his thirty-sixth birthday with Alicia at his side, he would not have dared to dream or imagine such an impossibility.

The day had started with Alicia coming over to his house with arepas and scrambled eggs she made for his breakfast. He still couldn't convince her to spend the night. She kept to that rule like it was a Dora Milaje weapon of defense. While they ate together, he fielded the usual social media and text message congratulations.

In the group of texts, one name stood up. April. The call with her about the apartment had been unexpected. She mostly communicated via text or email, and he had expected an email back in reply. She had ended the call, asking to see him, to talk to about "them." The disconnect between them for the year and a half they dated was even more apparent when he heard the words she used to describe their time together.

April: Happy Birthday, honey! I miss you so much. It has been so long. I'm looking forward to seeing you at the apartment tomorrow. Maybe we can have a drink afterward. Get to reconnect. ;)

As always, April laid it on pretty thick. She knew he wouldn't be overtly antagonistic, he respected her too much for that, and he was never rude or disrespectful to old partners. He saw no reason for it.

Gabo: Thanks, April. I'm hoping you are well. I'm flying out tomorrow, so I'll see you in the apartment to review the cash offer and the verifications. I don't think I'll have time for drinks.

A niggling nudge told him he should say something to Alicia. Knowing how Alicia could react, today was not a day he wanted to open up this conversation. April held a special place in his life, but unfortunately he hadn't seen a long term future with her. He wanted time to explain everything to Alicia once he reviewed the closing process.

His trip to New York to close out his storage unit and sell the few items he had left behind was God-sent. It allowed him to take a step back from his time with Alicia and think things through with a clear head. Once he returned, they would sit down and have the talk they needed to have. But today was his birthday, and he intended to enjoy himself to the fullest.

"Gabo! Come look at this picture your Mom has of us." Alicia's rich voice called him across the house. He sat with his Pops and Mason, both enthralled by the Tigers vs. Seminoles game.

The two most influential women in his life sat together at the kitchen table, giggling and speaking rapid-fire Spanish. Probably making fun of another unfortunate picture his Ma had taken of him when he was a pre-teen. He looked at them, and everything else faded from view. How could he let Alicia walk away from him after finding her and being brave enough to love her as she deserved?

His throat tightened at the thought of many Sunday afternoons spent just like this. The two of them visiting her Mother in Panama, spending the afternoon with her Tío Toño and his family. Friends coming over to hang around their pool.

He realized he'd never let himself think of having that with any other woman in his life. He'd spent his last fifteen years trying to replicate the closeness and connection he felt with Alicia, to end up with many disappointing results.

He walked over to them and saw the picture. It was the two of them in bathing suits in his parents' pool, Alicia already growing into her teenage body and him lanky and awkward, making a cross-eyed face to the camera.

"Do you remember that day? We stayed in that pool for hours," she said.

"Yeah, you were so preoccupied with classroom assignments and making new friends besides me."

"Was I wrong to worry? I wasn't the favorite of many of our classmates," she reminded him.

His mom scoffed at him and held the picture up. "They could sense what we all sensed, that the two of you are special together. Alicia, when are you going to put him and me out of his misery and tell us you are planning to stay here?" His mom was not one to waste an opportunity offered. The topic was too perfect for her not to ask. And she took full advantage of the moment.

"Mrs. M, why are you putting me on the spot like that? No se todavía, no he tomado una decisión final." Alicia's eyes flickered to his, and for a second, he felt she was willing him to say something, then she looked back down to the pictures, and the moment passed.

The doubts crept in right after. After telling him about her job offer, Alicia had retreated to her work and their goals for the center. Every time he brought up the subject, she reminded him she had a week or so more to think about it and that "they should focus on this menu for the reception" or "let's read that last chapter" or "I want you inside me right now," all very effective ways to distract him without having to deal with her pending decision.

After years of indecision with regard to her, he owed her this time. She needed to get to a place where she decided for herself, without any pressure from him. He had taken his sweet time to realize he could not live without her, and now the walls were pressing around him. He could only watch as she made a decision that would affect both their lives irrevocably.

"So you and Alicia." Not a question but a statement. His pops waited for dinner to finish to talk about this. Mason just left, and the night was coming to an end. It had been a great day, filled with good food, laughter, and, best of all, the people he loved the most in his life. He could not ask for a better birthday.

"We are figuring things out together."

They were in the kitchen washing the dishes. Alicia and

his mother had protested, claiming he shouldn't have to do anything for his birthday. He made sure they stayed in the living room, both having a drink before Alicia and he headed back home.

"You lost her for years, son. I want to make sure you know what you are doing. I know your mother is convinced this is the right path for you and Alicia. Still, after what happened last time—" His Dad loaded the dishwasher while he put away the leftover food in the fridge using his mother's reusable containers—old ice cream and take-out containers she saved through the years.

"It took you fifteen years for this 'I told you so.' Alicia and I are both in different places in our life now. What happened back then, let's just say we both learned our lesson. We're not kids anymore."

"What exactly happened? You never did say."

"It doesn't matter now. All that matters is we are back on track. And I'm not about to mess it up again," Gabo responded.

His dad stood up after the dishwasher was loaded and looked steadily at Gabo. He stood easy, the usual nerves and concerns about disappointing his father, interestingly not there. He did an internal search and realized somewhere along the line since returning, his compass had shifted away from the fear of risk and disappointment.

His dad was going to do his thing, and there was no changing him. That didn't mean he needed to let the man rule his life without his point of view.

"Good," his dad replied.

"What?" he asked, surprised. He was expecting Pops to berate him, to give him a lecture about friendship and values.

"Gabo, you were a young man when we last spoke of this, and I—I was wrong to interfere. I don't regret giving you the advice I gave you, but I should have framed it better."

"Did Mom get to you?" he asked incredulously.

Pops laughed, mirth making his face look years younger.

"Yes, she did, son. I think she understood better than I ever did, how much you love Alicia, and how much our words mattered to you. When I give you advice, I want you see it as one more aspect to consider, and not as a life imperative. That was my mistake as a parent, not to see that clearly."

He took everything his father said and let it sit for a while. It helped, and it made him realized how much he had mythologized his father in the past.

***

"De la vela la luz, solo anhelan decir, que tú cumplas muchos años, muchos años feliz!"

The voices of her mother and Alicia mingled with the baritone of his father in his accented Spanish. In front of him sat a beautiful cake with fluffy white peaks. Alicia made his favorite, a tres leches, which she had managed to smuggle into the house without his knowledge.

She sat beaming at him, her eyes bright and illuminated by the candles on his cake. His ma had exaggerated and added eighteen candles claiming she had to place half to not burn the house down.

"Go ahead, Gabo, make your wish!"

He blew all his candles, succumbing to the moment of making a wish, for he and Alicia to find their way together so he could make her his, and for him to be hers.

"Feliz cumpleaños mi vida! We bought you a present, your dad and I." His mom gave him a new waterproof watch. Great for swimming. "Thank you, Ma!" He gave her a kiss and hug, then turned to his pops on the other side of the table and hugged him as well.

Alicia sat across him and stood up and went to the living room, coming back with three small wrapped gifts, which she placed in front of him. Two of them were silver wrapped with a white ribbon, and one was in a black paper with a gold bow.

"The silver ones you can open right now, the black and gold one, wait to open it at home."

Her eyes twinkled in excitement and a little mischief.

He opened the first box, and it was a CD.

"That is a playlist of all the songs you and I have loved before and now. I thought to update your list. I burned them in a CD for nostalgia, but I also have a Spotify list I'll share with you." The back part of the CD had the list of songs from now and the past, all telling their story.

He gazed at her. His chest expanded. This playlist was her way to bridge the past with the now and still telling him without words that this was a beginning for them, same as that first night they hung out and listened to their favorite music together. Alicia stood up and walked over to him, wrapping herself around him and sitting on his lap. The soft weight of her body melded with him, and she pressed a kiss to his head.

"Your Pops and I are still here, you know. The way you are looking at Alicia right now. Dios Mío, if these two don't figure things out..." His Ma shook her head in exasperation and threw her hands up in despair. His father burst out in laughter.

He opened the next present, his hands were full of Alicia, so she helped him rip the paper, and again his heart contracted and expanded further in his chest. It was a picture of the two of them on the day of their BBQ on his pool terrace. Mariana must have taken it. Close to the end of the afternoon, they had all been sitting on a table playing dominos and shooting the shit. Alicia had sat on his lap, just like she was sitting now, to help his game. She was leaning against him, the two of them looking at each other with laughter in their eyes.

"I figured we have so many pictures of us, before... we have one of us now, you can thank Mariana also for that gift. I have the same one in my room."

He looked at her, and they held each other's stare for a while. Everything faded away. The noise from the TV, the dishes his Mom was picking up while they still sat at the table. Everything faded away. He realized at that moment that he could not let Alicia decide without telling her how he felt. Tonight.

ALICIA

Alicia stood in the threshold of Gabo's bathroom, a bathrobe covering her body. Tonight, she wanted to forget everything that was an obstacle and focus only on him. He sat on his bed, a look of pure anticipation on his face. Gabo was wearing only grey sweatpants and looked like he needed unwrapping. He bit his bottom lip and let it go slowly —this man.

"You can open your gift now," she told him.

"Are you my gift? I would love you spread open, thank you." His voice was rough and raspy. Every single cell on her body was vibrating, chasing each other across her skin. Her hand came over her collarbone and rested there, her pulse a rapid staccato under her fingers.

"No, not me, not yet, at least. Open the gift next to you."

He had already placed their picture on his nightstand and had the wrapped gift next to it. He reached out and ripped the paper open to reveal a book of short erotica stories.

"I found this book years ago and have read it and come to it so many times. When I close my eyes, the person with me has always been you. I want to gift this book to you as a promise." His eyes penetrated her the way she needed him inside her. At the moment, she thought he could hear all her thoughts.

"Come here, Alicia."

She sauntered towards him while he sat up on the side of the bed, swinging his legs down to the floor. She stood in between his legs, the soft satin whispering against his skin.

"Which scene do you want to do tonight?" He brushed his lips to hers. She loved his lush lips, always wanted to take a bite off his bottom lip, but he was not in that mood yet. He kissed her softly, and her eyes fluttered closed.

"It's your birthday, you should pick," she breathed into his mouth.

"It would be a gift to me to fulfill one of your fantasies. I want to see you unravel for me tonight." He coaxed her and held her in place until she relented.

"There is a story about a wife and her husband, and the first time they do anal."

His hands tighten on her hips, and she could tell he approved of her choice.

"Is this your first time?" He massaged her, over the silk robe up to her thighs, past her hips, and basked in her warmth. Her wetness coalesced between her legs. Her face was inches from his, the scent of his breath sweet and all his against her.

"No, but it hasn't been my favorite before. I know you can make it good for me. I want to feel your dick entering me slowly, and then I want you to give it to me so good."

"Oh, I'll give it to you good." His voice was low and deep. His lowest vibrations connected directly to her pussy.

His hand shifted paths slowly, and he palmed her ass. He kneaded her flesh over the robe. Then gave her a light tap on her left ass cheek.

"So you want me here?" His hands continued to lull her; his voice hypnotized her.

"Yes, God, yes."

He stood up, and his body crowded her, his hands never leaving her ass. Her lush curves felt abundant and luxurious under his heated touch.

"Do you feel me?" He pressed himself against her, his hardness against her soft belly. "Do you feel what you do to me?" His voice was rough with a tinge of desperation.

"I want to take it slow for you. But you stand here, with your sweet face and your filthy thoughts, and I want to you fuck so hard and fast until you pass out." Her knees weakened at his words. Her warmth pooled inside every inch, touched by this need for him.

"I don't want you to take it slow. I want you to fuck my pussy first then, fuck me from behind."

"When you get this filthy and confident, I—" He stopped talking, and in one swoop, he turned her towards the bed. She giggled. Her belly and face hit the mattress, and she felt his hot body on top of hers.

"Your laugh," he said reverently. He pushed her robe all the way up to reveal the lingerie she wore underneath. It was all lace, just enough to almost cover all the crucial parts—well, not all of them. He groaned at the sight of her lace-clad ass with an opening wide, right at the crack, and ran his hands reverently over her heated curves.

"I need to get you ready first Ali, did you bring any lube?" In the haze of their passion, she had forgotten an important detail. She reached in her robe pocket and handed it to him, getting herself on hands and knees.

He inhaled sharply. He'd noticed the crotchless portion of her lingerie now, easy access for all entries. A slap to her right ass cheek made her body contract, and a gush of warmth trickled down her pussy. She loved when he got like this, almost desperate in his need. She curved her back, ass up asking for more.

"Do it again," she panted.

"You like that, *wife?*" Oh he was giving her the whole immersive experience. His tone was low and curious, and then *slap*. He spanked her again, now on her left cheek.

"Ah yes!" she moaned.

"I love it when you get so fucking hungry for me." The click of the lube opening was loud in the room, and just that sound had her heart racing in anticipation. Her body was attuned to every single move that Gabo made, and it wanted, demanded its due.

The cold sensation of the lube battled with the warmth of her skin. Gabo's finger penetrated her, his large finger working slowly, getting her ready for the main course.

He brought some of his weight onto her, making her relax down to the bed, with her hips raised. The cool sheets slid across her nipples and belly, making her sensitive all over. "Estas bien amor?"

"Sí, keep going."

Another large finger joined the first, his slow movements preparing her for his girth and length. She didn't want to overthink it. That dick of his was thick enough she had to gather the courage to suggest this to him today. Despite her reservations, she knew she wanted him, all of him everywhere.

She pushed back slowly, looking for more friction. Kisses rained all over her back, and his other hand was caressing her right breast, playing and plucking her nipples, spiking her temperature and her need.

The moan that escaped her was loud in the quiet room, "More."

"Not yet. I need you panting for it, asking for it. Begging for my dick," he growled as he nuzzled her neck. He played with her breasts and fingered her ass which had her hot and bothered; she could not be more ready for him than this. Her hand skated down her belly to her clit and circled the wetness until she was overwhelmed by sensations. He pushed her hand away and took over for her, playing with her in tandem.

"Fuck Gabo, I'm ready."

"Not yet, not until you beg for it," he groaned. His dick was hard against her thigh, and she wanted it inside. Now. He did something with her clit, then inserted another finger, and she mewled in pleasure; her climax was right there, so close, looking to sweep her away.

"Ask for it, fuck—I need you to ask for it, baby!" His urgency matched hers, and she moaned in response, "I need you to fuck me now. I need you inside me now!"

She whimpered when she felt his fingers exit her tunnel, then his dickhead was there in place, his hands on her hip possessively holding her still for his invasion. The invading thickness of his shaft filled her little by little, stretching her and making her expand to accommodate him. She gasped when he bottomed out, and they both groaned together at the tight sensation of her ass hugging his length.

He moved, slow, measured, and languorous. The emptiness of her soaking pussy drove her wild, enhancing each and every thrust he made. He thrust all in, grinding against her ass, his hands massaging her flesh, telling her how good she felt. The dual feelings of emptiness and fullness made her feel electric, like a conductor of heat and light missing one last element to turn on and become infinite.

"Alicia, you—fuck, you feel so good, love. Fuck!" Gabo was barely coherent. She couldn't help herself; she started pushing back.

"You are so beautiful, Alicia, so fucking beautiful." His

pace was nonstop. Somehow he worked his way up to these fast thrusts that had her legs shaking.

He wrapped his body around her and brought her all the way down the bed, one hand holding her across her breast, the other on her clit, and she just moved with him. Her body yielded to all he had to give, and soon she was mindless, helpless to her relentless desire. When she came, her orgasm was a blissful eruption of pleasure, leaving her boneless.

She felt him go wild, her body somehow still meeting his every push and thrusts, his movements unmeasured and primal.

"Ali—I'm going to—fuck this is too. I'm coming." He was speaking nonsense, all growls and moans, and with one last thrust, he spilled in her pulsing in desperate completion.

Ragged breaths filled the room. Their climax ripped them of all sense of civility. They laid sprawled in bed, Gabo softening inside of her body.

"You are trying to kill me, and on my birthday no less." He pulled gingerly away from her body, sweat making their bodies slick to the touch.

"I thought it was the other way around! I think my legs just completely gave up on me, but I need to shower."

"I'll go get the wipes." He started to get up, but she stopped him.

"No, this will take more than wipes, all the lube..." He laughed as she got up and did a duck-walked to the shower.

BOTH OF THEM WERE SHOWERED AND LAYING DOWN IN HIS BED. "Thank you for today. You made my birthday extra special," he said, his voice low in the quiet room. It was as if he didn't want to disrupt the gentle peace that had surrounded them both.

"Oh love, it was my pleasure, it has been many years since we spent a birthday together. I was amped up to plan lunch and dinner with Mrs. M."

"Seeing you both sitting together, talking, laughing, I realized how much I want that for us. I want you in my life all the time."

"Gabo..." Her heart started to speed up; she was not ready for this conversation. For some reason, now that he was saying what she wanted, fear rushed through her. She'd poured herself into enjoying this day with him. No worries, no thinking of tomorrow.

"No, I need to say this to you. You and I, we do this. We avoid speaking of the truly important things."

"You are right, you are very right, but it's your birthday, and I envisioned the day ending in each other's arms. Tomorrow is another day."

"Tomorrow, I leave for a few days to New York, remember? I have to get things settled on my rented storage and closing. Then I'm back for the sponsor reception."

"Ok. So when you come back, we talk. Right now, you are touching me, and I can't think properly." It was the Goddess honest truth. After a brief respite, her body was vibrating again, the nearness of his heat, of his large body, holding her, making her needy.

"So you are trying to kill me on my birthday!"

She chuckled and pressed her lips to his. Their kiss started sweet, mingled with laughter, but soon the heat returned, and they were hungry for each other.

"I need you again," he said. He got on top of her. His mouth and hands were exploring her. He kissed, licked, sucked, and touched every single part of her skin. Her breast heaved with deep breaths, his warm breath coasting along with her nipples and making her shiver.

Her hands were not idle, his body was so large, wonderful

in its contrast of hardness with areas of softness, and she made sure to touch all his sensitive parts. She bit and sucked right between his neck and shoulder and made his whole body shiver. She had figured how to do that to him one lazy afternoon they had spent in his sun porch. She felt him gasp, then groan at the sensation, both of them knowing each other intimately, inside and out. This man who had known her since she was twelve, who she had lost for years, knew who she was.

He would be able to pick her out of a lineup with the lights off and no sound because her heart would reach out to his. This man was her past and was asking now to be her future, and she feared if she let him go, she'd never be able to heal.

In the night's quiet, in this dark room, they joined, his hardness sinking into her silken wetness with the ease of long-lost lovers. The pace they kept was steady, slow, and deep. She felt him everywhere inside, around her, in her heart.

"Ali. Baby, look at me." She had not realized she had closed her eyes. "You feel like home," he whispered.

His eyes were telling her what she didn't allow to be said at loud. *I love you. I need you.*

She whimpered when he hit that spot inside of hers. He kept his steady pace, ignoring her pleads for speed. The intensity that they were creating together, the longing of years, all mixed inside of her, threatening to explode in a shower of want and passion.

"I love you. I know you are not ready to say it back, and that is ok. I love you," he said.

The tingling of her spine spread all through her body, and she buckled under him. Her orgasm sneaking up on her, exploding in a powerful wave that swept her away—Gabo's name in her lips and his heart in her hands.

She tightened around him and took him with her; he pumped into her with no sense of coordination and flooded throughout her with warmth, her name clear and loud on his lips: a promise, a plead, a vow.

———

THEY LAID QUIET IN BED, GABO'S WORDS STILL AN ECHO IN THE silence of the night. Her heart was brimming with emotion, to hear his words, to know he loved her…but something was still holding her back, she desperately kept that flame alive, nurturing it with air and everything it needed but it was not ready yet to shine as bright as Gabo needed it.

"Gabo, you know how I feel about you right?" she asked, not wanting his words to go unnoticed.

"Shhh, it's ok. I did not tell you so that I could hear it back. I told you because I need you to know. I'm here whenever you are ready."

"Ok." She whispered.

After a while he broke the silence. "When you see your future. What do you see?"

"I…" She took the time to truly think of his question, to give it the importance it deserved. "I see myself working in a non-for-profit, doing good work, having a good place to live, and having the time to spend with my family and friends, chillin', baking, just having a good time.

I see myself being the favorite auntie to the nieces and nephews that my cousins will give me. I love kids, but when they are someone else's. My mom has still not come to terms with the fact I don't want babies.

And I see myself in a plane at least every four months. I want to travel all over the world." She said quietly her heart pounding, the recognition that that dream was closer than she realized, even here in Florida.

"Yeah, I saw the map you have in your room, with all the color-coded lists of places you want to visit. Who are you with in all of this dreams?" he asked, and she held his hand because the vulnerability of the question was as delicate as a crystal figurine. It deserved a vulnerable answer.

"I'm not going to lie, usually I'm alone, but sometimes, late at night, when I drop all my defenses and just let myself be…you are there holding my hand." Her heart ached when he pressed a chaste kiss on her forehead then gathered her closer to him, his breathing lulling her to sleep, as she let her walls down, if only for tonight. The last thought that flicker to her mind before succumbing to sleep, Gabo also felt like home.

FIFTEEN YEARS AGO

GABO TWENTY ONE YEARS OLD

"**A**licia is driving down this afternoon. She will arrive around dinner time. She decided to surprise us, and is coming a day early. If you like, I can leave the gate door open so you can check once she is here?" Mrs. Powell invited him into her house and offered him a glass of lemonade. She had a kind smile on her face, and her patience with him was appreciated. This was the third time he'd checked on Alicia's arrival today.

These past months of summer into the fall had been a revelation to him. After fighting his feelings for Alicia for so long, he had realized he was no longer willing to continue to do that. The summer had been periods of frustration mixed with the best days with her. Alicia. She had stopped getting mad at him and his mixed signals after that first encounter they had in the summer. Their hang outs had become a balance rope for him, making sure he was not putting out any signs while dying to kiss her.

Whenever they just laid on their porch, listening to music

and chatting, his mind and body would gravitate towards her. He just wanted to hear all she had to say, her take on any subject, and most of all, kiss her. Just one taste of her lush lips would be heaven.

But the fear he had of losing her, of attempting anything that would risk their overall friendship, was terrifying. He had made her promise she would never freeze him out, but the reality was, he realized that was not a fair ask. No matter how he wanted her to make a vow if he told her about his feelings, he knew there would be no turning back.

Then Tariq kept hanging around. They would go to parties, and Tariq was there. To the beach. Tariq was there. Even their hangouts in the pool became a group affair, their friends and Tariq's friends forming a summer clique. She was moving on from her romantic feelings of him. It scared the shit out of him.

So here he was back from school and had decided he could no longer continue like this. He was going to lay his cards on the table to her. That there wasn't a night he would go to bed without thinking of how she was doing. The days she had exams, he would keep his eyes trained on his cellphone to make sure he would answer her text as soon as she needed any encouragement. That he had not been able to concentrate this semester trying to imagine how it would be to explore her and have her explore him. All the way.

"Oh look, she just texted me and said she is on her way down with Tariq. It seems he stopped by to pick her up. That boy is so nice, and he is so into her." Mrs. Powell stood by her kitchen island, lemonade jug in her hands, the same smile going extra soft.

Dammit. If he was a guessing man, odds were Mrs. Powell suspected he had feelings of more than friendship for Alicia. She and his mom were very close and talked all the time, and his mom was very vocal in her thoughts.

"Oh, that's good. That way, she is not driving by herself. Gracias por la limonada Mrs. P. I will see you later once Alicia is here."

The knowledge that Tariq was driving her twisted his gut and made him want to throw something. He hated she was showing any interest in him, even though Gabo had no rights to his anger.

He walked to his house, preferring to take the long route back vs. taking the offer from Ms. P to walk through the gate. He needed to clear his mind and doing it at home with his mom hanging around was going to be complicated.

After an hour and fifty laps on his pool, his head remained as unclear as before. Knowing Alicia was in the car with Tariq pissed him off. But he knew as of now nothing was happening with them. She would have told him something.

He reached for his blackberry, which was on the side of the pool, and with his heart on his throat and all his alarm bells ringing, he wrote her a message:

Alicia,

I know you are on your way home. I want to talk to you tonight if you have time. I have been thinking a lot lately, and I want to tell you my thoughts. You are the first person I think of when I go to bed, and you are still in my mind when I wake up. I'm not running anymore. I want to be with you. For real with you. Call me when you get here.

Then he deleted all of that and typed instead:

Powell, we need to talk you and me, private. I want to tell you something about us. And I want to tell you tonight.

He pressed send. Then he waited.

CHAPTER 20

ALICIA

"You asked me to stay home with you tonight, and you've been quiet, eating your popcorn," Mari said, exasperated.

It was ten at night on Sunday, and Alicia and Mariana lounged in Mariana's bed. "Just cause you took the week off it doesn't mean I don't have to work tomorrow, so spill it." Mariana turned on her side to face her cousin, who laid flat on her back, or as flat as her behind would allow it, looking at anything but her cousin.

The room was another extension of Mariana's personality, with vibrant colors, deep blue walls, and sewing items and fabrics all set like a collection of dolls on shelves. Dark wood furniture complimented the contrast of colors, and there was an assortment of hair products, sex toys, and design books strewn around any available surface.

"Who said I wanted to talk?" Alicia scoffed, "I wanted to hang out with my prima."

"Ay por favor, you love me, Alicia. But you and I are out and about on town when you feel like going out, or..."

"Or I'm at the salon. I know." Alicia finished for her.

"Do you? I want to be there for you, but sometimes you —" Mariana plopped back to her back, looking to the ceiling as well. "Are you still planning to leave, Alicia?"

"No se, Mari." An audible sigh escaped Alicia. She was tired and could only imagine how the rest of her loved ones felt about her indecision.

"They called me about the job again. They've given me until next week to decide."

"So why are they calling? Are they pressuring you?" Slight outrage would be the best description for Mariana's protectiveness right now. Alicia smiled at the sight. She was not without people in her corner; she often forgot that.

"No, no. It's not like that. On the contrary. The same organization has a South Florida office, and now they have an opening here as well, the same position."

"That's amazing." Mariana sat up abruptly and jumped on the bed with her contained excitement.

"No, it's—look, I don't know. I still think about how I have been these past few years, and I cannot go back to that. I wasn't happy here." The movement of her head had her twists rubbing back and forth against the smooth satin of the pillow. Her thought tightened, and for a moment, she felt the weight of this decision that would dictate her future. How could she decide something that would determine her course in less than a week?

"Keyword, 'was'. Alicia, you have to admit things have changed for the better for you. I see it, Daddy sees it, Aayala sees it, Mason sees it." Mariana said.

Ignoring her turmoil for a second, she didn't let pass the opportunity to rib at her cousin, "Mason, y tú qué? What are you not telling me?"

"You think you are funny. But you are not. Don't distract me. You've changed prima. I see it, and I'm glad for it every day. Since Uncle passed away, you have been a shell of yourself. And I get it. I know everything sucked for a long time. But you are giving yourself an opportunity."

"You. The one that tells me that no man should define me. You are now telling me you think I have changed because of what, of Gabo?" Alicia's annoyance was evident in her tone.

Mari raised her eyebrows. "I didn't mention his name, not once. Look—" Mariana laid back down, faced her, holding her damp hands with her dry comforting ones. "Gabo, might have been the starter of the match, but you are the phosphorus. If you weren't ready to light up, you would have stayed just as in the dark as before. I didn't mention Gabo because this change I see, it's all because of you, chiquita."

Alicia shook her head yet again. "I had a whole plan, and it was all falling into place. Gabo coming back into my life at the tenth hour shouldn't be the thing to make me stay. I should look at this job offer with full pros and cons. Not with my heart because my pumpum got some fun times."

"Denial, tu nombre is Alicia."

Alicia took the pillow right under her head and threw it at Mariana. The yelp of surprise gave her untold satisfaction.

"Oh, so it's like that," Mariana sputtered in laughter. "You know I have a wicked arm. I don't care about your superwoman strength."

To leave this behind, Mariana, her little cousin Mila, her uncle, and auntie would hurt. She would miss them all so much. She had refused to put a name and a voice to that in the past because she couldn't continue risking her mental well-being for them. But things were different now. She liked it here. She actually is living her life to the fullest now.

Would it be so bad for her to suspend logic and reasoning

for a period of time and just trust that it would all be well? Was Mariana right, and had she changed for the better?

IT WAS MIDNIGHT, AND MARIANA WAS LIGHTLY SNORING NEXT to her. She looked at her cousin with love and quietly stepped outside of the room to text Gabo.

The living room hummed subdued with the usual electrical noise of any household in America. She sat down on the comfortable sofa and threw the blanket Mariana had for TV watching, over her.

Alicia: Are you awake?
Gabo: Wrong number.
Alicia: Don't you remember me, Papi?
Gabo: I told you I have a girlfriend, now stop texting me, please!

Alicia's body shook in silent mirth.

Alicia: Ohhh, you have a girlfriend. Tell me about that heaux
Gabo: She is not a hoe. Please respect my amazing, witty, living in her head, dedicated, stubborn, loving, sexy as fuck, beautiful woman.
Alicia: I miss you
Gabo: I've been gone for a day.
Alicia: Yeah, but I had to cook tonight, and it was not fun.
Gabo: I knew you only wanted me for my ramen.
Alicia: Don't forget your mom's arepas as well. Big Bonus.
Gabo: Oh, I will give you my Big Bonus next time I see you. I miss you too.
Gabo: Have you decided?

She was that person. The indecisive 'thought bubble then left you in read' type of person. She did not want to be that. She wanted to make a logical decision that made sense for her life and make sure she did not break any hearts. Not Gabo's, especially not his.

Alicia: Not yet, but I am honest to the Goddess, thinking it all through
Gabo: Ok...I wish I were there so I could worship you with my body. Show you with actions what I know I can never do justice with words.
Alicia: Just hurry and get back home, ok?
Gabo: Home...I like how that reads. Sleep well, Ali.

GABO

He loved this airport. People of all walks of life meandered at different speeds and purposes on the corridors leading them to their destination. He power walked with his roll-away bag behind him, focusing on the exit by the luggage claim. It had been an early morning flight, and he hoped to catch some rest in the middle of what promised to be a hectic day.

He'd been sure that scheduling his trip right before the sponsor reception was going to be manageable. He had not accounted for the nerves that were currently coursing through him. He hated this uncertainty, having to host an event to ensure their organization stayed afloat wasn't the best use of their time. It all felt so transactional and artificial, but unfortunately necessary. Especially now that Alicia had shared with him and Mason that her job would stop their funding by year-end due to "other responsibilities."

Stepping out of the sliding doors, the relentless Florida heat combined with that ever-persistent humidity hit him, causing some sweat to form on the back of his shirt.

He checked his phone, pulling up his Uber app when he did a double-take. A woman in jeans and a loose blouse leaned against a Lexus with her hands folded under her chest. His woman.

"To what do I owe this surprise?" He approached her car and leaned against her, his worries dissolving with her presence.

"I came to pick up my man. Have you seen him around?"

He growled at her and, in a fast move, dropped his luggage and tugged her close to him. Flush curves embraced him, and their mouths touched each other. His hands were full of her behind, and he squeezed, enjoying the faint moan that elicited.

Then she was laughing, and that sound filled him up with warmth and joy that made everything else seem attainable—the fundraising, the center, solidifying things with her.

"I missed you, Gabo," Alicia said.

"I was just gone for a couple of days," he said with a laugh. "Here look, I got you a little present. Even though my trip was short, I missed you dearly." He opened up his bag and showed her five romance novels he wanted to read with her.

"You know the way to my heart. I cannot wait to read them with you. Come, let's get you home so that you can get some sleep before we have to get ready to head out." She detached herself from him, and his body was already bereft, missing her warmth.

"You know we aren't going to sleep, right?" He picked up his fallen luggage and walked to the back of the car to place it on the trunk.

"I don't know what you are talking about." A look over a shoulder and a wink told him she knew exactly what was going to happen once they got to his house.

CHAPTER 21

ALICIA

Alicia laid on Gabo's bed, wrecked after the morning they had together. The things they did. Thank you to the Gods of romance novels for introducing all types of sexual experiences to Gabo. He had been hungry for her and her body. It had been fast first, the yearning of being apart for a couple of days driving them forward. Then slow once they had both orgasmed once, then filthy because they couldn't help themselves. Four hours later, and she was wondering how to walk straight.

Gabo had been so anxious for everything this evening that he decided to head out early to the center to discuss talking points and overall strategy with Mason. She had zero incentive to move from the bed. She was stretched out naked and boneless after that good dicking Gabo provided in the morning.

Her goal for the week was to pack all the items she had left in the later pile before she had moved to her parents' home, knowing she wouldn't need them until closer to the sale. With Tio Toño's crew moving efficiently along, there was no more time to procrastinate the inevitable.

Whenever her mind trailed to the sale and to move, a ball of pure anxiety ran through her veins, it was sharp, with tiny teeth, and it seemed to have a vacuum in its behind because the feeling of sudden emptiness was a little violent.

Anxiety and restlessness had now taken residence. Goodbye to the day of leisurely rolling in Gabo's sheet naked. It was a shame she couldn't enjoy his bed for much longer. Lying naked on his sheets should be a national pastime. The fabric smelled of him—a hint of sandalwood, lavender, and this smokiness that was all Gabo. She couldn't have detected what the smells were, she just checked his cologne bottle, so she could get candles with the same scent. She wanted to luxuriate in it for longer, but her mind was being an asshole and wouldn't let go.

She picked up her phone and called the hotel, making sure all final details were ready and checking that the Director of Events would be there to greet her before the event start. She had asked Gabo not to worry about the logistics of the actual planning of the event, and she meant to follow through.

After the call, which did nothing to her calm anxiety, she called her mom. Clearly, she was feeling a little destructive today.

"¿Mami, en que andas?"

She could hear Samy and Sandra Sandoval in the back, which meant that her mom was doing some cleaning.

"Aqui mamita, cleaning a bit before going out to get some groceries, y tú mija?. How is your week off? Did you finish the packing already?" Alicia rummaged in her assigned drawer that Gabo had given her when she kept having to walk across backyards for clean underwear.

"Yeah, almost. Most rooms are all packed up and ready for donation. Are you sure you don't want me to save anything else?"

"No, memories are all I need. The little things I asked you to save are small enough not to be in your way once you move out. I don't want to impose on you more than I already have, Alicia."

"It is not imposing, Mami." She put the phone on speaker on the dresser while she put on her clothes.

"Have you decided what job you are going to take?"

"How did you know?"

"I'm your Mom. I had a feeling this is why you called in the middle of the day outside for a regular call schedule."

"I don't have a call schedule!"

"You always call me when you are driving, from work to home. That seems like a pattern to me."

"You know, never mind, Mami."

"No, no, you called because you needed to talk, and I'm glad for it, Alicia. You haven't wanted my opinion on something in a long time."

Alicia sighed, sitting down on Gabo's bed.

"Yes, Mami, I decided, I want to—" The doorbell rang, and Alicia's train of thought was lost.

"Was that the doorbell? That doesn't sound like the house's one."

'Yeah, because I am at Gabo's. That's weird, I wonder who it is. Probably someone was dropping up a package. They'll leave."

But the doorbell rang again. And then a third time.

"Mami, let me let you go so I can get this door."

She ran down the stairs wondering who could be visiting Gabo in the middle of the day. She checked the peephole, wondering when Gabo was going to get an electronic doorbell. He was living in the nineteenth century here. There was a tall and attractive light brown-skinned woman at the door.

She opened the door with caution.

"Hello?" Alicia answered.

"Hi, oh sorry, I'm not sure if I have the right house, is this Gabo's parents' house?" the woman asked, all perkiness and smiles.

"Yes, this is The Miller residence." This woman was giving her major rich lady vibes, but she tried her best not to make assumptions.

"Oh. Good. I'm April, Gabo's—" she smiled even wider, "—good friend, I was hoping to stop by and surprise him, hopefully, go together to the fundraiser?"

Gabo had not mentioned any April to her. She frowned. "Ohh. That's...nice. You missed him, though. He went to prep with Mason at the center. Do you know where it is?" She was trying to glean as much information as she could without being obvious, but this woman was giving her some major "some shit is gonna go down" vibes.

"Sorry, you are worried your employer will get upset about letting me in, but it's ok. Gabo and I go way back, like relationship way back, and hopefully again in the future. So you won't get in trouble at all."

Goddess forgive her, but Alicia was having uncharitable thoughts right now.

"Oh, don't worry, I won't be in trouble." She made sure her face was placid, a slight smile on her face, but her eyes were giving her away because April made a tiny step back in self-preservation.

"Oh, so sorry, I'm...I didn't know he had family staying with him..." The lady said. Again, she was grasping at straws to explain who Alicia could be, but none hit the mark.

"I'm not family, or better yet, I am family to him but not blood related." Another smile, this one a little more feral.

This was an unreasonable reaction to a misunderstanding that was probably innocent. But this woman was just rubbing her the wrong way.

"Oh...well. Could you tell me where the center is? I did not get your name...?" April's demeanor changed slightly. She went from bubbly and sparkly to flat, like a soda opened for too long.

"I didn't give you my name. To be honest, you have given me just enough public information to make me think I should not share his current location."

"Oh, well, I can help with that." The glint in April's eye was unmistakable. She thought she had something. She pulled her phone and showed her a photo of her and Gabo in some type of gala. They were awfully close, and the date was less than six months ago. A month before he returned to Florida. And he had said nothing to her.

They had talked about Tariq and previous people they were involved with, and when was the last time they had sex with someone. And he had not said a thing to her. A chill ran through her body and her muscles all contracted, and her breath left her in whoosh.

"And I knew the house address as well. I was just with him this weekend. He is considering putting the sale on hold now that he is thinking of returning to New York." April's eyes searched her. She was studying her reaction to the final piece of news.

Breath still out of her body, there was no additional air to escape her with that news. Hands prickling, stomach bottomed out, she still managed to keep her composure through it all.

She could tell that April was equally perplexed by her response, or lack thereof. She didn't know Alicia and how well she could mask her concerns. In the end, this was not about April, anyways. The dislike she felt for this woman was all because of being blindsided by her presence and the information she just conveyed. It had nothing to do about April's character, even though she disliked she had just brandished all that information in such a petty way.

No. In the end, it was not about April. It was about the knowledge that, again, Gabo had kept things from her when he knew how that had hurt them in the past.

"Ok, well, to be honest, he is probably heading over the hotel. I assume you have that address?"

"I do. Thank you. I am guessing I will see you there?" A note of apology in April, voice. An attempt to smooth things now that she had guessed that Alicia was important in Gabo's life.

"Your guess is as good as mine."

ALICIA WENT TO HER HOUSE AND GOT READY, AN ODD CALM running over her. The memories of all the conversations in the house followed through her as she took a shower, put on makeup, and picked out a white jumpsuit with black phrases of empowerment in italics. It was a statement outfit with wide legs and a plunging neckline that was appealing and powerful at the same time.

She thought of all the moments her family and Gabo had kept vital information away from her. Kept her out of the loop for reasons they had claimed were for her good.

Her rational mind always thought she had understood those reasons, that they all came from a place of love. But right now, another force came into play inside of her. Something that was always ready to expand and feed on her insecurities and her doubts. This force was forever clouding her judgment, gray, thick and nebulous, a mass of gas and pain. It was insidious, sometimes colorless. It made her not notice when it was taking over.

She managed to realize the physicality of it after years of letting it simmer in the borders of her mind. These last months, where she let herself just live and love and be herself, had revealed to her how much it had been present in her everyday life.

Because of her newfound self-awareness, she realized Gabo had to have a reason he had not explained things to her. Heck, that woman April could have been making things bigger and grander than they really were in her mind. It all had an explanation. She only needed to talk to Gabo. To listen and stay open-minded. She knew he would not hurt her, not now. Not when she had decided to be fearless, to take a leap of faith with him. She hoped she was right.

She felt almost herself again when she walked out of her house. Her car ran smoothly on the highway, and for a second, she wondered if it was a good idea to go to this event tonight with a turmoil of emotions inside. But she had promised Gabo and Mason she would ensure all was running well throughout the cocktail event. And now was not the time to let personal feelings distract her from the reasons for the event—the youth.

She sat in the office of the banquet team, hiding in the back of the hotel's house. Somehow she had got herself in a place of utter and focused calm. She was good at this, at keeping things out in the periphery and focus on what was necessary.

"The banquet lineup is done, and all the banquet servers are ready and in place to start greeting guests. We have a mix of champagne, red and white wine, and a nonalcoholic spritzer to greet guests when they walk into the atrium."

The banquet captain talked to her, walking her through all the service points of the evening, ensuring with words and confidence that all was ready for this important event. She nodded along, absorbing all the comments, while her mind picked at the exchange with April earlier on today.

"Let me know when Mr. Miller and Mr. Brathwaite come upstairs."

She had arrived through the back of house entrance, wanting to avoid bumping into Gabo. She was not ready for the conversation they needed to have. The questions she wanted to ask. This was not the place.

She also knew he had been anxious when he left, and he would pick up on the icy exterior that surrounded her right now. They had been greeted by the general manager, and he had invited them to a quick cocktail in the lobby bar before guests started to arrive. Better like this. It gave her more time to woman up.

"I will, Alicia. Are you staying back of the house for longer?"

"Yes, all looks good outside, and I know I am in great hands with you, Charles, and your team."

Time passed. It could have been minutes or hours, as her gut continued to churn, and she kept trying to keep thoughts at bay.

"Alicia...they are upstairs, and there are some guests with them already."

"Thanks, Charles."

She approached the event space, standing in an in-between alcove that separated the back-house entrance from the front, a large atrium on the hotel's top floor. The area took over most of the floor, excluding the back-of-house space she had just walked out from. It was all glass and steel beams on the top and floor-to-ceiling glass windows reinforced by steel. The views of the floor were breathtaking, with the entire city of Fort Lauderdale bathed in gold as the sunset for the day.

The middle of the floor had a large round bar, which was open to hotel guests for evening cocktails and light fare. Tonight it had been privatized to host the Fundraiser Cocktail for The Gifted Athletes Center of Broward. She stood behind the nook, which had a frosted glass material that allowed her to look out so that servers got the lay of the land before heading into the front of the house but blocking the view of the service entrance.

She saw Mason and Gabo at the opposite side of the space, talking and socializing with a group of about ten guests. He looked a little tense, but only she and Mason would know that he wasn't the epitome of confidence to the casual eye. Gabo stood tall and comfortable among his potential donors, a bright smile on his face as he shook hands and greeted guests.

More guests were coming out of the elevator, and she stood there, rooted on the spot, watching through the glass, something compelling her to wait.

She saw her as soon as she walked out of the elevator. She must have changed clothes, or maybe had the change of outfit with her because April was now wearing a different dress than when she first saw her. It was a black, long sleeve dress that went mid-thigh and showcased her slender figure.

She saw when Gabo saw April, and a broad smile blossomed on his face. He shook a couple more guests' hands then gestured to her, his hands inviting her to approach.

The way she stood beside him and reached up to kiss him, then left her hand on his chest showed how familiar she was with him. She saw him sidestep a bit after he greeted her, but then someone stood in between her and covered her line of sight.

All the sound of the atrium, the jazz music playing, the clink of glasses and plates, the voices of the banquet servers as they walked out with replenishments of drinks and food faded away. Her heartbeat was fast, loud, and became a soundtrack, a deep base in her ears that did not allow her to hear anything else.

When the person in front of them passed by, she saw Gabo, who now had his hands on April's waist and was introducing her to an older couple, as she smiled and laughed. Mason seemed to be very keen to greet the couple and was working his charm on both of them as well. The whole tableau showed her that Gabo had still managed to keep her in the dark about things, somehow had managed to present himself as the open book he always was to her, and still have this fucking plot twist waiting for her. It was fifteen years ago all over again. The bass got louder, the gray mist of past hurts grew colder and thicker as she watched.

She saw April reach and get a glass of champagne from a passing server and then saw her offer some of her drink to Gabo. There must have been a moment where the pause button was pressed because Gabo seemed to stop and look at April, a bit of disbelief in his expression, then with a laugh, he took her offer.

She walked back to the banquet office team and asked Charles to let Mr. Miller and Mr. Braithwaite know she was not here.

GABO

Mason and Gabo were standing with their back to the bar, drinks in hand. This was the first time they had been able to speak without being surrounded by people. The room had thinned out, from about seventy-five guests at the peak of the reception to about twenty guests remaining in the atrium.

"Where is Alicia?" Gabo asked.

"I don't know. I could have sworn I'd seen her walking by the service entrance earlier."

"This is weird. When I left her at home, she was planning to come early," Gabo said, worry starting to form in his gut.

"Did you try calling her?"

"I did, also text, no answer..."

He spent the last two hours talking, smiling, and greeting prospective donors. He felt like he had a five-hundred-pound weight on his shoulder, and sandpaper in his throat. He was going to need a full day of not talking, and hopefully Alicia's company to recuperate from such a long two hours.

"Can we talk about it now?" Mason turned his body to him, his entire attention focused on Gabo.

"I don't want to talk about it here."

"Why is April here and acting like she is your woman?" Mason, being Mason, ignored his request.

"It is like I am speaking to a wall," Gabo murmured.

"If you mean serious business with Alicia, you need to talk to April. Unless you are doing an open relationship which then I have nothing to say." Mason shrugged.

"Again, you are just having a whole conversation over there on your own." Gabo could feel Mason's scrutiny. The intensity of Mason's stare and the heaviness of that five-hundred-pound weight moving to his chest was not helping his mood.

"Does Alicia know about April?"

He scoffed and took a swig of his drink. "There is nothing to know."

"Really?" Mason's eyebrows climbed up in his face, "Where were you last Sunday and Monday?"

"Fuck Mason, I can't do this right now." The weight in his chest made his breath shallow.

"Speak of the devil..." Mason whispered.

April approached them with a smile on her face. Her

familiar scent of expensive perfume, musky and floral, attacked his senses, and he thought to sneeze to make some space between them. She had attached herself to his hip since the minute she had arrived, not leaving his side while he mingled and networked. It all felt oddly familiar to their previous life, and he resented having to pretend with her and keep civil while in public.

So much was at stake for this reception. After Alicia's news to them, he could not afford any fuck ups. April, knowing he had not much rope to give, had taken advantage of the vulnerability of his situation. The need to appear in control and worthy of the donations of these people. They should be compelled to donate for the youth and not because of his character.

"Sweetheart, this was a success!" April's hand went back to his chest, and for the first time in the night, he took her hand and moved it away from his body. She breezed right past that very pointed gesture and kept talking.

"You both are going to get an influx of donations for the center! And to think you used to hate going to these types of events with me in the past! I can't wait to attend more with you in the future," she chirped.

He heard Mason's mumbled expletive and took another swig of his whiskey. The conversation they had last weekend about not having any chance of reconciliation had gone on deaf ears. He needed to talk to April in private. And he could not postpone the conversation any longer.

"Mason, I'll be back," Gabo said.

He escorted her to a corner of the room that was clear of guests and hidden behind a few indoor tropical plants. It was not the ideal place, but he needed to make sure this didn't happen again.

After she sat down at the cocktail table, he sat next to her.

"April..." He began.

"I know what you are going to say. Sorry I just, I get carried away sometimes." An innocent smile, the kind that used to work on him because he had never been invested in anything serious with her.

He knew she'd been hurt badly in the past by her previous boyfriend, he'd cheated repeatedly and taken her for granted. He understood she'd been working on trauma and insecurities when she met him and somehow she projected all her dreams onto him. It hadn't helped that he'd been sitting there letting it all happen to him, not refuting any of her plans. He'd failed and for that he was sorry.

"Look, I thought we had a good conversation on Sunday?" he asked.

"I just think you should keep your options open, Gabo. I know you said that you did not see a future between us. And well, you not wanting to have sex was a big turn-on for me. I have never been with a man that was so respectful of my thoughts and feelings.

"The usual society men I have dated in the past...well, let's just say you have been the highlight of many years. I owe it to myself to ensure I gave it my all. Plus, you are considering going back to New York. That's perfect."

"But you are completely ignoring my feelings in the matter. I don't see a future with you. The fact we did not have sex...well, that was a big tell for me. And I tried to explain this to you on Sunday, I have to feel a full connection to someone to take that step."

"Yeah I guess, I wasn't fully listening," she grimaced, "but I get it now. Today, I could tell how uncomfortable I was making you. I'm sorry."

He looked at her and saw genuine remorse, and then she winced and bit her index nail. Seeing her do that made his stomach drop.

"Actually, I am sorry, not just for this afternoon..." she said.

"What do you mean?" he asked, his skin crawling.

"There was this woman in your house today."

Gabo froze.

"What happened with the woman in my house today?" he asked.

April bit her nail again. "You didn't tell me you were seeing someone!"

"April..." he warned. He was fast losing patience with her.

"Fine. There was this woman, who I thought was your maid, but I don't think she was. Because when I said something to that effect, her eyes got angry. But she was very composed besides that. I don't know her name. She refused to give it to me, but I may have implied that..." She looked around as if someone nearby could save her.

"April!" he urged.

"I told her we had seen each other this weekend but left it very vague. I could see that news took her aback. Then I told her you were planning to move back. I am guessing she did not know who I was."

That anvil fell right through his chest, into his stomach, and out of his body. Behind it, a cold rush had him standing up, his sense of urgency making him raise his voice to April.

"What did you do, April? What did you say?"

"Nothing else, I just wanted to surprise you. We exchanged a few words, that was all." April shrugged, back to her normal "I don't have a care in the world" self.

"I have to go." He started walking away from April. He wished he had said something about April to Alicia before he left for New York. He should have said something. Fuck. That she was his realtor. And a past interest. She was going to think this was like before. But it wasn't. Was it? He walked so fast he was by Mason before he registered to move across the room.

"I have to go. Are you good with greeting the last guests?" He was frantic to get out of there.

"What happened?" Mason's face transformed, and his brow furrowed when he saw that Gabo's hands were shaking.

"Alicia...April...they met today."

"Oh, shit...sure go, fuck, I was hoping that wasn't the case. But Alicia not being here..."

"I know, I know, man! Fuck!"

"This is not like last time," Mason reassured him.

"This is exactly like last time!" He shook his head, knowing deep down she was going to take it as such. A dereliction of his duty as a friend. To tell what was going on with him.

"No, it is not because you are a grown-ass man now. And you are not afraid of taking risks anymore." Whatever face Gabo made had Mason rethinking his sentence because he nodded, "Correction. You're less afraid of taking risks now, so make sure you explain yourself this time."

"Ok, ok." Gabo felt a hand on his shoulder and whirled around to see April's face, contorted, eyes teary eyes, mouth pinched.

"Gabo, I am so sorry. I fucked things up for you, didn't I?" she said, wringing her hands as if she was an eighty-year-old grandma.

"Look, April, it's—well, don't worry, this is between Alicia and me."

"Oh, shit, that was Alicia?" Alicia's voice peaked high, mirroring the increase in his blood pressure. "I feel so bad. I know what she means to you. Go, I am delaying you. Go."

Both Mason and April got him out of the atrium and in his car. The only thought in his mind was to reach Alicia without crashing on the way because of driving one hundred miles per hour on the highway.

He did not bother going to his house. He parked the car on Alicia's front porch and knocked on the door.

"Alicia." *knock knock knock*

No answer.

"Alicia." He pressed the ringer, hoping that would do the trick.

No answer.

"Alicia, please open the door. I have been calling you!"

No answer.

Her car was in the driveway. He knew she was there. He pounded on the door now, loud, not caring if the other neighbors could hear him. He was sweating through his shirt and his heart was trying to escape his chest.

After three more tries and no answer, he got back into his car and drove to his house.

His house was quiet, but he spared not even a second to check if Alicia was there. It was pointless. His legs were carrying him now; the pull to her was relentless. He needed to talk to her, needed to ensure she heard him before she jumped to any hasty conclusions.

He reached the gate at his backyard and hesitated. If the gate were closed, that would tell him the state of her mind. How closed off, she was to any type of conversation.

For the first moment since leaving the hotel, he paused. Took a deep breath. Felt the air rush through his lungs, giving him a little clarity. It was going to be ok. He and Alicia had grown up and evolved. He could trust her not to jump to conclusions that would end up hurting them both.

With his chest tight, he opened the gate and felt the air whoosh from his lungs when he realized it was open. Twenty more steps, and he was inside of her house.

The sound of bass guitar, percussion, and the cadence of

her dad's reggae albums. Another breath. He hesitated on the base of her stairs. Then the adrenaline that had carried him through the journey home gave him one more boost, and he ran up the stairs to see Alicia.

He knocked on the door and heard her voice, faint underneath the loud volume of Beres Hammond's "There For You".

"Come in."

CHAPTER 22

ALICIA

Alicia sat on her bed, a reel of the day running on repeat in her mind. She alternated between wanting to answer Gabo's desperate calls and texts and burying her head in the proverbial sand.

When Gabo returned to her life, she knew deep down that the best thing for them was to be just friends. It almost seemed like they were cursed, forever destined to get close to their nirvana, just for it to fall to pieces right before reaching their pinnacle.

She heard his foot pounding up the stairs, the noise matching the urgency she saw in his text. There must have been a moment in the night when April told him about their meeting. His messages had gone from flirty "I can't wait to hold your hand tonight" to concerned, "Is everything ok? Are you on your way?" eventually, to "Please pick up, we need to talk. Don't jump to conclusions."

She kept trying to stop her mind from going there. Keeping her sanity in check was as pointless as keeping a group of butterflies inside an open box. She felt hollow, the pit of her stomach burning with a simmering disquiet. The mist was ever-present, there waiting to cloud her completely.

She invited Gabo into her room. She deserved to hear what he had to say about today. About what she saw.

God, did he have to look so handsome? He was imposing in her childhood room. The simple act of coming into her room had her sucking in her breath. Same as he sucked in the numbness that had clung to her this past hour she had been home. The music in the background became garbled noise, and her heartbeat increased while he stood there taking a breath from his sprint into the room.

He was sweating. His shirt clung to his torso, still in his slacks. The only note of incongruity was his bare feet. Somehow he had the presence to remove his shoes before coming into her house—the habit of many years.

Gabo looked at her, eyes focused on her face. A question mark etched in his expression.

"Alicia..." he hesitated.

"How was the fundraiser? Did you get to the goal?" she asked, her voice calm.

"I—" He ran his hands through his hair and walked, pace measured and hesitant. "Can I sit down?"

"Is this going to take long?" she asked politely.

"I'm hoping we can talk, so yes, it might take longer," he answered back, a bit of annoyance coloring his tone.

"You are sweating." She pointed at him.

He ran another hand through his hair, his other hand clenching and unclenching. For a minute, she thought he was going to stay standing and was surprised when he stripped down to his boxers. Then yanked open his drawer, he'd just earned the privilege of having one a few days ago, and pulled on a pair of sweatpants and a t-shirt he left in her house.

"There, I am in clean clothes. Can I sit down?"

She gestured to the bed, and he took her invitation and sat down next to her. The gulf between them wide was as the expanse of the space in the bed. She pressed herself to the backboard and pulled her legs up, as close as her body would allow.

He looked at her for a moment, eyes wide, and a hand reached for hers. He realized his involuntary move and pressed his hands back to his side.

"April was a woman I was dating before moving back home," he started.

"I don't think she understands the meaning of the verb *was* is past tense," she replied.

"I—" He was visibly shaken, and for an instant, her hand mirrored his movement just minutes ago. The need to reach out to comfort him was strong, but the mist was starting to rise around them.

"I agree with you. But she understood what it meant tonight."

The music kept playing and served as a needed third party, helping to keep things from going nuclear. The need to say several things at the same time had her throat clogging up. A breath. Then she spoke,

"Tonight, while she stood by your side and greeted people with you?" she asked.

The mumbled "malparidez" told her how bent out of shape he was at the moment.

"Alicia, I don't know what you saw."

"It doesn't matter what I saw."

"You are right. It does not matter because I was not doing anything with her. She came to the fundraiser to show support. She was a little enthusiastic in her show of support, but that was it. Yo no quiero nada con ella." he finished.

"I don't really care," she replied—some of the calm leaving her.

"Shit, you could have fooled me. You have been the paragon of communication today," he said, exasperated.

"Oh no, Gabo. You aren't turning this on me, you know why I am upset. You know why this is a big deal. I don't care that she was showing her support." She used her hands to do air quotes, which she knew would piss him off. "I think that if you were serious about us, you should have marked your boundaries a little more clearer with her, but I want to believe you would not be so overt in an event I was meant to attend.

"The problem is I did not know about April. After the whole conversation about Tariq, after what we talked about before having sex the first time..." Her voice broke at the end of the sentence, and she cleared her throat, chasing away the burning sensation behind her eyes and her throat.

"You are right about almost everything. I should have said something. But you are wrong about one thing. I did not omit any information the day we had sex the first time. I told you the truth. I had not been with anyone for more than two years."

"So you and she had been separate for two years?"

"No."

She laughed, the sound bitter in her mouth.

"No, she and I broke up less than a year before I moved, but we stayed close. We never slept together. What I told you that day is also true. I do not sleep with people if I do not feel a connection bigger than a simple attraction."

"You know Gabo, that is none of my business," she said, a little shaken by the news he hadn't had sex with his ex-girlfriend and what that meant.

"But it is your business. Please make it your business. I want you to care."

"Why, for what? For this?" Her hand moved between them back and forth a gesture of exasperation and helplessness. "This is what you want? To keep things from me and expect me to care and rail to the world and then stay your friend and girlfriend. The one thing I needed from you, I needed from anyone, you were incapable of giving me. I should have known better."

"Alicia, come on, I messed up, I know, but it's not like you had not told me about Tariq before we bumped into him," he countered.

"That was before. Before you convinced me to take more than a chance between the both of us. Besides, once we saw him, we talked about it. You saw this woman this weekend!"

Her voice rose in volume. She got off the bed in a tangle of legs and pure momentum. The mist was starting to grow, and she could not see. It was choking her, surrounding her, suffocating her.

"You are right. I am an idiot. I wanted to stay something before traveling, but the night of my birthday was so perfect, and I..." he trailed off.

"What, Gabo, tell me what was preventing you from saying something to me?"

"This! What we are doing now. Exactly this! Every single time we have spoken about you staying, you put a guard up. I swear you are worse than la defensa del equipo de fútbol de Colombia. No ball gets into the goal line.

Do you think I was ready to make such a pass before being sure I had you? Before you agreed to give us a chance? Alicia, you know I want you. I want you more than anything. I was ready to move back to New York for you. Te amo. But you are not ready to commit."

She whirled around to face him in the bed, nostrils flared. Her body was tense as she pointed her finger at him.

"I was right not to give in. I was right not to make a hasty decision. The one thing I needed from you was not love. I know I have always had that. The one thing I needed from you, from anyone, was full honest, unvarnished truth! I needed to count on you!

And by the way, the whole moving back to New York thing. The worst offense. How am I supposed to trust you?" Her voice broke, and she could not help the tears escaping her eyes. The mist was gray and thick, and she could not see him anymore, only anger and despair and the certainty that this would not work between them.

She moved through the mist and went into her bathroom. Tears escaped her with no permission whatsoever. She washed her face, the cold water making the tears stop.

"Alicia Marie, Ali, please come out." His voice was full of pain and sorrow. He stood right outside her door. He sounded like she had ripped something out of him, and again that pull to comfort him, to try to dislodge her from the mist came over her, but there was too much around her. She was too far gone.

She walked out of the bathroom, sensing a cold deep inside her. She sat back in the bed and curled herself, knees up. She could not even feel herself moving, she could not look into his eyes. There lay pain and trouble.

"Gabo, I need you to leave."

"Alicia, please." She could hear him.

"Gabo, I need you to leave, please."

"Por favor Alicia, don't do this again."

"I'm not doing this again. I just need space. I need to think, and I am closing off. I don't want to hurt you, and I don't want you to hurt me. So we need to pause this conversation for now, ok?"

"Ok." The defeat was coming from him in waves, and she wanted to reassure him it would be alright, but she needed to take care of her first.

The sounds of his tattered breaths followed him down the stairs and out of her house. After she heard the sliding door open, she walked downstairs to her patio, numb to the world. She listened to his sliding door close with a loud thud that reverberated through the night. After she was sure he had left, she quietly closed the gate and locked the entrance.

GABO

"You are going to carve a path in my living room floor."

Gabo's mom looked at him while he kept walking in his living room with his blackberry in hand.

"Que pasa hijo?"

"Nada, I am good."

"Oh, great. I don't want to see how 'not good' looks on you. Do you really think I believe that?" his mother said.

No more words. He used all of his allotment in that message he sent to Alicia. The message she had yet to respond to. The uncertainty of not knowing if she had seen it and decided not to answer versus not reading it yet was killing him.

He knew she had her phone before driving down with Tariq because her mom had received a message. But Alicia was notorious for leaving her cellphone anywhere but next to her. So she could have put it in her bag and forgotten about it.

So, more pacing. He looked outside and wondered if he should just swim some laps to get some of the edge off.

"Maybe you should take a swim, Gabo."

Bruja. He was convinced his mom was a witch.

"Or you can sit down, and I can make you some stuffed arepitas?"

A good witch, surely.

"No, I don't think I can eat."

"So something is happening?"

"You know, I am going to head over to Alicia's." A quick look at his watch told him she had been on the road with Tariq for about five hours. She should have arrived by now.

"Why don't you just cross the backyard?"

"Nah, I'll wait for her by her porch. I don't want to bother Mrs. P."

A cool breeze met him when he walked out of the house, and it soothed him for a while. All things blended together. Beige, green, white lines were streaking across his eyes as he jogged to Alicia's. There was no sense of objects, just color and the cool breeze meeting him while his feet pounded the pavement. Ten minutes later and he was on her street. He turned the corner, his breath shallow and quick, he saw a blue sedan in front of Alicia's house, six houses away. Tariq was getting out of the car and walking to the opposite side to open the door for her. She got out of the car, and seeing her again hit him in the solar plexus, a rush of pure warmth running everywhere. There she was, carefree, hair in a riot of curls, smile wide, dimples fully activated as she thanked Tariq.

A word from him, a laugh from her. Then they both froze, and she listened to whatever Tariq was saying with full attention. A dip of her head then a surprise as Tariq pulled her closer. There was a noise in his ears that was making his head hurt. Instead of breathing better after the jog, it felt air was in short supply, and somewhere inside him, a force told him to move. To make himself known. But he could not. He stood rooted in the spot as he saw her relax against him and then accept his kiss.

BACK IN HIS HOUSE, AND IN HIS ROOM. TO STORM INTO HIS house like he did, and ignoring his mother as he had, was undoubtedly going to earn him a stern talking from his father later. What the fuck? He did not understand how Alicia could kiss another guy after his almost declaration. Like a fucking idiot, he had sent her that text for this to happen.

A niggling voice told him Alicia might not have seen the text yet. But fuck that. He was hurt, he was angry, he felt abandoned. He had loved her for years. That was the reality. But his fear of losing her, of risking everything they had, was bigger than that romantic love. And the moment he had decided to take a risk. This happened.

Hurt and restless, he changed his clothes and went swimming. He swam as the sunset and the night turned dark and quiet. He must have been in the pool for more than two hours when he got out and dried his body. His parents were upstairs, giving him space, so he quickly dropped his wet trunks and put on a pair of sweatpants and a t-shirt.

And that is when he heard her.

"Gabo."

He had very few words to describe what he felt when he heard her voice. Something had pulled him in the way she said his name. Something was wrong. Very wrong.

He turned around and saw her tear-streaked face. He also

saw a tentative smile. And when he looked down, he saw her cellphone in her hand—screen on pointed towards him.

"Alicia. You are home." He was Captain Obvious.

"Yeah. Sorry I didn't come over right away. I was...never mind that. I'm so glad to see you."

He thought he felt pain before, but now, knowing something was wrong with her had all of his insides twisted up on top of his misery.

"What's wrong, Alicia Marie?" He tried to soften his voice, but some of his turmoil must have come out because he saw her visibly recoil.

"I just fou—" She took a minute to compose herself, "are you upset or something?" she asked instead.

"If I'm upset? No, I am fine," he assured her even though he was not okay. It was like his body had taken over the task of answering with no care of what he was happening inside, what he actually wanted to say to her.

"You seem upset, though."

"I am fine. You, on the other hand, were crying. Why?"

"I was coming to tell you, but I am thinking now is not a good time after all." She shook her head.

All this time, she had stayed right by the gate door. She started turning around towards the door. Whatever energy he was putting out there was upsetting her. But dammit, he was hurt and scared too. He did not want to lose her.

"Now is a perfect time," he said to her, willing her to turn around and look at him.

She turned back and looked at him. His mother's witchiness was catching.

"Your text message." If he had not been looking at her intently, he would have missed it. She spoke it so soft.

"Oh, that? Sorry I was being mad dramatic. I just wanted us to hang out tonight," he said, trying to be calm about it.

"You know we were going to hang out anyways, no need

for such a cryptic text. Knowing you as I know you, I thought this was bigger; it was more."

"Nah, you are reading a lot into it." he shrugged.

"So talking about you and me, that wasn't something important?"

Her shoulders were squared, and her mouth turned down. She was emanating hurt, and confusion and he wanted to reach out to her, but his own hurt and confusion were holding him back. His hands, which had dried in his towel, were damp again, and he could barely swallow.

"Alicia, look, I just wanted to catch up. That's all."

"Fuck, what are you keeping from me?!" She raised her voice.

Wow. She was not a screamer, at least not with him.

"Alicia, what is wrong?" he asked, palms raised towards her in peace.

"Tell me what you are hiding from me."

"I'm not hiding anything. What the fuck? Are you hiding something from me?"

"I tell you everything!" she said.

"Really? Everything, *everything*?" he asked, knowing that couldn't be possible. Not with what he now knew.

"Yeah, I do," she responded. So sure of herself. Pain lanced through him, at the lie, at the manufactured disappointment and rage she was projecting at him.

Whatever this was had to do with Tariq and the fact she saw that text and couldn't care less what he felt. All of a sudden, all of his fears actualized at this moment. He was mad that she had put him in this position. He had told her he did not want to risk them, but she kept talking about feelings and more, and he fell into that fantasy.

Now here they were screaming at each other, and he needed to fix it. She had no idea that he saw her. Maybe she felt guilty and needed some type of absolution. That was probably it. She did not want to feel bad that she had moved on.

He realized what he needed to do. He sat down and reached out his hand to her, inviting her to sit down.

"Tell me what is wrong, Powell. You have been crying, and I'm here for you. Whatever you and I need to talk about, we can do after." She sighed at his words, and he let some of the tension go.

"My dad, he is sick, Gabo. He has cancer. And they kept it from me. And I don't know what is going to happen. This hasn't even been the first time he had it. And somehow, I'm finding out now. I'm so hurt."

His heart dropped, and a sense of dread overcame him. "Fuck I'm sorry, Ali, they were probably trying to protect..."

He trailed off when he heard a gasp come out of her mouth.

"You knew, didn't you? You aren't surprised. How long have you known?" The hurt on her was unmistakable.

For a minute, he was tempted to lie, but that wouldn't be right. This had spun into a minefield, and he had both feet on a mine. "I, yes. I knew, but I couldn't—"

He stood up again and walked towards her while she walked backward. "My parents slipped and told me but made me promise not to tell you because that was your dad's wish. It killed me inside. I even asked your dad, but he knew you'd focus all your energy on him and possibly stay here instead of going away for college."

Her face was a mask of pain and rage. She kept walking towards the gate while facing him. "You know what, Gabo? This is bullshit. Fucking bullshit. I'm done. I'm done with your wishy-washy behavior and your teasing and lack of balls, and now this. You kept this from me all along. So I am ending it. Everything. I don't want us to be friends anymore. Don't come by no more."

"What no, no Alicia, what are you talking about, no." He was rambling and hurried towards her, but she was now almost pressed against the gate. "You promised me we would always be friends, that you would not freeze me out!" His insides were crumbling.

"I came to you, hoping for my friend to comfort me today. Guess what? You knew all along. On top of that, you were trying to pull some of your usual fuckery. I can't even go back to the house right now. It had already been the most horrible day in my life, but then I saw your text when I opened my backpack. And for a moment, I felt lucky to have you, Gabo, and even though I am hurting and scared, I thought at least this day was going to bring one good thing. But no. You just showed me how I could not count on you to take care of my heart nor me as a friend."

Every word was a stab. Every sentence made him want to scream to the heavens. How the fuck did this day go so upside down? All the pain he felt could not compete with the visceral need to hug her, hold her, and make sure she was okay. She was hurting so bad.

"Alicia, I'm so sorry about your dad. God, tell me what you need, what do I need to do to make this right? To help you through this."

"There is nothing to say. I'm leaving. Let me go."

He hadn't realized he was holding her until she asked him to let her go. His need to hold her was so strong he'd already had her in his arms. Every instinct told him not to let go. If he did right now, he would lose her forever.

"Gabo Let. Me. Go. I'm done. I'm done with you and this so-called friendship."

"Don't do this, Alicia Marie."

"I'm done!" Her voice was urgent and low, and he was surprised by the soft shove as she moved away from him. She opened the gate door, and before he could respond, she was on the other side, and he heard her put the lock on.

The sound of that lock was what really did it for him. He wanted to scream, but there was nothing inside right now. All was cold and frozen and empty.

Disbelief. In a flash of confusion and words, he had lost his best friend and the love of his life all in one afternoon.

<h1 style="text-align:center">CHAPTER 23</h1>

ALICIA

ifty missed calls. Ninety-four text messages. A dozen visits and knocks on her door. That is how she had spent her Thanksgiving week—ignoring the world outside of her parents' house. She focused on packing, and that helped her keep her sanity. Whatever was left of it, at least.

She walked around the house, and all the ghosts of moments past crowded her. All the reasons she wanted to move had reared their ugly head, and it was becoming hard to breathe easy. Hard to process things, hard to find her center.

Everything was gray. She had for a while let herself think and believe that staying here, in this place where her parents betrayed her by keeping her out, and then her friend had compounded the wound by also showing his feet of clay, had showed she needed to protect herself at all costs. To trust the people you loved the most was asking for heartache and trouble.

But she was wiser now and knew to stop and listen, hear the other side. These moments didn't revolve around her only, and with years of experience, she realized she owed Gabo more than angry and hurt words.

She walked into her parents' bedroom and saw everything in boxes piled in the corner. All this time, this house had stood empty of love and warmth. Five years. And for five years, her Daddy's clothes and items remained in here like a museum to his memory. Mami left her here to deal with it all by herself. And she was done with it, done with the waiting, done with the hoping that she could find a way to feel better. Her daddy was gone, and nothing was going to bring him back.

Her knees felt weak, and she sat down by an open box in the corner. The last box was open and had one of Daddy's last books. She had been reading them to him as he was going through the treatment from the last bout of cancer. The one that took him away. She opened the book and touched the pages, feeling the soft paper with her fingertips, the smell of must and old clinging to everything in the room.

Eyes closed, she brought the book close to her and closed her eyes. A vision of the last time she read the book to her dad.

The room was a cacophony of beeps and machines all there to keep her father's organs from completely shutting down. The rehab center had sent him home, the quiet part being said out loud. It is time. Death is coming.

Her mom was taking a nap in her room, and she was holding vigil by her father's side while she read to him.

He looked a fraction of the man he used to be, all bones and skin hollowed to his frame. His lush black coils had turned gray wisps, patches covering his head. His eyes, currently closed, were glassy and disoriented. There had been many a night that she wished whatever force made the world go round, just to let him slip easily in the night. Then she would cry herself to sleep, knowing she would never be ok without him. His soft faint voice startled her from her reading.

"Alicia, when you gonna call that boy?" her dad whispered.

"What boy, Daddy?" She closed the book and leaned towards him, the smell of disinfectant and stillness.

"You know what, boy. Gabo," her dad said.

She scoffed a brief smile of affection, visiting her otherwise serious face. "Daddy, when are you gonna stop badgering me about that?"

"Until you call him."

"No, Daddy, it has been too long. Too much time has passed to heal those wounds." She shook her head and put her book aside.

"Stubborn like your grandma."

"Oof, really, Grandma? So you're not stubborn?"

"I don't know what you talkin' 'bout, girl."

"Riiight." She carried her hand soft through his head, brushing the soft scruff while he took a few breaths. Talking was hard for him. It pained him to speak, but he took time each day to talk to both her and her Mom—his way of closing chapters, leaving things as done as he could.

"I'm sorry, ya know," he whispered, closing his eyes for a moment.

"You are sorry about what, Daddy?"

"We should have said something. We should have talked to you. You're wiser than your years, and we..." The air was still, the entire room all waiting for his words. "We were a unit, the three of us, and by keeping you out. We damaged that."

"It is ok, Daddy, you were doing what you thought was right," she shrugged, trying to dislodge the sharp corners of her pain.

"You somehow have managed to forgive me, but your Mom?"

"It is fine, Daddy."

He sighed. This sigh was not of pain, or maybe it was. "Just like your Grandma. Call him Alicia Marie. Call him."

Tears flowed out of her eyes into the book, her chest was heavy, and for a moment, she wished she was the type of person to rail to the world. To scream and shout and get it all out and feel cleansed. She figured Mariana would mourn that way; Aayala would dance the day away and think of the good times. She wished she could. But the ball of all that was hurt and disillusioned sadness stayed there. Unlogged to be dealt with another day.

Her phone chirped in her hands, and she looked at the text. It was Reg.

> Reg: Hello Likkle Alicia, you got a cash offer at asking price, and they know your uncle is still working on the house. They're willing to buy while the work is still ongoing. It ain't gonna get better than this child. Call me when you have time to talk

She took the longest time to process. Then she picked up the phone and called her mom. It was time to say bye to this house.

GABO

Four days and no answer. Alicia was ignoring all types of communication. He had considered for a brief instant to send her a pigeon, a la historical romance, but knew the humor would fall flat on his face.

Hopeless. For a while, he'd dared to reach with both hands for what he wanted, Alicia. He lived in fear of not trusting himself with her love. He always thought he would mess it up because he was too young or inexperienced in life, then too fickle in relationships. So he waited and thought she would be there, for him as a friend. He took her for granted and lost all those years ago.

When he saw her again, he knew deep down he could not wait any longer. What he wanted from Alicia from that first day was always more than friendship. So he took a risk, and in doing so, he lost again. He lost her love and her affection. Her dances when she thought he was not watching. The way her eyes grew heavy when she was reading a steamy scene, how serious and dedicated she was to helping the center, her inhibited love of sex. How the love for her parents bled into everything in her life, the little ways she made sure he had a good morning by being around even if she had not slept over. Their dinners and their hang outs. He lost all of it.

Thanksgiving sucked. The end.

His mother tried to cheer him up while making sure to check in on Alicia as well. His Pops gave him disappointed glances while he carved the turkey. Mason came through later in the evening and sat with him in silence while they had some beers. All he could think of was Alicia. How he had fucked up again with her, how in the heat of the moment, words didn't seem to work for him, and he tripped over his own fucking sword.

Fifteen years ago, the fear of losing her friendship caused him to trip on his own sword when she was hurting and needed him the most. He knew of her enough now that they both had been young and foolish. He had not been equipped to deal with the emotions she was going through while dealing with his feelings of inadequacy.

So he thought to talk to her. This time he was ready to deal with what she was dealing with and what he needed to. He checked the gate door back home to find it locked, same as that fateful week fifteen years ago. Then he got shitfaced and woke up on Black Friday with mosquito bites all over his arms.

It was now Saturday, and his overthinking had him exhausted. Work was his friend. It always had been.

He sat in front of his computer, working on his latest project for a small private college in Louisiana that needed a consultant to review the new curriculum for a few new degrees they had added in tech. The act of getting lost in the prospectus and the soothing black text and white paper helped. The couple of bites of leftovers he ate for lunch sat heavy in his stomach. Even leftovers were ruined this Thanksgiving.

He loved them. He waited a year to taste his Mom's Pavo Asado, the rice and beans, and the pernil she made especially for him. It all sat sad and lumpy in his stomach. He was doing worse than the heroes in the mushier books Alicia made him read. He couldn't even enjoy some good food.

He knew Alicia was hurting, and he realized she was letting herself stay in this frozen place where she thought she could not trust those who loved her. She had plenty of reasons to believe that, and he understood. He understood fear. He had felt it for years about to her. It hurt so much to be on the other side of that coin. For all the hurt he caused her as a young woman, he wanted to ask for forgiveness. He wanted, no, needed to talk to her.

A thumping on his door interrupted his thoughts.

He came downstairs, knowing it could only be two people. His Mom or...

"Open up! I let you mope enough."

Mason.

Gabo opened the door mid-knock, which left Mason with his hand in the air and a humorous look on his face. Any other time he would have laughed and made fun. He still enjoyed the little perverse satisfaction of fucking with him, but his heart wasn't fully engaged.

"I do not mope."

"I thought I was going to find you prostrated in your

boudoir, crying for your lost love. I came prepared with these," Mason said.

A six-pack of Aguila and a bag full of artisanal chips and homemade dips. Maybe Mason's dips were the ticket to getting his appetite back.

Mason's idea of comfort watching was "Something Great." The movie was the story of a breakup, and he high-key wanted to punch his friend for this selection. It was messing with his confidence. Confidence he needed right now.

"So you good?" Mason asked while eating chips.

"No, I'm not."

"But you seem way more...centered that I expected you to be."

"Because I refuse to believe it's over," he shrugged and laid back further on the couch.

"Oh, ok, we are going with the denial strategy. Smart."

The line of Mason's lip was almost an upside 'u' while he nodded in pretend awe.

He had a flash vision of Mason spluttering in laughter after falling in his pool. Fully clothed and drenched, after a push from Gabo. Visions like this sustained him in moments of low patience.

"No, I'm not in denial. Alicia and I are grown-ups; we can have a conversation; we can work this out. She said she needed space, so I'm giving her that."

"Has she answered your calls?"

"No."

"Is the gate-" Mason continued.

"Closed, yea."

"Bruh..."

"I know, I just can't give up this time, ok. I have to try," Gabo said, holding on to faith,

"Ok, I hear you. I don't blame you. Alicia is..."

"She is everything, and she is it for me. Spending time with these few months, and I know what a mistake it was not to try with her all those years ago. This can't be it for us. I'm sure she'll listen."

"Ok then, I'm glad I don't have to hug you and dry your tears. But you know I'm here if I need if you need me to," Mason said, his voice sincere.

"I know. Love you, bruh," Gabo answered, glad his friend came through.

"Love you too."

CHAPTER 24

ALICIA

"You need me to get, what? But Tío, why can't you —" Alicia was interrupted by her uncle's voice on the phone.

"Alicia, vé a Home Depot and get me a twenty foot by thirty foot tarp and chalk reel. I have too many jobs going on right now, and the guys will be there early tomorrow, and this saves them a stop."

Her uncle spoke fast on the other side of the phone, his voice a bit of a proverbial shove on her behind. It was Sunday; she looked down at what she was wearing and saw her three-day-old outfit. She did a pit check, and the smell hit her hard.

"I gotta take a shower first."

"Please don't be going to Home Depot stinking like the tall heaven."

"It's high...never mind. Bye Tío."

"Bye Mija, Bye."

Regret washed through her, the murky water mingling

with the mist to make it a humid fog. She had been doing good in not answering her phone. Her Tío's calls were one she could not afford to ignore, with him working on her house and all. So when she heard his ringtone, she knew she had to pick it up. After speaking with him, though, she'd drained the little energy she had gathered with meticulous dedication, just like finger detangling her tender-headed niece on wash day.

She took off her favorite t-shirt, from NYU, a gift from Gabo, even in her misery she found ways to be sappy. She took a quick shower, ensuring she washed well all the essential areas and threw on a new sweatsuit. Then with her energy levels in minus thirty, she went to the worst place on earth, aka a hardware store.

Aisle ten was her destination after using the website that told her where to find the tarp her uncle had asked to buy. At least technology was her friend. As she walked down the main aisles her insides jumbled, and slight nausea rose inside. The thought of Gabo not walking here by her side made her physically ill.

She needed to call him soon. Things couldn't stay up in the air like this. She wanted to talk listen to him. Work things out. But she lacked the courage. That and an intense allergy to the serious conversation they needed to have. Her wanting to be with him did not erase the fact he kept things from her. It was all a mess in her brain.

Retched and miserable, she turned the corner looking to her right for the damn tarps, and accidentally bumped another cart. "Sorry," burst out of her mouth before her eyes had even connected with the person pushing the other cart. She gazed up, and there he was. Gabo. The person who should have been by her side in the fucking hardware store if this was a romance novel, but this was reality. And life sucked.

"Alicia Marie." Eagerness and sadness all combined in two words. How did he do that?

"Gabriel Ernesto." Her voice betrayed her feelings, and the words sounded full of need and sorrow.

"I've been standing in this aisle for about an hour now."

"Why would you? Oh, *oh*. Wait till I see Tío tomorrow," she said.

"Don't kill him, he definitely was against getting involved, but Mariana convinced him."

"Oh, she will get it too, wait and see." The nausea that had been roiling around the pit of her stomach suddenly lifted and transformed into warmth. That warmth grounded her and helped her see the mist for what it was and not something that was part of her. Clarity was not there yet, but self-awareness suddenly arrived. She wanted to touch him, his hands rested on the cart, one finger tapping up and down his arm, which was currently tense and coiled, or the corner of his lips which had a sad turn downward.

The knowledge of the cause of all of this was no comfort to her; she had wanted to be his panacea, not his tormentor. She had not wanted anything, but here they were.

"Gabo, I don't think this is the place and time."

"I disagree," he said with a smile.

"I don't have much to say."

"Good. Then you will hopefully listen."

She crossed her arms over the sweatshirt, remembering in a peak of *idontgiveafuckery* she had eschewed wearing a bra. Big mistake. Like two big mistakes.

"I don't think—"

"Alicia, we did this years ago; like idiots, we stayed apart instead of talking."

"It was more than that, and you know it. And idiots? Speak for yourself," she smiled, letting him know his accurate assessment did not offend her.

"Fuck, yes, of course, it was more than that; you went through a horrible experience with your parents and found out I knew at the same time. It colored everything that happened, including us. I get all of that now, but there are things you do not know. Can we please talk?"

"You know I'm going to say yes, right? With your mysterious 'there are things you don't know?'" She deepened her voice to imitate his baritone.

"If this is what it takes for you to come with me..." he shrugged, but his eyes told her how on edge he was feeling.

She walked towards the end of the aisle then looked back.

"Did my uncle really need this tarp?"

"Oh yeah. He very much needs it. I don't want him to kill me tomorrow so let's pick it up and go."

THE MOMENT THEY CROSSED THE THRESHOLD OF HER HOUSE, she turned around and looked at Gabo. A tall wave was coming her way, and she was not equipped for what it would do to her once it came to her shore. She was petrified of hearing what he had to say, and for a minute, she had the urge to run to her room and lock herself in there, wanting to keep his words at bay.

Her defenses were down, and glancing at Gabo, the determined set of his sculpted jaw, and the way he was almost crowding her, she wanted just to wave a white flag and scurry back to her hiding hole.

"I froze when you needed me the most," Gabo said, face serious.

"What? When?"

"Fifteen years ago. I failed everything that our friendship stood for because I was hurt." His words were coming fast and furious, and she wished it was because it was a Vin Diesel movie and not because he was bringing up old hurts.

"I saw you. I know it's not an excuse, but I saw you and Tariq that day when he dropped you off. Do you remember?"

She tried to jog her memory of that day. All she remembered was the horrible moment when she found out her father was sick and the utter betrayal she felt for both of her parents, especially her mom, for keeping her in the dark.

She remembered her foundation crumbling and needing Gabo to ground her and then finding that enigmatic text. The one that said he wanted to talk. The spark of hope, the light that turned on after the darkness of her parents' deception carrying her to his house. And then more deception. More cover-ups for the sake of her sensibilities and the person who was supposed to keep her from sinking had carved the foundation open for her to fall in.

"I don't remember much of what happened with Tariq that day," she said cautiously.

"He kissed you. He kissed you like he wanted you, and you responded. And I was standing there by Mrs. Johnson's house, and I remember thinking someone was screaming loud and harsh, but it was just all in my head. It was a gut punch to see that. To realize I was too late."

"I'm so confused. What does that have to do with everything else?"

"That's why before you told me about your father, I was acting weird. Then you told me, and I wasn't ready for that, and I fucked it all up," he finished, sadness in his tone.

They were still standing by the entrance of the house. She walked away towards the TV room. She needed some distance from him right now. Alicia needed to walk away because she did not know what she would do if he stayed close.

"Did you hear me, Alicia?" His steps behind her, making

sure she would not escape this time.

"I did hear you." She sat on the couch and curled herself in, taking in how stupidly they let time pass on things left unspoken.

She had no time to process what all of this meant. What would she have done if she knew this back then? Could she have had the maturity to realize he was hurting too and taken time to talk things over?

He saw her and Tariq. She had not remembered that kiss but now the memory bloomed in the back of her mind, soft and ethereal. Action but not a feeling, she saw in her mind how she responded to his kiss but nothing more, no heat, not excitement. She did not even remember what song had been playing when he dropped her off.

Gabo remembered, though, he recalled in a way that had contours and weight, and Goddess help her she understood. She understood how he went from that to trying to save face and pretend he hadn't meant anything by his text. They were young and foolish, and she couldn't front and act like she did not understand. If only he knew she had already planned to let Tariq down gently. What Gabo saw had been as new to her as it had been to Gabo.

Gabo knelt in front of her and took her hands in his. His were warm and solid and dear. Hers...

"You are so cold. You are shaking."

She focused on looking at their hands. Right now, words were not her friend. Words were going to hurt him if she tried to use them now. All she could do is feel. Let his words do what they must. Wreak the havoc of what-ifs and recriminations. The regret of not giving him the time of day to explain after he called a million times and texted as much washed over her. She hated that she ignored her parents' pleas to reach out to him after the years had passed and her father was in between treatments.

And at last, when he reached out with that token of love and connection, an olive branch after years. But grief had overtaken her by then, and she no longer was the Alicia he loved. So, what was there to give him?

"Talk to me, Alicia. I need to hear what you are thinking. What are you thinking?"

"All the what-ifs," she said quietly

"I know. They are mad heavy, but we have to work on letting it all go," he said. "I've thought about it, and I don't know if I'd have done a thing different about your dad's news. It was something he explicitly asked me to keep to myself. So I tried my best to be there for you, even if in silence. The grilled cheese, the hangouts, all of that was my way of supporting you. Supporting them. It's all I had to give in a fucked-up situation. And I got to spend time with my favorite person." Conviction strong in each word.

"I can't say I like it. But I get it. I've made peace with all of that. I've also had to sit with the fact I made it about myself when my dad was hurting." It was still tough for her to contend with how stubborn she could be.

"Everything I explained about April on Tuesday stands. I don't know where things went so fucked up with her, and I should have told you about her. But you need to know April was my realtor, and she took information about my consideration and made it bigger in her mind. New York was an idea in the back of my mind. A Plan Z.

The only fear I had was of fucking things up by even bringing her up and muddying the waters of our past. But now," he pointed to the floor with emphasis, "our present, it's only you. If I'm keeping it real, in our past, it was only you. It has always been you." His breathing was hard after bearing his soul all in a platter to her, and she could not take her eyes away from him.

And he wasn't finished. "Please tell me you feel the same? Please tell me you love me too?"

She wanted to reach to him and hug him and kiss him and take away that haunted look he had. She tried to assure him, of course, it was only him, always him, and how could he have ever doubted that. Words should have been their friends fifteen years ago, but emotions were carrying them both, young and restless and inexperienced.

"Of course I love you! I've loved you for years, even when I was angry," she said, eyes watering.

There were tears in his eyes too, and she ached for him.

She realized how right this all was. How much her true self came to life when she was with him. How he complimented all the good things in her and soothed all the dark parts in her. She didn't need him, but life sure as hell was a million times better in how he complimented her every step of the way.

She'd decided in her pain that a place would be the answer to her sorrows instead of love and community and him. The wave came through her and washed her to shore, leaving clarity behind. It left her wet, raw, and cleansed. She also realized she needed to do some healing.

"I know we will figure all of this out. But first, I need to work on myself a little. I'm here. But I have to figure some things out first, ok?"

"You are gonna make me wait for that answer, aren't you?" he said.

"No, don't think of it as an obstacle, but as a key for me to unlock what's blocking me. I don't want to hurt you or us ever again," she told him, willing him with all she had to understand. This was different. This was her realizing some things needed change.

He sighed. "Ok, then Alicia. Do your thing. I'm here."

CHAPTER 25

ALICIA

Mari was whispering about her again. She thought Alicia was born yesterday, and with everything that was going on in her life, she felt Mariana might be right.

Alicia sat in the guest room just having finished her virtual session with her new therapist. It had been three weeks since she'd spoken to Gabo, and she had dedicated herself to get her life together. She explained she needed to get her head straight because she didn't want to keep hurting him. After all, she was hurt. Things were tentative between them since then.

Her therapy sessions had been revelatory, so much hurt she had been keeping inside that she spent her first two sessions in a burst of speech and tears. It would take time to sort through everything, but it felt good to know she was taking concrete action for her well-being.

Now that she had a therapist working with her, she knew she could go to Gabo with no uncertainty still bothering her.

She just did not know how to approach him. She tried approaching the conversation a week ago, but he assured her he would be good with whatever she chose to do. They would figure it out together. She could feel him holding back, though, and she didn't know how to reassure him.

After putting her tablet away, Alicia approached the door, and Mariana's voice rose in volume. Mari probably thought she was still in her session with her headphones on.

"Mason, ok. Yeah. What do you want me to do about that? She had told him she was selling the house from day one."

Pause. What was that about? Had Gabo met the new owners? Her chest constricted in pain to imagine how that must have felt for Gabo. He knew about the sale, but with her staying at Mari's, he would be more exposed to the house than she was. She had had her own time of mourning for the sale.

"Yeah, I know, but... but I told you she needs time." Pause. "She'll make the right decision." Longer pause. "And that's between them!"

She could kiss Mariana. She understood what Alicia was trying to do before committing Gabo and their future.

"I know. Well, what do you want me to do, rush her? I mean, you and I know this has been a fifteen-year saga, and now he is wavering on the finish line. Nah." Pause. Alicia's palms were sweaty. What did she mean by that?

"Ok, ok, I get it, I know, Mason, ok! I get it. She is working on some things before making any decisions, yeah. Yeah, I am coming to the holiday party. Ok. Yeah. Ok."

Alicia could not in good conscience continue eavesdropping. She made a big show of opening her door and walking out to the living room.

"Oh, speaking of la Reina de Roma... Mason says hello. He also says...no, no hold on Imma put you in speaker."

Mari was exasperated, her afro looking like the living

animation of her mood, wild and free today. Mason's voice boomed in the living room, and she decided to sit down to listen to what he had to say. "Little sis. You both need to get your shit together. I realize you are working through shit, but you have to talk to him. He is in the worst mood I have ever seen him be in, and clearly, the possibility of you moving is still messing with him. So fix it. Y'all getting on my last nerve."

The call abruptly ended, telling her Mason ended the call. Mariana put the phone down on her kitchen counter and looked at her. "Don't let him rush you."

"No, he's right. I can sense Gabo is uneasy."

Mariana just nodded, not saying much more. "You want to go to the center's holiday party?"

"Yeah, I'll let Gabo know I'll meet him there."

"Ok, girly, start getting dressed then. It starts at six, and you take forever."

SHE WAS NO BACKSEAT DRIVER, BUT TODAY SHE HELD THE "OH shit!" handle as if it was her ticket to safety. Mariana drove recklessly through the highway, weaving in and out of lanes. Nervous energy coursed through her, and the radiations must be affecting Mariana as well if her driving was any sign.

"Chiquita, I'm going to need you to relax."

Alicia attempted to relax her hand on the handle. She failed miserably.

"No worries, I will get you to this party safe and sound."

"Safe and sound are looking like a pipe dream at this moment," Alicia replied.

"You could have driven yourself," Mari said, annoyed.

"We would have crashed. I don't know why I am so nervous," she said honestly.

"So then, don't come complaining about my driving now. It's ok, Alicia, you will see him soon. He is not going anywhere."

Alicia knew Mariana was rational, but something inside her had snapped to attention when she heard Mason's words. Gabo and her had kept things transparent and somehow had still failed to share what was most important to each other. Fear had driven them both to knuckle-headed decisions, but she could own up that the walls she had erected to keep herself safe were now threatening to cost her, and the cost was too high for her to risk.

She looked at her phone and rechecked the time— 6:30 p.m.

The event had started already, and she'd hoped that they arrived before everyone else for an opportunity to speak privately with him. This seemed like the wrong time to start a conversation, but she couldn't shake the thought that she could wait no longer. Maybe the thought wasn't because of him. Maybe it was her. Talking to her therapist she'd realize she had stop trusting people after her parents' deception, but the worst part was she has stopped trusting her own instinct.

Gabo had always been there when she needed him the most. Even while they spent years without talking, an odd sense of ownership and entitlement colored all her thoughts about him.

Gabo was her person. He was her teenage best friend, the man that saw her grow up to a young woman and knew all her hopes, dreams, quirks, and ugly corners. That she knew the same of him made her feel protective of what they had together. And all throughout her instinct had pointed her directly to him, and for once she listened.

Life had created obstacles, and somehow she had lost sight of her true self, that girl that loved with no restrains and understood that people were flawed. That her people were flawed. She had created this perfect persona around her and expected perfection from everyone else, and somehow the walls she built had caused her unbearable pain.

Mari got off the highway, and soon they were navigating the known streets that would lead them to the Center. Her heart sped up in her chest as they made the last turn to their destination.

Her hands were damp, and she took some tissue paper to dry them. A quick inspection on her sweater dress, and she hopped out the car as soon as Mari had shifted to park. The crisp cool air blew through her braids, and she felt a brief respite. Mari was already standing next to her, her hand extended to her.

"Are you ready?"

"Hell yeah, I'm ready," Alicia replied.

She was ready. Gabo had seen through those walls and had reached out to her in a way no one else had been able to for years. Her stubbornness had prevented her from reaching back as he deserved. To see the walls he erected through the years to protect that soft inside of his. How could she have been so self-centered? But she was shedding all of that. She needed to show him she was now ready to be fully vulnerable with him—a deep breath and Mari's hand in hers as a show of support.

She could do this.

They walked to the door and opened it to full-blown holiday mood. Green garlands were all around the welcome counter, with touches of gold and silver sparkling in the dimmed entrance.

Lights twinkled all around the door leading to the main hall, the smell of pernil greeted her, and the voice of Hector Lavoe singing "Aires de Navidad" soothed some of her nerves. If she wasn't so nervous she would go attack the pernil, her mouth watered at the lovely scent, but she knew she couldn't take a bite right now.

People were milling around, laughing and talking. The spirit of the holidays was almost a thing she could touch. This Christmas had been such a hard one for her. The house sale and grief took hold of her in ways she was not prepared for. It made her miss that feeling in the air that came with every holiday season. She felt it now. In this room were friends and family of Gabo and Mason were all around in addition to the kids from the center with their families.

The air was a little lighter, and for a moment, she took stock of all the good that surrounded her life, even in the most difficult of times.

Then she saw him. Gabo was standing next to Mason, talking to Mason and his parents. He was wearing a burgundy sweater on top of a white shirt and slim black slacks. Today was one of those Florida winter days where you had to layer to combat the drop of temperatures in the evening. He was doing the complete opposite to her. Her temperature spiked, and her heart started dancing a whole choreography to the song's beat playing on the sound system.

He looked good. Her entire body yearned to be surrounded by his big, strong frame, to be held by his arms and feel cherished by him. A smile adorned his face while he bantered with Mason and their families, but there was an air of sadness around him that tugged at her heart; she felt the same way. The hesitation, even after her declaration of love, had taken a toll on him. Mrs. M, ever the intuitive mother, was bringing what comfort she could, her hand moving in soft motions over his bicep.

Mariana stood next to her, her presence an emotional buoy keeping her moored.

"Look at these two knuckleheads; they are both wearing matching sweaters in different colors, no puedo."

Her eyes reluctantly moved away from Gabo's face to look at Mason, and a strangled laugh escaped when she saw that, indeed, Mason had the same sweater and white shirt as Gabo but in a deep royal purple. Mason's dark skin looked luminescent under the warm amber lights, and for a minute, she saw her two friends, gentle giants standing side to side, and a rush of pride overwhelmed her.

"They look amazing."

A mumbled "I guess," was all that Mariana contributed to that statement.

"Ok then, are we going to stand here, or are we going in?"

At that exact second, the music went low, and everyone started murmuring, looking around. Makayla and Rob, two basketball seniors, stood by the sound system, fidgeting as they waited for everyone to settle down.

"Hey, what's up? I'm Rob, and this is Makayla." Makayla did a quick royal wave, and some of their friends snickered and laughed.

"We just wanted to take the time to say thank you to Mason and Gabo for opening this center." they said.

"Yeah, there is a lot of people that say they have their best interest in their hearts, but the two of them..." Makayla extended their hand towards where Mason stood with a warm self-deprecating smile, and Gabo with an uncomfortable grin that showed more teeth than required and all his discomfort., "...have been working with us for a while now, giving us advice, and access to information and knowledge that have allowed us to prepare for the next steps even if we don't get scholarships. There is nothing to it for them, and the fact that they both have put this as a priority, well, it means a lot. We see you, and we are thankful for you. We wanted to extend this moment to say thanks and also to put you on the spot to give us some words." Makayla finished their speech and smiled at their friend Rob.

Her heart swelled for the two of them, and she was so glad they had this opportunity to get their accolades. She knew they did not do this work for prestige or attention, but it is always good to be appreciated.

"Thank you, thank you! Thanks, Makayla and Rob, for putting us on the spot like that. Gabo and I are here because our community doesn't have the same opportunities for our athletes to move on to the next phase of their life after high school. We saw it happen to many of our friends when we were in school, which was the seed that created the center. We want to thank all of you for trusting us, for the families that have trusted us to guide your youngin's. It is a privilege and a responsibility that we do not take lightly."

Then Mason turned to Gabo, and it was his time to speak. She could tell he was visibly moved and had to clear his throat a few times before starting to speak. "I usually don't have much to say because Mason has always been the talkative one of the two of us." A few chuckles and laughs spread through the people. "I have learned so much from all of you this year. There's perseverance and courage to live each day to the fullest that you have transferred to me, and for that, I will be forever grateful. Many times when I was your age, I was afraid of taking risks. But you all taught me that ain't it."

More laughter from the crowd.

"Thank you for trusting us, and I cannot wait to see what every one of you accomplishes after high school. You never needed us, nor do you need us now. Each of you have what it takes, but you needed resources, and I hope we have done right by every one of you. To your health and success." He raised his glass to all the students and their families.

Then Makayla spoke up again.

"Oh, look, there is Ms. P! Ms. P, I know you are not part of the fantastic two, but we see you too! Thank you for all you have done to help Gabo and Mason. You should speak too!"

Her body flushed, and cold trickled all over her when all eyes turned to her and Mariana standing by the doorway. She saw when Gabo looked at her, and she realized he had known all along she was there, no surprise shown in his eyes; instead, his eyes bored into her, and she felt like he could see everything. Expectation showed in every face, and she had no choice but to speak even though she hated being in the spotlight.

"Thanks, Makayla, I swear you knew exactly how I would feel being on the spot like that." She hoped the smile she tried to pull looked genuine and not a grimace of an excess of emotions. She attempted to keep eye contact with the young adults, looking at each of them while she spoke. Seeing their smiling cheerful faces.

"I'm only here today because you all are amazing. Even though this was an intimate Gifted Athletes of Broward family affair, I want to believe that I'm an adopted Auntie to ya'll. The work you have accomplished in these short months and what you will accomplish next year is inspiring. I'm always in awe of all of you every time I have had the opportunity to be in the center and hear you working on new opportunities and learning new skills. Coming here and being with you has inspired me as well. I have lived in fear of the full potential of what my life could be if I only opened up to the people close to me. I know many of you might have had fears of trusting these two men and what they offered for your future when so many have only cared for your athletic skills and nothing else."

Her throat was dry, and her heart had decided to rearrange the space in her chest. She looked at Gabo, and her heart stopped. His face was completely closed off, and she could not tell what he was thinking. She kept eye contact with him because what she had to say next was for him. She wished she was giving him this news in private, but she would not be a coward. She laid her hand on the table.

"So I want to say thank you, some of your courage has rubbed off on me, and I have decided to stay in South Florida and work with a great non-for-profit organization which will allow me to volunteer here more often. I want to stay all of y'all's adopted aunty for years to come. I hope you will have me. I raise my imaginary glass to your health this holiday season and new year. *Salud*"

Gabo's face made no changes while she spoke. Even once she was done, and her little pantomime of raising her glass made people laugh and clap, he made no move to smile or even acknowledge what she said. Mason clapped his back and pulled him towards the door where she was standing with Mariana, and she saw him brace his body against Mason's hand. Her heart dropped, and at that moment, she realized how much she had taken for granted. She broke eye contact with him and turned back towards the entrance.

"Licy, wait, he is just in sh—"

"I know, bebita. This is his moment thought. I should have known that. He and I will catch up."

She was out of the center in a second. She pulled her phone as she walked away and found an Uber two minutes away. A white Yaris pulled up in the corner, and she quickly hopped on the car. She closed her eyes and let the image of Gabo's impassive face take over.

GABO

"What the fuck was that, dude?"

A punch on his arm jogged him back to his body.

Alicia was staying in South Florida. She was not moving. What did that mean? He sensed her arrival as soon as she walked into the entrance and had spied her standing there with Mariana while she hesitated to come in. Then Rob and Makayla had started the whole speech thing, and embarrassment mixed in with all the rest of his feelings.

Once he realized she had also been put on the spot, he almost spoke for her. His heart jumped on his throat, and he had wanted to protect her. Somehow, even though he knew she was leaving, he could not help but want to be close to her.

She hated public speaking, so he did not know what to make of her words once she started talking. Was that her diplomat persona trying to put a pleasant face in front of everyone? He doubted that. Her face had been open, and the Alicia Marie he knew and loved had shone through each word as she looked straight at him. Not knowing where he stood with her, he kept his face neutral even while she shocked him with the news of her staying.

"Earth to Gabo!"

Mariana punched his bicep again and tried to do a third punch, but Mason held her hand.

"Mari, give him a minute." Mason tried to reason with her.

"Nope, I have no minutes to give. I brought her here with her raw ass feelings to talk to him, and he stood there like a statue and let her make a fool of herself."

"I did not ask you to bring her to do a grand speech," Mason replied.

"So you should have spoken up then and not let her be put on the spot like that."

The bickering between Mason and Mari was entertaining, but he could not handle it right now. With his heart in his throat, he made a move towards the door, wanting answers from Alicia. He needed to understand what this news means for them.

"Are you ok, *mijo*?" His Mom's soft voice stopped his determined walk towards the exit.

"I don't know, Ma. I just need a moment with Alicia."

"She left," Mariana interjected, walking right behind him next to Mason. He heard Mason swear.

"She left? Why did she leave?" he asked. Things were moving a little too fast.

"Well, I don't know, probably because you looked at her like she had grown antlers or something." Mariana's tone dripped with unconcealed sarcasm.

"Fuck." He ran his hand through his hair, frustrated with himself for being so slow to react to Alicia's declaration. All of her message had been for him, and in his confusion and hesitation, he let her get away.

"Gabo! Te voy a lavar esa boca. But later, go get Alicia. Your dad tried going after her when she realized you were having a moment, but he missed her. This was just like the time you had that poem recital in the fourth grade talent show, and you just froze there staring at everyone like a deer in headlights."

"Son, I tried. Sorry." He noticed his dad breathing a little hard next to his mother.

"Here. I'll stay with my parents tonight. But make sure you don't defile my apartment. Actually, she needs some so, just wash the sheets in the morning." Mariana placed a cold object in his open hand, which he instinctively held. Her apartment key.

"I got this, go." Mason soft shoved towards the door was all the push he needed. He looked at his parents, at Mason and Mariana, and warmth filled him once more. Only one person was missing, and he was going to make sure she was never missing again.

ALICIA

"Alicia, are you here?"

Gabo's voice filled the otherwise quiet, dark apartment. She heard his footsteps then felt him standing in front of her. She was sitting on the living room floor with the lights off, illuminated only by the string lights that were set outside of Mariana's balcony.

His voice unencumbered by doubt felt like a soft breeze on heated skin.

"Gabo, what are you doing here? You should be at the party. We can talk later."

He bent down, his large body graceful as he arranged himself to sit on the floor in front of her. His long legs came around her, and his hands reached out to hers.

"I came after you, but you left so fast."

"I saw your face…."

He moved one of his hands to her face, cradling her cheek so delicately. "Yes, I know, love, you took me by surprise. I couldn't believe my ears. For a second, I thought you said you were staying, and I knew I was bugging."

"Stop." She cradled the hand that was touching her face. "You heard me right."

"Why are you staying?" His voice was so tentative.

"I am staying because I was wrong in my reasons for leaving. I thought moving away from home would be the solution to all my hurt, to all my loneliness. But the truth is the solution lies in me. I hadn't realized how much I isolated myself from everyone after discovering Daddy's diagnosis.

I channeled all my anger into how I felt about my parents keeping that from me and in part into how I felt about you. I alienated my favorite people because I did not want to feel that anger again. So when you came back to my life, ready to take a chance in us, I was scared. I retreated to my comfort zone, and I doubled down on the idea of moving. I thought that was going to fix me. But I have to work on fixing me."

"Ali, you are so brave. You know this, right? There is no fixing to be done. You were not wrong in your feelings, just how you were channeling them. I just want to be here with you for the ride, no matter what. You are my person," he said.

His thumb swiped her cheek, and she realized she was crying.

"You are my person too. And I want you in my life always and forever. Even if the right thing had been to move, I wanted us to work it out, whatever it took, long-distance, super commuting. Whatever worked because I realized that having you by my side has always been my dream and will always be my dream," he told her.

"It doesn't have to be a dream, though. I am right here," she said between sniffles—Goddess, this man made her soft.

"That you are, let me pinch you." His laugh was so full of joy. She felt his joy embrace her and become hers.

"I'm so sorry it took me so long, babe. I put you through the wringer."

"Ali…haven't you figure it out yet? You are worth it all. It took me a while, though, so you are in good company," he chuckled.

"I think deep down I have always known we belong together. I was just scared to trust that instinct. But I trust it now, and I trust you above all."

The beauty of his smile brightened her from inside. Her lips responded to his happiness, her cheeks aching from her wide smile. There was a twinkle in his eye that made the chime in the back of her mind go off, alerting her that things were about to take a turn.

"Come, you are too far," he said, voice changing from sweet to filthy in less than sixty seconds.

"What do you mean too far? I'm right here," she protested.

He let go of her hand and face, took a handful of her ass and pushed her forward, and had her straddle him. She quickly opened her legs to accommodate his frame. She wiggled in bliss in her new position. All that power, all Gabo.

"That's better," he said with a smug smile.

The joy of having him close. His breath mingled with hers. Both their chests rose and fell together. She sighed, and a small smile coasted her lips as she closed her eyes. She felt his full lips graze hers, a delicate touch. Another closed mouth kiss. Then another. Then, with no warning, he took over her mouth and consumed her. His lips punished her, his tongue lashed at hers, asking for her surrender. She mewled when she felt him suck her tongue into his mouth and moaned when she felt him grow hard against her parted legs.

His hands grabbed her ass, fervently massaging her closer to him. In a bit of holiday magic, he got her dress off in a matter of seconds. The growl he made when her bra came off and her chest pressed against him lit a fire within her.

"First, I'm going to fuck you hard and fast, and you will come for me because I won't be able to hold it much longer. Having you in my arms again..." He bit her lower lip with enough force to make her gasp. "And then I'm going to give it to you real slow until we both forget these past weeks."

"Yes." She said in more of a moan than any recognizable word.

He captured her mouth again and thrust his covered dick against her damp underwear in case she had any doubts about what was coming next for her. Silly man, he did not need to threaten her with a good time. She had already surrendered to all his demands. After all, she had always been his to love.

CHAPTER 26

ALICIA

Alicia stood in her wrap dress, applying her lip gloss next to Gabo's bed while she looked down at him. His face was turned towards her, those full lips of his slightly open, and his powerful arms and shoulders were hugging the pillow below him. For a second, she wished they could stay in bed the whole day, just like after they got back together. The only break they took was to spend Christmas with his parents. Just thinking about the past week made her feel languid and made her legs wobble a little.

"Gabriel Ernesto, I'm going to need you to wake up."

They needed to get going. Besides, the flutter of his lashes against his closed eyes told her all she needed to know.

"Gabo, please, we have about forty minutes before we need to head out. I gave you plenty time and took a shower first." If he stopped pretending, he would have seen the eye roll she sent his way, with the dimpled smile that followed.

One minute she was standing, applying the last of her makeup. The next, she was underneath a very naked and aroused Gabo. He was braced on his arms on top of hers, and all his delicious weight was settled on her below the waist.

"I thought you were sleeping?" she laughed.

"I was until I heard we have forty minutes before we have to get out the house."

Gabo kissed her through her laughter, slow, drugging kisses that made her forget everything.

She was in kiss-induced trance until her second alarm went off.

"If you don't stop with your sexy fine ass. Stop trying to get me to forget that we have to leave. Come on, we need to go, Gabo."

"Convince me," he said, his voice, pure temptation.

That smile alone was going to convince her to stay in bed. This was her favorite pastime. After their night together in Mariana's condo, she had moved in with Gabo into his parents' house. The move was temporary as they had decided to buy a house together with the money they both made from the sale of their respective homes. They were in no rush. Finding the right place for both of them to make fresh memories was the most important thing.

"Oh, I can convince you real quick," she replied.

"Oh, can you? I don't think I like that smile. You look smug," he said, raising an eyebrow.

She didn't answer. She got him on his back with a gentle shove and then showed him how smug she felt about her convincing. He grasped the white sheets, groaning her name less than five minutes later.

She got off the bed and straightened her dress, which looked just as good as before he pulled her to bed. A quick swipe of her thumb against the corner of her mouth made sure nothing was left behind. Then she bent over and gave him a quick peck as he laid there, gasping for breath.

"Fuck Ali, that was— whatever you did there at the end

with your... fuck me, the vibration— just for the record, I wasn't ready," he babbled.

"Sure, thank God I know you can hold on longer than that if not..." She started to walk away from the bed.

"Oh, come here and let me show you how much I can hold," he growled.

She ran out of the bedroom laughing, a sexy, naked, and hard again Gabo chasing after her.

GABO

He held her hand while he navigated the way out of their neighborhood. "Are you nervous?" he asked.

She stayed quiet, then answered, "No, I don't think so, more anxious."

"I know it is a lot, but I'm so glad you asked your mom to spend New Year's Eve with us. I've missed her since she moved."

"Yeah, I am too. I was glad to speak with her to clear the air between us. Or, at least we started to clear the air."

Gabo squeezed Alicia's hand and raised it to his lips, leaving his soft imprint on her hand and sparkles of magic that traveled through her and lowered her pressure. He had that way on her.

The car's music transitioned to a ring that Gabo answered.

"Yo, what's up, my dude?" Mason's voice boomed.

"What's up, Mason. You're on speaker. I'm in the car with Alicia."

"What's up, sis? You good?" Mason asked Alicia.

"I'm good, Mason. We are on our way to the airport," Alicia responded and squeezed Gabo's hand.

"Yeah, Mari told me Mrs. P is coming for New Year. Are we gonna link up?"

Gabo squeezed her hand again, a small smile on his face.

"Actually, yeah. Gabo is letting me entertain in his house."

"Our house till we get our place," Gabo interrupted.

"Well, as I was saying, we are doing a little get-together at the house for New Year's Eve. Just us, the fam," she said.

"Sounds good. I'll tell my parents and my sisters too if that's ok?" Mason asked.

"Of course! I said, the fam didn't I? Dr. & Dr. Braithwaite, the ladies and the twins are more than welcome," Alicia said.

"So, what's up?" Gabo asked, bringing back Mason's attention.

"Oh, nothin', I was just making sure I got my invite. Catch you both later," Mason said.

"Later," Gabo said. Alicia felt a snort escape her as Gabo shook his head, smile still firmly in place.

THERE WAS SOMETHING TO SAY ABOUT HOW FULL HIS HEART felt right now. Too bad he had no words. Instead, he started writing down some places he wanted to visit with her from her list, to fulfill her lifelong dream of traveling the world. He'd put it all in a journal, and bought her a matching journal for her to document their travels once they started. He had plans to give it to her tonight, with the first ticket to their first adventure. He could not wait to see her response.

Alicia walked around checking on everyone, making sure their glasses were topped off, refilling the platters of the different pastries and assorted appetizers they made for tonight.

She looked luminous, her brown skin glowing under the lights of his parents' living room. Her hair was a riot of tight coils, his favorite hairstyle of hers, and her smile and dimples in full display. The strapless sparkly dress she was wearing draped over her in just the right way, and he was already picturing her on his bed while he came into her slow and steady to bring in the new year doing his favorite thing in the world.

He saw her mother walk towards Alicia. Mrs. Powell was a picture of how he had a blessed future if her looks were any indication of how Ali would look when they were older. To be honest, he did not give one fuck how she was going to look; the only thing that mattered was that they were going to be together.

Mari was working her phone; she had been placed in charge of the playlist and hit all the right notes with a mix of old and new that covered from his Bostonian father to her Trini mother and all the in between.

Whatever Mari had been looking for was a success, she gave a high-pitched *yiii*, and the drum entrance of "Working My Way Back To You" by Sanchez ft Flourgon came on. She turned the volume up, pulled Mr. and Mrs. Torres up, and started jamming to the song.

Everyone got up, and soon the entire group was dancing. Dr. Braithwaite was doing his old man two-step while dancing with a laughing with Mrs. Powell. His mom and dad were slow dancing to the song like it was a ballad. Mari's sister danced around everyone doing her own personal dance train with Mason's sisters and Aayala. Mason twirled his mother around. In the middle of all of that, Alicia stood smiling, letting the rhythm sway her.

To walk towards her was as inevitable as breathing. He held her from behind, placed his face on her shoulder, and let her lead him wherever she wanted. After all, he was hers to love today and always.

EPILOGUE

Light streamed through the window, illuminating the main bedroom. The sun was setting, and her eyes were focused on the serene waters of the lake behind the pool terrace of the house. The windowsill of the bedroom had a wide wooden white ledge. A seat cushion would fit there perfectly for both of them.

Reg did well. He'd found the house for them.

Reg and Gabo's voices came to her ears from some other room of the house. She was in no rush to join them. She knew he would find her. She stood still, letting the sounds of the house become second nature until she sensed him. His arms came around her waist, and his mouth pressed a gentle kiss to her temple.

"I don't even have to ask. This is it," he said.

"You know me well." She turned her head up and gave her a soft kiss on the lips.

"It has three bedrooms, one as our joint office, the other for any guests."

"And our book collection," she reminded him.

"And our kinky romance book collection, which will have our families blushing."

"Nah, I think we are pretty vanilla compared to other members of our fam," she said, laughing.

"No lies detected there..." They stood looking at each other with identical grins. He kissed her again, helpless to hold back. This kiss was longer, deeper, and they lost themselves in each other. After what could have been hours, they looked out the window again.

"You like the pool terrace?" he asked in a whisper.

"I absolutely love the pool terrace. I cannot wait for you to turn it out there," she whispered back.

"I love you, Alicia Marie."

"And I love you, Gabriel Ernesto."

This kiss was soft. There was urgency at the borders of it, but when were they not hot for each other? At the core of it, there was unadulterated love—a promise for all that was to come.

WANT MORE?

Want more? If you want to read more about Alicia and Gabo's formative years, head to my newsletter for additional scenes! You will get different exclusive scenes of their friendship before Alight starts...Remember that night Gabo mentions when Alicia got drunk?... It's in there!

https://www.subscribepage.com/alight

ALSO BY A.H. CUNNINGHAM

The Firecracker Cousins Series

Alight

Ablaze

Embers

Toying with Temptation

Holiday Shorts

'Tis The Season to Release

Anthologies

Current: An Anthology for Jackson Mississippi - Vol 1

Wicked Moves Series

Plié

A Turn in The Air

Hidden Desires Series

Jardel

Check out the A.H. Universe website to see how it all connects!

ACKNOWLEDGMENTS

Alight is the culmination of three years of learning, daring, and dreaming.

This book would have never happened without my family: to my husband, thank you for patience and encouragement and for always believing in me. To my daughter, thank you for being the first person to call my writing time "Mami's other job." and celebrating each milestone with enthusiasm and passion. And thank you to my son, who has no idea what's going on, but gives me the best hugs ever. Thank you to my sister who has supported this venture from day one.

To my parents, family and close friends...you should have just bought it and not read it. Can we please not talk about what you just read next time we see each other? Deal? Love you all!

Writing and learning alone can be isolating; I am so thankful to have found two amazing communities that opened their doors to this baby author with acceptance and kindness.

Thank you, Tasha L. Harrison, and all of the wordmakers! Tasha, the community you've built and your support have been a gift. This book flourished under the many days and nights I wrote in our sprints. I am so grateful to have found you all. A special shout out to the #nightowls. Thank you for embracing the newbie and all your wisdom.

Thank you to the Inclusive Romance Project and Kharma Kelley for creating a group where our voices are a priority, and we get to learn in a safe space. To the WIP critique group, you were the first to see the pages of this manuscript, and your feedback was instrumental to this book. To Melanie Greene, thank you for your endless support, knowledge, patience, and for grounding me when I got too nervous.

Thank you to Gabrielle Brown, Katrina Carruth, KaSandra Vincent, Cielo Bellerose, your feedback gave me the courage to keep going.

And Thank You, many people in our romance community supported this book with a share, a recommendation, a review, a purchase, and I am in awe and so grateful.

Dear Reader, thank you for reading Alight. I hope you enjoyed it as much as I did! Self-published authors depend on reviews to get the word out there. If you have the time and capability, a review in your favorite platform would mean the world!

A.H.

ABOUT THE AUTHOR

A.H Cunningham is an introvert that weaves lovey-dovey contemporary romance and erotica. Her characters are Black and Multicultural adults, trying to navigate their grown folk lives while contending with all the horny feelings and falling hopelessly in love in their journey. In her writing, you will find a deep love for the entire Black Diaspora and all the ways we connect through our heritage. When she's not writing, you can find her reading, snacking at odd hours, dancing some Panamanian song, and playing the metaphorical Tamborine as her family navigates a new move.

Alight is her debut and the first book in the Firecracker Cousin's series.

Join A.H's newsletter to get all the latest updates!
http://www.ahcunninghamauthor.com

9 781737 859710